喚醒你的英文語感！

Get a Feel for English !

喚醒你的英文語感！

Get a Feel for English !

English Writing Guide

→ 升學　→ 證照　→ 連續性成功

英文寫作
高分指引！

Use advanced word-substitution techniques to improve the accuracy, logic, and persuasiveness of your writing.

翻譯大師寫作要訣無私公開

To sum up... → To summarize; / better than... → superior to
it is... → it is... inferior to / According to... → Allegedly

作者 / 翻譯大師團隊　郭岱宗、鄒政威、盧逸禪

☑ 優化句構關係創造段落整體性及連貫性，
　　　→ 以關鍵詞支持有力論述架構。

☑ 活用高級換字修辭技巧提升語句精確度，
　　　→ 強化邏輯、呼應文章主軸。

 貝塔語言出版
Beta Multimedia Publishing

 高點 登峰美語系列

　　我們可以這麼看英文寫作：它初步的價值在於創作一個好作品；它進一步的價值在於讓寫作者有一個和自己心靈交會的機會；而一篇好作品最大的價值則在於能讓閱讀者產生更多、更好的共鳴。

　　寫出一篇優美的英文作文是一個腦力和感情兼用的工作，因為如果沒有經過深思熟慮，作品就可能缺乏見解、欠缺深度；如果沒有置入感情，作品就難以扣人心弦、引起共鳴。所以寫作與我們的心智相輔相成：只要專心一致地寫，任何一篇文章的寫作過程都將會使我們變得更成熟，因為我們的思緒變得更縝密、心靈變得更敏銳，理性與感性得以兼具。

　　在這本書中，我們將用循序漸進的方式帶領讀者一步一步進行寫作訓練，先從基礎的英文寫作紮穩腳步，然後進步到高級英文作文。其實所謂的高級英文作文不過就是進階英文作文，一點也不難！在本書中你將先學會如何鎖定方向、如何下筆，接著學習如何發展主文，最後學習如何收尾；每一次進展，都有豐富的實例和練習帶領各位學習英文創作。只要遵循書中所提供的方法，確實學習，必能在數個月之內掌握訣竅，輕鬆下筆；之後就有如千軍萬馬，氣勢難擋；自然水到渠成，圓滿收尾。

　　鄒政威和盧逸禪曾是我同步口譯和英文作文班上的好學生，現在則是英語教學界成功的好老師，實實在在作育英才，我很高興邀請他們共同寫作此書。學習首重方法，方法對了，自然就會了！感謝讀者與教學同仁使用本書，並敬祝各位健康順利。

　　英文的聽說讀寫四項能力中，恐怕所有教學和學習者有志一同皆認為，寫作是這四項能力最困難的一環。在大學和補教界深耕多年，學生最常問的問題之一就是：「老師有推薦的英語寫作書籍嗎？」然而最難習得的能力，卻是學習資源最匱乏的區塊。

　　企圖自學的學生，經常發現坊間的寫作書多半都是給予大量的範文。但這些範文水平參差不齊，而且這種學習方式也漫無章法。學生只能透過記憶、背誦，碰碰運氣，看考試是否能碰巧遇到類似的題目。對於英文文章組織沒有任何理解，也經常寫出過度中式的英文。

　　選擇坊間補習班補習，通常使用寫給母語人士學習的原文書。這類書籍，因為是設計給英語能力進階者閱讀，省略許多核心基礎觀念，並且過度偏重文體的教學，使得部分想要單純增加書寫能力的同學，句構尚未熟悉，便被趕鴨子上架，強學文體的風格，本末倒置。

　　所以本書集結三位老師的力量，決定編寫適合國人的英語寫作書，亦即一本不論從學術、考試甚至培養書寫實力的各種角度，都能提供讀者全方位養成的英語寫作指南。從基本的句構文法開始，再到文章組織的學習，接著提供優良範文的分析並對文體的架構做介紹。最後進入進階的寫作觀念，協助讀者調整單字和句構，擺脫中式英語，寫出連母語人士都會驚豔的優美英文。本書循序漸進的引導讀者，從初階到高階的英文寫作。任何程度的英文學習者，皆能在閱讀本書的過程有所收穫。書中點出多數學習者在英語書寫中常見的問題，並且提供了全面向英語寫作的知識。

　　能完成一本連筆者自己都衷心喜歡的書，必須感謝另外兩位老師的通力合作。希望本書為台灣貧瘠英語寫作資源，注入一脈活泉，並且幫助不知從何提升寫作實力的學習者，引出一條清晰的路徑。

　　很多有一些英文基礎的人常常會問：「英文口說」要如何進步？「英文詞彙」要如何增加？英文文法到底要怎麼學，才能建構出所謂的「文法概念」？針對以上問題，如果我說：「那就開始學寫作吧！」你們會不會在那一瞬間出現「黑人問號」的表情呢？我會這麼說，肯定不是為推銷這本書。

　　對一般人而言，「寫作」的目的，多半都跟「自己」有關。不論是描述跟自己有關的故事，抒發自己的感受，發表自己的觀點，總之，離不開自己內心想表達的東西。正因為跟「自己」密切相關，比起單純「背單字」或「學文法」，「寫作」能帶出一種不同的溫度。在寫作的過程中，為了忠實且流暢地呈現事件發生的過程、時空背景或因果關係等等，我們自然會需要透過種種的文法架構來建立出文章的雛形；這個過程不僅強化了我們的邏輯思考，也同時既被動又主動地讓我們「不得不學習應用文法」。為了能更細膩、更具體、更貼切、更生動的描繪，或許主動，或許不得不，終究，我們會因為需求，在一番腦力激盪過後學會掌握更多的詞彙用語、句型結構，並逐漸進入英文的思維和模式，讓文法概念滲透到每一句我們說出來的英文。

　　所以，拿起筆或是鍵盤，開始寫作，就對了嗎？不，不，不！「寫作」是需要「學習」的，更何況我們談論的還是英文寫作呢！絕對不是「有寫東西出來」就會讓我們的英文寫作進步的。一篇好文章的誕生，有著它一定的結構。從美好正確的句子開始堆疊、拓展，在適當的地方做修飾、美化，讓句子既細膩又俐落，讓文章架構完整、流暢有深度，既富含情感又兼具邏輯。為了帶領大家實現這樣的美好，這本書於是問世了。

　　從「基礎英文寫作」到「高級英文寫作」絕對不是一條輕鬆的路，但是我們要帶各位一步一步盡可能輕鬆地走。熱衷英語教學的我們，對英語本身有一份熱誠真摯的愛，所以我們衷心地期盼能透過此書深入淺出的剖析和專業用心的引導，來帶領讀者們戰勝英文寫作，進而造就多方面的成長，豐富英語學習的世界。

盧逸軒

CONTENTS／目錄

Chapter 2 | 寫出好文章

☑️ 從基礎英文寫作進步至高級英文寫作

本書共分為四章，Chapter 1 至 Chapter 3 將帶領讀者由淺入深地將英文寫作常用的基本句型及英文作文的基本架構做完整學習。而在 Chapter 4，則將進一步討論難度較高的英文寫作，即所謂的高級寫作。其實，高級英文作文並不難，只要遵循以下的寫作技巧，就可以從基礎英文寫作紮紮實實地進步到高級英文寫作：

1. 單字較成熟。
2. 句型較靈巧。
3. 邏輯較完整。
4. 思想較深邃。
5. 探討較具宏觀。
6. 文筆較細膩。
7. 氣勢較磅礡。

為了讓各位更清楚地抓住重點，我們用簡單的比較表來說明初級英文作文以及高級英文作文的異同：

初級英文作文和高級英文作文的相同之處
1. 鎖定主題，打死都不離題，自始至終都圍繞著 main idea。就像一個孩子黏在母親身邊，無論怎麼走、怎麼繞，無論別處的誘惑有多大，都以母親為中心軸。
2. 不但用腦，也用感情，理性與感性必須兼具。正如一個「有腦無情」的人無論有多麼聰明和理性，仍會令人不耐，而「有情無腦」則缺乏致命的吸引力。
3. 起、承、轉、合，一個不少，才有邏輯。就像開車，若是突然啟動（因此起得不好）、隨時轉變（因此承得不好）、隨便轉彎（因此轉得不好）、隨意煞車（因此合得不好），都令人感到莫名其妙。
4. 文法正確，時態清楚，作文才讓人看得下去。

初級英文作文和高級英文作文的相異之處		
	初級英文作文	高級英文作文
用字遣詞	比較幼稚	成熟靈巧
句型	比較簡單	精簡、有力、活潑
邏輯	合理	穩健而且精緻
結構	制式	靈活卻仍仔細融入「起、承、轉、合」
內涵	較淺薄	很有深度
文筆	平順	十分細膩、令人感動
氣勢	一般	令人震撼

　　看了以上這些標準之後，請確實跟著本書一一來執行，一起把文章由初級英文作文蛻變為高級英文作文！

Chapter 1

沒有好句子，就沒有好作文。

句子的基本構造

　　一篇文章是由一個個的句子所構成，所以寫好文章的第一步，就是必須先學會正確活用英文句子。

　　主詞是句子的頭，而動詞是句子的靈魂。所以我們在寫作時，就要先找出恰當的主詞和動詞，一但主詞和動詞被用對了，有了頭，也有了靈魂，句子就一目了然，清楚呈現。同樣地，當我們在閱讀時，第一步也必須先辨認出一個句子的主詞和動詞，閱讀才會正確而迅速。

　　不同類型的動詞帶給句子不同的變化，我們先看看英文句子有哪些變化：

📑 簡單句：主詞 + 動詞

　　一個最簡單的句子，可以只有一個動詞。不過一般來說，句子至少具備一個主詞和一個動詞。

① 只有一個字的句子：命令句

> **(You) Run!** 快跑。
> **(You) Look!** 看哪！

② 主詞 + 動詞的句子

> **She sings.** 她唱歌。
> **I run.** 我跑步。
> **Birds fly.** 鳥兒飛

📑 補語將句意補足

　　補語也常出現在句子裡，把句子的意思「補足」。

① Be 動詞 (is, am, are) 常須要補語：

⊠ I am ... 我是……（句子不完整，所以不對。）

加上一個補語就完整了：

☑ I'm home. 我到家了。（副詞作補語）
  ★ home 在這表示我「所在之處」，既表示地方，就是副詞，不是名詞。
  ★ I want a home. 這個 home 才是名詞，作 want 的受詞！

> She is happy. 她很開心。（形容詞作補語）
> They are students. 他們是學生。（名詞作補語）

② 連繫動詞也常須補語

最常見的連繫動詞有：sound（聽起來）、smell（聞起來）、taste（嚐起來）、feel（感覺起來）、look（看起來）、seem（似乎）、get（使得）、become / turn（變得）、keep / stay（維持）……等。

⊠ The idea sounds. （句子不完整，所以不對。）
  這個點子聽起來……

加上一個補語就完整了：

☑ The idea sounds great. （主詞補語）
  這點子聽起來很棒。

> The salad tastes funny. （主詞補語）
> 這沙拉嚐起來味道怪怪的。

> Ice feels cold. （主詞補語）
> 冰摸起來涼涼的。

Tom seems angry with me.（主詞補語）
湯姆似乎在對我生氣。

Her face turned pale.（主詞補語）
她的臉色變得蒼白。

You have to stay calm.（主詞補語）
你必須保持冷靜。

📝 受詞：「接受」動詞所發出的動作

受詞也常出現在句子裡，它的角色就是接受動詞所發出來的動作。值得注意的是，只要是受詞，不管長什麼樣子，必然是「名詞」。

☒ I love. 我愛……（句子不完整）

加上一個受詞就完整了：

☑ I love you. 我愛你。（受詞 you 是代名詞）

My sister likes cats.（受詞 cats 是名詞）
我的妹妹喜歡貓。

I don't like dancing.（受詞 dancing 是動名詞）
我不喜歡跳舞。

I don't know what his name is.（受詞 what his name is 是名詞子句）
我不知道他叫什麼名字。

一個動詞後面必須加受詞的，我們稱它為「及物動詞」，不需要受詞的則稱為「不及物動詞」。不過，有些動詞既可以作為及物動詞，也可以作為不及物動詞。請比較以下兩個句子：

She can sing.（動詞 sing 後面不須接受詞，所以是不及物動詞。）
她會唱歌。

She can sing the song.（sing 是及物動詞 + 受詞 song）
她會唱這首歌。

受詞分為直接受詞和間接受詞。我們看以下同時含有「直接受詞」與「間接受詞」的句型，就可以輕鬆地分辨兩者。

I gave her a flower.
我給她一朵花。
★ 給的東西是 a flower（花），所以「花」才是動作的直接受詞。
★ her 則是間接受詞。

這樣的句子也可以加上一個介系詞，變成另一種型態：

= I gave a flower to her.

Miss Lin asked me a question.
= Miss Lin asked a question of me.
林小姐問了我一個問題。
★ 所問的是 a question，所以 a question 是直接受詞。
★ me 則是間接受詞。
★ 加一個介系詞，就可以改成等號右邊的句子。

My mother bought me a new computer.
= My mother bought a new computer for me.
我媽媽給我買了台新的電腦。
★ 買的東西是「新電腦」，所以「新電腦」是直接受詞。
★ me 則是間接受詞。
★ 加一個介系詞，就可以改成等號右邊的句子。

還有些句子則稍微複雜，不但有受詞，還有受詞補語，用來補充受詞：

☒ **I made my mother.** 我讓我媽媽⋯⋯（句子不完整，所以不對。）

加一個補語，就完整了。

☑ **I made <u>my mother</u> angry.**
 我讓我媽媽生氣了。
 ★ my mother 是受詞，angry 是受詞補語。

We elected <u>Tom</u> our class leader.
我們選湯姆當我們的班長。
★ Tom 是受詞，our class leader 是受詞補語。

Judy kept <u>us</u> waiting for hours.
茱蒂讓我們大家等了好幾個鐘頭。
★ us 是受詞，waiting 是現在分詞作形容詞用（形容 us），也就是這一句的受詞補語。

EXERCISE 1

【一】請運用創意，完成下列不完整的句子。

① Mr. Brown is _____.
   （主詞補語，補足 Mr. Brown 的狀況）

② Mr. Brown teaches us _____.
   （做 teach 的直接受詞）

③ Eating vegetables keeps you _____.
   （受詞補語，補足 you 的狀況）

④ The leaves turn _____ in autumn.
   （主詞補語，補足 the leaves 的狀況）

⑤ Jerry didn't buy _____.
   （做 buy 的受詞）

⑥ I'm glad to lend _____.
   （lend 的直接受詞 + lend 的間接受詞）

⑦ The food tastes _____.
   （主詞補語，補足 the food 的狀況）

【二】句子分析：請在完整的句子前寫 ○。不完整的句子前寫 X，並將句子改正。

① _____ She didn't tell me the truth.
② _____ His shoes are really.
③ _____ This apple tastes.
④ _____ Mary stood in front of the classroom.
⑤ _____ My brother drives me crazy.
⑥ _____ My parents sent me last week.
⑦ _____ Tom looked yesterday.
⑧ _____ I visit my grandparents every month.

⑨ _____ They named the newborn baby.

⑩ _____ Jerry lives in the country.

【三】短句翻譯，並請細膩地分析句子結構。

① 我媽媽每天做早餐給我們吃。

例 <u>My mom</u>　<u>makes</u>　<u>us</u>　<u>breakfast</u>　<u>every day</u>.
　　主詞　　及物動詞　間接受詞　直接受詞　　時間副詞

② 他的爛成績讓他父母很生氣。

_____

③ 我發現 Jerry 是一個很有趣的人。

_____

④ John 每天打掃他的房間。

_____

⑤ 魚在河裡游。

_____

📖 EXERCISE 1 參考答案

【一】

① an English teacher

② English

③ healthy

④ red

⑤ anything（或 us any drinks 或 any drinks for us）

⑥ you some money（或 lend some money to you）

⑦ delicious

【二】

① O

② X　His shoes are really big.

③ X　This apple tastes great.

④ O

⑤ O

⑥ X　My parents sent me a postcard last week.

⑦ X　Tom looked sad yesterday.

⑧ O

⑨ X　They named the newborn baby Jane.

⑩ O

【三】

② His poor grades　made　his parents　mad.
　　　主詞　　　及物動詞　受詞　　受詞補語

③ I　　found　　Jerry　an interestingperson.
　主詞 及物動詞　受詞　　　受詞補語

④ John　　cleans　his bedroom　every day.
　主詞　　及物動詞　　受詞　　　時間副詞

⑤ Fish　　swim　　　　in the river.
　主詞 不及物動詞　介系詞片語，作地方副詞

★ Fish 本身單複數同形，當作魚的統稱。單數，只有一條魚則前面加 a。但當 fish 加上 es，則涵蓋各式
各樣的魚類。

UNIT
02

寫句子常見的錯誤

我們寫英文句子時，經常犯以下的錯誤。

📝 錯誤一：一個句子中有兩個動詞

☒ I *am like* English very much.
> ★ am、like 兩個都是動詞，不能同時出現，依照意思，應該把 am 拿掉。

☑ I like English very much. 我很喜歡英文。

☒ I like *swim*.
> ★ like、swim 同為動詞，不能同時出現，解決的辦法有兩種：一個是加上 to 隔 開；另 一個是把第二個動詞改為動名詞 V-ing 形式。大部分的動詞遇到下一個動詞都用 to V，少部分必須使用 V-ing，而 like 剛好兩者都可以。

☑ I like to swim.

☑ I like swimming. 我喜歡游泳。

📝 錯誤二：雙重否定

☒ I *didn't* eat *nothing*. （否＋否）
> ★ didn't、nothing 都是表達否定，兩者選一個就夠了。

☑ I didn't eat anything. （否＋正）

☑ I ate nothing. （正＋否）
我沒有吃任何東西。

☒ He has *barely no* money to live on. （否＋否）
> ★ barely（幾乎不）本身就具有否定意思，而 no（完全不）更是如此，二者只能取其一。

☑ He has barely enough money to live on.
他幾乎沒有錢可以過日子。

📝 錯誤三：主詞和動詞不一致

☒ She *like* dogs.
　★ 主詞是第三人稱單數，應該使用單數動詞。

☑ She likes dogs. 她喜歡狗。

☒ My brother *don't* smoke.

☑ My brother doesn't smoke. 我弟弟不抽菸。

☒ Hair *protect* our skin.
　★ 雖然毛髮數量很多，但整個毛髮多得數不清，所以 hair 在此是「不可數名詞」，應該被視為單數，必須使用「單數動詞」。

☑ Hair protects our skin. 毛髮保護我們的皮膚。

☒ Eating vegetables *are* good for your health.
　★ 雖然 vegetables 是複數，但其實真正的主詞是 eating vegetables（多吃蔬菜）這件事情。「一」件事情，自然要配合單數動詞。

☑ Eating vegetables is good for your health.
吃蔬菜有益身體健康。
　★ 以 to V 或 V-ing 開頭當主詞時，因為都是指一個動作，所以被視為單數。

To see is to believe. / Seeing is believing.
眼見為憑。

Teaching and learning are two different things. / To teach and to learn are two different things.
教與學是兩回事。

☒ One or two days *is* enough.

☑ One or two days are enough.
一兩天應該就夠了。
　★ 當句子主詞中有 or、nor 或 not only … but also，動詞要依「最靠近」的主詞作變化。這一句的動詞靠近 "two days"，所以該用複數動詞。

⊠ <u>Not only</u> you <u>but also</u> I *are* wrong.

☑ <u>Not only</u> you <u>but also</u> I am wrong.
不僅你還有我都錯了。

<u>Are you or</u> he Jerry?
你跟他誰是 Jerry ？
★ 問句中 Be 動詞倒裝到主詞前，變成比較靠近 you，所以應該用 are。

關於單複數的變化，還有更多例子：

① each, every, many a ... 接單數

主詞前面有 each、every、many a ... 這類單數形容詞時，後面只能接單數名詞，當然也只能搭配「單數動詞」。

Many a student has made the same mistake.
許多學生都犯了同樣的錯。

Every boy and girl enjoys the movie.
每個男孩和女孩都享受這部電影。

② both, several, many, a few, few, a large number of ... 接複數

主詞前面若有 both、several、many、a few、few、a large number of 這些複數形容詞，其後都得接複數的可數名詞，所以動詞一定得用「複數動詞」。

Both men are good at playing basketball.
兩個男人都很擅長打籃球。

Several books are now on sale.
幾本書現在正在特價。

Many people believe in God.
許多人相信上帝。
★ people 本身就是複數形，a person 才是「一個人」。

A large number of workers often work overtime.
很大量的勞工經常得加班。

③ **a lot of, plenty of, half (of), some (of), most (of), all (of)** 出現在主詞前，需視
主詞是否多數，決定動詞是單數或複數

    a lot of, plenty of, half (of), some (of), most (of), all (of) 等，因爲可修飾單數亦可
形容複數名詞，所以動詞得隨著它們所帶領的「主詞」是單數或複數而變化。

> Some rice grows in the Americas, but most of it grows in Asia.
> 有些美洲地區有產米，但大部分的稻米生長在亞洲。
> ★ rice 不可數，所以動詞用單數。
>
> Some of these students are good at playing basketball, but most of them
> aren't.
> 這些學生中有些很擅長打籃球，但大多數是不會的。
> ★ 學生為複數，所以動詞用複數。

📝 **錯誤四：用 There is、These are 或「地方」開頭時，單複數常被混淆**

> ☒ At the bottom of the stairs *are* standing *a girl*.（主詞與動詞不符）
> ☑ At the bottom of the stairs is standing a girl.（單數動詞搭配單數主詞）
> 在階梯底站著一個女孩。
> ★ 以 there、here 開頭的句子，或以地方開頭的「倒裝句」，真正主詞是在主要動詞之
> 後，因此動詞必須向右看齊。

> In the box are several books.（主詞與動詞相符）
> 盒子裡有幾本書。

    在結束這個單元之前，我們順便看一下基本而重要的簡單式和進行式的句子。

何時使用簡單式？

① **陳述一個真理或事實**

> The sun rises in the east.
> 太陽自東邊升起。
>
> My name is Avery.
> 我的名字是 Avery。

② 表示習慣

因為是「習慣」，所以常伴隨所謂的「頻率副詞」出現，例如：every day（每天）、always（總是）、often（經常）、usually（經常）、sometimes（有時候）等。

> I watch TV every day.　我每天看電視。
>
> She always eats breakfast before school.　上學前她總是會先吃早餐。

何時使用進行式 (Be + V-ing)？

① 特定時間點當下正在進行的動作

> 現在進行式 (is/am/are + V-ing)
>
> Sam is sleeping right now.
> 山姆現在正在睡覺。

> 未來進行式 (will be + V-ing)
>
> Sam will be sleeping when we arrive.
> 當我們抵達時，山姆將會在睡覺。

> 過去進行式 (was/were + V-ing)
>
> Sam was sleeping at 11:30 last night.
> 昨晚十一點半的時候，山姆正在睡覺。

② 習慣上，越來越多的英語人士喜歡用「現在進行式」，來表達「即將發生」的事情

> I'm leaving for Taipei tomorrow.
> 我明天「即將」出發前往台北。
>
> Christmas is coming.
> 聖誕節「即將」到來。

EXERCISE 2

【一】請將下列空格填入正確的動詞形式。

① He _____ (do) his homework now.

② My brother _____ (walk) to school everyday.

③ I always _____ (take) a shower before I go to bed.

④ Every dog _____ (have) its day.

⑤ There _____ (be) no money in my pocket.

⑥ Eating fruit _____ (make) you healthy.

⑦ To exercise every day _____ (help) you to stay slim.

⑧ Either you or I _____ (be) wrong.

⑨ Most of candy _____ (have) too much sugar.

⑩ A few students _____ (be) lazy.

【二】分析下列句子，在正確的句子前寫 ○，不正確的句子前寫 X，並將句子改正。

① _____ I'm wanting to buy a new shirt.

② _____ There is a lot of flowers under the tree.

③ _____ My brother is like swimming in summer.

④ _____ Jerry and I am good friends.

⑤ _____ Are you or he Kelly's brother?

⑥ _____ I'm going to Kaohsiung this afternoon.

⑦ _____ Reading books help you get smarter.

⑧ _____ The earth is round.

⑨ _____ Butter contains a lot of fat.

⑩ _____ My brother and his friends play basketball now.

【三】短句翻譯，並請細膩地分析句子結構。

① 我的爺爺奶奶明天要來拜訪我們。

_____

② 買一部新車是我的夢想。

_____

③ 在抽屜裡有一枝筆跟一本筆記本。

_____

④ 我朋友跟我正在玩牌。

_____

📖 EXERCISE 2 參考答案

【一】

① is doing

② walks

③ take

④ has（★這句照字面上是指，每隻狗都有自己走運的一天。所以此句諺語的意思是：「風水輪流轉」。）

⑤ is

⑥ makes

⑦ helps

⑧ am

⑨ has（★ candy 是不可數名詞，所以應該當作單數主詞來看。）

⑩ are

【二】

① X   I <u>want</u> to buy a new shirt.

　　　★ want 是描述想要的一種心態，沒有所謂「我正在想要」，所以使用簡單式。

② X   There <u>are</u> a lot of flowers under the tree.

③ X   My brother <u>likes</u> swimming in summer.

④ X   Jerry and I <u>are</u> good friends.

⑤ O   ★ 動詞靠近 you，所以用 are。

⑥ O   ★「即將」發生之事，可用現在進行式代替未來式。

⑦ X   Reading books <u>helps</u> you get smarter.

　　　★ 雖然 books 是複數，但主詞是 reading books 這件事情，應該作單數看。

⑧ O   ★「不變」的事實用簡單式。

⑨ O   ★「不變」的事實用簡單式。

⑩ X   My brother and his friends <u>are playing</u> basketball now.

【三】

① <u>My grandparents</u> <u>are visiting / will visit / are going to visit</u> <u>us</u> <u>tomorrow</u>.
       主詞   及物動詞   受詞 時間副詞

    ★ 如果使用進行式 (are visiting)，則有強調「很快就會」來看我們的意思。

② <u>Buying / To buy a new car</u> <u>is</u>   <u>my dream</u>.
         主詞   不及物動詞 主詞補語

    ★ 主詞可以用動名詞 (V-ing) 或不定詞 (to V)

③ (1) <u>In the drawer</u>   <u>lie</u>   <u>a pen and a notebook</u>.
       地方   不及物動詞   主詞

      ★ lie 意思是「平放著」。此句 lie 也可以改成 are。

    (2) <u>There</u> <u>are a pen and a notebook</u> <u>in the drawer</u>.
    地方副詞   主詞

④ <u>My friends and I</u>   <u>are</u>   <u>playing cards</u>.
      主詞   不及物動詞   主詞補語

    ★ play cards 意思就是「玩撲克牌」。

UNIT 03

用連接詞輕鬆地替句子瘦身

透過連接詞，可以把兩個句子合併，並且清楚地表示前後兩句的關係。也就是說，善用連接詞可以讓句子的意思更清楚活潑、加強句子之間的關聯性，在寫作時，文章自然更流暢。

連接詞分為「對等」和「不對等」

連接詞分成兩大類，一種為「對等連接詞」，它所連接的前後句子地位平等，例如：and、or、but、so、for 等。另一種不對等的，就叫做「從屬連接詞」，它所連接的句子一主一從，例如：after、before、when、since、because、although、though、even though 等。請看以下的例子。

對等連接詞

下列例子中，因為 and 是對等連接詞，它所連接的兩句地位平等，所以每一句都可以單獨成立。既然可以單獨成為一句，前後兩句如果用句號分開也算正確。

> My name is Avery, and her name is Phoenix.
> 我的名字是 Avery，而她的名字是 Phoenix。
> My name is Avery. And her name is Phoenix.

不對等連接詞

既然「不對等」，就必有輕重之分。下列例子中，不對等的「從屬連接詞」所連接的兩個句子，其關係就好像一個是主人，另一個是隨從。「主要子句」都可以單獨成立，但「從屬子句」卻無法獨立存在。我們以 because 連接的句子為例，其後所連接的句子就不可獨立存在。

☒ He went to bed early. *Because he was tired.*（從屬子句，不可單獨存在）

☑ He went to bed early because he was tired.

　　因為他累了，所以早早上床睡覺。

☑ <u>Because he was tired</u>, <u>he went to bed early</u>.

　　　從屬子句　　　　　　　　主要子句

Ch
1

認識了「對等」與「從屬」連接詞之後，現在讓我們進入連接詞的細節！

連接詞 and

① 表示「而、還」

Steve cleaned his bedroom, and he also helped his mother to do the laundry.

史提夫打掃了自己的房間，還幫他媽媽洗衣服。

My brother is taking a shower, and my sister is watching TV.

我哥哥正在洗澡，而我妹妹正在看電視。

② 表示「然後」

My mother washed the dishes, and I put them into the cupboard.

我媽媽把碗洗乾淨，然後我將它們放進碗櫥。

Jane moved to Taipei, and she has lived there ever since.

珍搬到台北，然後從此就住在那了。

連接詞 or

① 表示「或者」

You can pay cash, or you can use your credit card.

你可以付現金，或者你可以刷信用卡。

You may go shopping with us, or you may stay at home.

你可以跟我們一起去逛街，或者你也可以留在家。

② 表示「否則」

> Get up now, or you'll be late for school.
> 現在就起床,否則你上學就要遲到了。
>
> I must help him, or he will fail.
> 我應該幫忙他,否則他會失敗。

連接詞 nor

表達「既不……也不」

通常與 neither 搭配出現。Neither ... nor ... 因為是否定連接詞,所以連接句子時,助動詞、完成式必須與主詞倒裝。

> Neither does he know any Taiwanese, nor has he been to Taiwan.
> 他既不認識任何台灣人,也沒有去過台灣。

連接詞 but、yet

but 與 yet 同樣都表示「但是、卻、然而」

> He did not study, but he still got good grades.
> 他沒有念書,卻還是得到好成績。
>
> Amy wants to buy a doll, but she doesn't have enough money.
> 艾咪想要買一個洋娃娃,但是她沒有足夠的錢。
>
> Sally dreamed of winning the lottery, but she has never succeeded.
> 莎莉夢想可以中樂透,然而她從未成功。

yet 常用來表示「還(沒)」,既表示時間,就是副詞;但 yet 也可作連接詞,用法和意思與 but 相同,請看下面的例子。

> I haven't finished my homework yet. (時間副詞)
> 我還沒寫完我的功課。
>
> He did not study, yet he still got good grades. (連接詞)
> 他沒有念書,卻還是得到好成績。

連接詞 so

表示「所以」

> Jim got a cold, so he went to see the doctor yesterday.
> 吉姆感冒了，所以他昨天去看了醫生。
>
> Jamie didn't have breakfast this morning, so she feels hungry.
> 潔米今天早上沒有吃早餐，所以她感覺肚子很餓。

　　中文常說「因爲……所以」，但是英文的 because 與 so 都是連接詞，因此不能擺在同句中使用。請看以下的例子。

> ☒ *Because* Sam forgot his wallet, *so* he didn't have money to pay for his lunch.
> ☑ Because Sam forgot his wallet, he didn't have money to pay for his lunch.
> ☑ Sam forgot his wallet, so he didn't have money to pay for his lunch.
> 　　Sam 因為忘記帶他的錢包，所以沒有錢付午餐。

連接詞 for

　　大家都知道 for 可以當作介系詞，表示「爲了」、「給」；但是 for 作連接詞時，意思、用法卻與 because 相同。也就是說，句型爲「..., for ...」時，for 是連接詞，表示「因爲」。

① for 作連接詞，表示「因為」

> You'd better put on your jacket, for it's windy outside.
> 你最好穿上你的夾克，因為今天外面風很大。
>
> He didn't show up today, for he was sick.
> 他今天沒出現，因為他生病了。

② for 作介系詞，表示「為了、對……、給」

　　for 作介系詞時，後面必接一個「名詞」，作爲它的受詞。

> Mom bought several new T-shirts for me.（代「名詞」作受詞）
> 媽媽買了幾件新 T 恤給我。

Smoking is bad for <u>your health</u>. （名詞作受詞）
抽菸對你的健康有害。

I love you for <u>what you've done for me</u>. （「名詞」子句作受詞）
我愛你是為了你對我付出的一切。

Thank you for <u>loving me</u>. （動「名詞」作受詞）
謝謝你愛我。

My aunt paid $1,000 for <u>the pearl necklace</u>. （「名詞」片語作受詞）
我阿姨為了買這珍珠項鍊花了一千元。

★ 小叮嚀：還記得主詞和受詞都需要用「名詞」嗎？

連接詞 When 與 While

表示「當……的時候」

When I <u>was</u> a boy, I <u>liked</u> to go to the beach. （過去的狀態，所以用過去簡單式。）
當我還是一個小男孩的時候，我喜歡往海邊跑。

When I <u>entered</u> the room, my brother <u>was watching</u> TV. （過去簡單和過去進行）
當我踏進房間時，我弟弟正在看電視。

While I <u>was doing</u> my homework, my sister <u>was taking</u> a shower.
（兩個句子都是過去進行）
當我正在寫功課時，我姐姐正在洗澡。

I <u>felt bad</u> when you <u>were crying</u>. （過去簡單 + 過去進行）
當你不停哭泣的時候，我感覺很難過。

連接詞 since

① 表示「自從」

It <u>has been</u> 15 years since they <u>got</u> married.
從他們結婚到現在，已經 15 年了。

★「結婚」這個動作是 15 年前的「一個時間點」所做的，故用過去簡單式 got married
★ 結婚狀態已經持續 15 年，故用現在完成式 has been
★「結婚」永遠是被動語態，所以用 get married 或 be married
★「嫁」或「娶」則是主動語態，所以後面直接接受詞即可。例：He will marry Jane.

She <u>has learned</u> English for 10 years since she <u>was</u> seven.
從她七歲開始學英文，至今已經十年了。

★「七歲」為過去的一個時間點，故用過去式 was

★ 已經持續學英文 10 年，所以用完成式 has learned

完成式的概念圖：

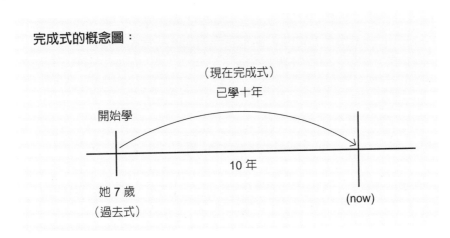

I haven't eaten anything since this morning.

從今天早上到現在，我都還沒吃任何東西。

★ this morning 是過去的一個時間點

★ 從早上到現在，所以用現在完成式 haven't eaten

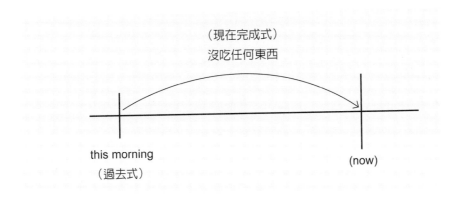

Mary has lived here since 2000.

從 2000 年開始，Mary 就住在這。

② 表示「因為、既然」

(陰影部分為主要子句，底線部分為從屬子句)

since 除了當作「自從」外，另還可以當作「因為、既然」的意思。用法和意思跟 because 相同：

Since you want to pass the exam, you have to study hard.
既然你想通過考試，當然得用功讀書。

Because Christmas is a holiday, we don't have to go to work.
= Since Christmas is a holiday, we don't have to go to work.
因為聖誕節是一個假日，我們不用上班。

連接詞 until (= till)

表示「直到」

I didn't cry until my parents gave me a hug.
我本來沒有哭，直到我父母給了我一個擁抱。

She was sleeping until somebody knocked on the door.
她本來在睡覺，直到有人敲門。

Mom didn't go to bed till I got home.
媽媽直到我回家才上床睡覺。

She didn't go to bed until 3 o'clock last night.（只有一個句子）
昨天直到清晨三點，她才上床睡覺。

連接詞 although (= though、even though)

表示「雖然、即使」，三者差別在於語氣強弱 even though > although > though

Although I like playing basketball, I'm not a good player.
雖然我喜歡打籃球，不過卻打得不是很好。

Even though she doesn't exercise a lot, she's in good shape.
即使她不常運動，卻仍然擁有苗條的身材。

Even though she has learned English for only six months, she speaks it very well.
即使只學了英文半年，但是她可以說得相當好。

中文常說「雖然……，但是……」，不過英文的 although 與 but 同樣屬於連接詞，不可用在同句中，請看下面例子。

☒ *Although* he's only 15, *but* he is now as tall as his father.
☑ Although he's only 15, he is now as tall as his father.

☑ He's only 15, but he is now as tall as his father.

雖然他現在只有 15 歲，但是已經跟他爸爸一樣高。

📑 連接詞的句子可以再簡化

我們開始練習替句子瘦身！當兩個句子的主詞相同時，帶有連接詞的那個句子可以簡化，來看下面幾種不同的例子：

「主動」的動詞，用現在分詞 (V-ing) 來簡化

When I opened the door, I saw a mouse running through the living room.

當我打開門時，我看見一隻老鼠跑過客廳。

= Opening the door, I saw a mouse running through the living room.

= When opening the door, I saw a mouse running through the living room.

（when 也可以保留）

When I was a student, I often stayed up.

當我還是學生時，我常熬夜。

= Being a student, I often stayed up.

= When being a student, I often stayed up. （when 也可以保留）

「被動」的動詞，用「過去分詞」來簡化

Because he was hit by a car, he stayed at the hospital for weeks.

因為被車撞，所以他住院好幾個星期。

= Hit by a car, he stayed at the hospital for weeks. （句首的 hit 是過去分詞）

完成式也可以簡化，不管是主動或被動，只要把 have / has / had 改成 having 即可。

Have / has / had + 過去分詞 ——(改成)—→ Having + 過去分詞

Since Peter had watched this movie before, he felt bored to watch it again.

→ Having watched this movie before, Peter felt bored to watch it again.

因為 Peter 之前已經看過這部電影，所以要他再看一次，他覺得相當無趣。

★ 注意：當句子因為簡化而使名字消失時，要把下一句中的代名詞改回人名。

否定句的簡化也非常容易，用 Not + V-ing 即可。

<u>Because John didn't want</u> to hurt her feelings, <u>he</u> didn't tell her the truth.

→ <u>Not wanting</u> to hurt her feelings, <u>John</u> didn't tell her the truth.（John 為主詞）
因為不想傷了她的心，約翰沒跟她說實話。

<u>Because I wasn't satisfied</u> with the grades, <u>I</u> made up my mind to study hard.

→ <u>Not being satisfied</u> with the grades, <u>I</u> made up my mind to study hard.
（I 為主詞）
我因為不滿意這次的成績，下定決心要認真念書。

※ 這種簡化不可以

再次提醒，句子簡化的條件，是必須「前後兩個主詞相同」。許多人經常一不小心，就會寫出下面的句子：

☒ After leaving the party, *Jack's car* wouldn't start.（Jack's car 為主詞）
　★ 因為縮減的句子必屬相同的主詞，所以這一句意思變成：Jack 的「車」離開 party，
　　意思不正確。所以這個句子不可以簡化，而是：

☑ After we left the party, Jack's car wouldn't start.（we 及 Jack's car 各為主詞）
當我們離開派對後，Jack 的車卻發不動了。

所以如果要重新簡化句子，我們必須讓兩個主詞相同。

第一步 先讓前後兩個主詞相同

After we left the party, we found that Jack's car wouldn't start.
當我們離開派對後，我們發現 Jack 的車發不動了。

第二步 主詞相同了才能簡化

After leaving the party, we found that Jack's car wouldn't start.

EXERCISE 3

【一】選擇正確的答案。

① (　) After _____ a shower, John went to bed.

    (A) she took　　(B) he take　　(C) taking　　(D) take

② (　) While everyone _____ the movie, someone's phone rang.

    (A) saw　　(B) was seeing　　(C) seeing　　(D) sees

③ (　) _____ Amy is 45, she looks young.

    (A) Since　　(B) Even though　　(C) Because　　(D) While

④ (　) Sam always drinks some water _____ he goes to bed.

    (A) after　　(B) since　　(C) though　　(D) before

⑤ (　) _____ I opened the box, I found several old books.（選出錯誤者）

    (A) When　　(B) After　　(C) Because　　(D) While

⑥ (　) She didn't put on her raincoat _____ it started to rain.

    (A) until　　(B) since　　(C) because　　(D) for

⑦ (　) _____ on the comfortable sofa, the little girl fell asleep.（選出錯誤者）

    (A) Sitting　　(B) She sat　　(C) Because sitting　　(D) After sitting

⑧ (　) John got wet on his way home _____ the heavy rain.

    (A) since　　(B) until　　(C) because of　　(D) and

⑨ (　) Steve _____ in Taipei since he was five.

    (A) lives　　(B) lived　　(C) living　　(D) has lived

⑩ (　) I _____ Mr. Jones while I was walking to school.

    (A) seeing　　(B) saw　　(C) was seeing　　(D) see

【二】請將下列各題中的兩句，用適當的連接詞合併。

① I can go swimming everyday.

    The weather is cold.

② My cell phone was broken.

I couldn't call you.

_____

③ I was listening to music.

My mother walked in my room.

_____

④ I brush my teeth.

I eat things.

_____

【三】將下列各題中帶有連接詞的句子簡化。（可視句意需要，決定是否留下連接詞）

① While Phoenix was walking home yesterday, she met her old friend, Avery.

_____

② Before I go to work, I always have a cup of tea.

_____

③ I have been living in this house for 10 years since I bought it.

_____

④ Because I've seen this movie before, I don't want to see it again.

_____

⑤ Because Jean was too poor to buy a new car, she had to borrow some money from the bank.

_____

【四】完成下列各句。

① Before going to ...

_____

② After having finished her ...

_____

③ Walking on the street,

_____

④ Not wanting to ...

_____

⑤ Being lost, ...

_____

📖 EXERCISE 3 參考答案

【一】

① C　★ 可直接用分詞（因為洗澡是主動的，所以用 V-ing）來簡化句子。如果不簡化，(A) 也不對，因為 John 是男生，所以不能用 she 代替。而 (B) 時態不正確。

② B　★ 過去進行式

③ B　★ 即使

④ D　★ 上床之前

⑤ D　★ While 習慣後面使用進行式，所以放入此句中不正確。

⑥ A

⑦ B　★ (B) 缺乏適當連接詞連接兩個句子。

⑧ C　★ heavy rain 是名詞，按照意思只有 because of 符合。

⑨ D　★ Since 表示「自從」時，代表經過了「一段時間」，應該使用「完成式」。

⑩ B　★ 瞬間動作，沒有「一直在……」的意味，應該用過去簡單式。

【二】

① I can go swimming everyday <u>even though</u> the weather is cold.

② (1) My cell phone was broken, <u>so</u> I couldn't call you.

(2) <u>Because</u> my cell phone was broken, I couldn't call you.

③ I was listening to music <u>when</u> my mom walked in my room.

  <u>While</u> I was listening to music, my mom walked in my room.

④ I brush my teeth <u>after</u> I eat things.

  ★ after 有三種詞類：

  副詞：I'll go after.

  介系詞：I'll call you after <u>dinner</u>.

  受詞

  連接詞：I'll call you after <u>I eat</u>.

  子句

【三】

① <u>While walking</u> home yesterday, Phoenix met her old friend, Avery.

② <u>Before going</u> to work, I always have a cup of tea.

③ <u>Since buying it</u>, I've been living in this house for 10 years.

④ <u>Having</u> seen this movie before, I don't want to see it again.

⑤ <u>Being</u> too poor to buy a new car, Jean had to borrow some money from the bank.

【四】

① Before going to work, I put on some makeup.

  ★ put on some makeup 意思是化妝。字面上的意思，是把化妝品穿上。

② After having finished her dinner, she did the dishes.

  ★ 洗碗的動詞可用 do 或 wash。

③ Walking on the street, she saw a car bump into a tree.

  ★ bump into 意思是撞上，也有突然碰見的意思。

④ Not wanting to fall asleep in class, I drank a cup of coffee before I came.

⑤ Being lost, she couldn't find her way home.

UNIT 04

把句子寫得更細膩
——善用關係子句

什麼是關係子句？

關係子句就是一個句子，它是一個「長的形容詞」，可用來修飾「人」或「東西」，使整個句子變得更精緻。試比較下面句子在加上關係子句之前與之後的差別。

沒有關係子句：

> Mr. Brown is talking to Avery's mom.
> 布朗先生正在跟 Avery 的媽媽說話。

有關係子句：

修飾

> Mr. Brown , who is our English teacher, is talking to Avery's mom.
> 布朗先生是我們的英文老師，他正在跟 Avery 的媽媽說話。

結論：

有關係子句的那個句子，把布朗先生描述地更清楚了：原來他是我們的英文老師。

一起來創造關係子句

在開始講解關係子句的用法之前，請先試著完成 Exercise 4-1 的練習，你將更清楚什麼是關係子句。

EXERCISE 4-1

【一】看完範例後，請你也練習用一個關係子句來形容下面題目每個「人」的職業。

例 A doctor is a person <u>who helps sick people.</u>
醫生是幫助病人的人。

① 醫生是幫助病人的人。

A barber is a person who

_____

② 司機是開車的人。

_____

③ 攝影師是拍照的人。

_____

【二】剛剛是形容「人」，現在我們試試看用關係子句來形容「物」。

例 **A fish is an animal <u>which</u> lives in water.**
魚是一種住在水裡的動物。

① 蜜蜂是一種會製造蜂蜜的昆蟲。

A bee is an insect which

_____

② 鳥是一種在天空飛的動物。

_____

③（請自己發揮）

_____

【三】下面有四個小朋友，每個人父母的職業都不一樣。我們先看例句，然後練習用關係子句來描述，「誰的」父親或母親的職業是什麼。

例 **Karen is the girl <u>whose</u> father is a fireman.**
凱倫就是那個爸爸是消防員的女孩。

① **Sam is the boy <u>whose</u>** _____.
山姆就是那個媽媽是女警的男孩。

② **Peter is** _____.
彼得就是那個媽媽是護士的男生。

③ **Cynthia is** _____.
辛西亞就是那個爸爸是飛行員的女生。

【一】

① A barber is a person who cuts hair.

② A driver is a person who drives a vehicle.

③ A photographer is a person who takes pictures.

【二】

① A bee is an insect which makes honey.

② A bird is an animal which flies in the sky.

③ A dog is an animal which is friendly to human beings.（狗是一種對人類友善的動物。）

【三】

① Sam is the boy whose mother is a policewoman.

② Peter is the boy whose mother is a nurse.

③ Cynthia is the girl whose father is a pilot.

Ch
1

📖 兩個囉嗦的簡單句，因關係子句而有新面貌

　　許多人在寫作時習慣用「簡單句」堆積成一篇文章，這樣的句子既冗長又無趣，而且無法清楚地表現前後兩個句子的關係，因而使句子與句子之間不順暢。我們先看較冗長的例句：

> **The man** is my father. **He** is sitting in the sofa.
> 這個<u>男人</u>是我的爸爸。<u>他</u>坐在沙發上。

　　關係代名詞這時就可以派上用場了。其實這兩個句子，只要透過關係代名詞 "who" 便可以把兩個句子結合，清楚顯示句子的重點：

　　　　　關係代名詞

> **The man who is sitting in the sofa is my father.**

　　　　　　　關係子句，修飾主詞 "man"

> 坐在沙發上的男人是我的爸爸。（「男人是我的爸爸」為主要子句）

　　我們在寫作文時，要把令人困惑無聊的兩個簡單句改寫成關係子句其實不難，只要幾個步驟，很快就可以活用關係子句。

第一步 找出在兩個簡單句中「相同」的人或物，這就是可以簡化之處。

第二步 判斷我們要修飾的是「人」還是「物」，並學會分辨主格、所有格、受格。

★ 修飾「人」或「東西」所需要配合的關係代名詞不一樣。我們前面已經練習過「主格」（「人」用 who、「物」用 which）、「所有格」（都用 whose）的句型，但是實際上還有「受格」的用法。先參考下面的表格：

	主格	所有格	受格
人	who	whose	whom
物	which	whose	which

第三步 把整個關係子句，緊連著第一句要修飾的對象（人或物）。

修飾「人」

（※ 以下範例陰影部分為主要子句，畫底線部分為關係子句）

例 1 我有一個朋友。她住在美國。

第一步 找出兩個簡單句中「相同」的人或物，此即可以簡化之處。

主要子句　　　　關係子句

I have a friend. She lives in America.

相同的人

第二步 從「關係子句」來判斷要修飾的是「人」還是「物」，並學會分辨主格、所有格、受格。

She lives in America.

★ She 是關係子句的主詞，所以應該用「人」的主格：who 來取代。

第三步 把整個關係子句緊連第一句要修飾的對象。

I have a friend. She lives in America.

→ I have a friend who lives in America.

緊連修飾對象

也就是：我有一個 住在美國的 朋友。

例 2 那個男孩正在哭。他的手斷了。

第一步 找出兩個簡單句中「相同」的人或物，此即可以簡化之處。

The boy is crying. His arm is broken.

相同的人，都和 the boy 有關

第二步 從「關係子句」來判斷要修飾的是「人」還是「物」，並學會分辨主格、所有格、受格。

His **arm is broken**.
★ His「他的」，應該用「所有格」：whose。

第三步 把整個關係子句緊連第一句要修飾的對象。

The boy **is crying.** His **arm is broken.**
→ The boy whose arm is broken is crying.
└──────→ 緊連修飾對象

也就是：那個 手骨折的 男孩正在哭泣。

例3 我遇到那個女生。你昨天談論到那個女生。

第一步 找出兩個簡單句中「相同」的人或物，此即可以簡化之處。

I met the girl. **You talked about** her **yesterday**.
└──────→ 相同的人 ←──────┘

第二步 從「關係子句」來判斷要修飾的是「人」還是「物」，並學會分辨主格、所有格、受格。

You talked about her **yesterday**.
★ her 是 talked about 的受詞，應該用「人的受格」：whom。

第三步 把整個關係子句緊連第一句要修飾的對象。

I met the girl. **You talked about** her **yesterday**.
→ I met the girl whom you talked about yesterday.
└──────→ 緊連修飾對象

或 **I met the girl** <u>about</u> **whom you talked yesterday**.

也可以把介系詞從後面搬到關係代名詞前

也就是：我遇見 你昨天談到的 那個女生。

★ 注意：口語中常用 who 來代替 whom，但此並非正規文法，寫作時宜避免。

　例如：I met the girl <u>who</u> you talked about yesterday.

　　　　　1. whom 才是最標準的文法
　　　　　2. 整個關係子句用來修飾 the girl（met 的受詞）

修飾「物」

剛剛舉的例子都是用來修飾「人」，現在我們來看修飾「物」的句子。其用法和步驟完全一樣：

例1 就是這本書。它花了我不少錢。

第一步 找出兩個簡單句中「相同」的人或物，此即可以簡化之處。

　　　　主要子句　　　　關係子句

This is the book. <u>It cost me a lot.</u>

　　　　相同的物

第二步 從「關係子句」來判斷要修飾的是「人」還是「物」，並學會分辨主格、所有格、受格。

It cost me a lot.
★ It 是 cost 的主詞，應該用「物的主格」：which

第三步 把整個關係子句緊連第一句要修飾的對象。

This is the book. <u>It cost me a lot.</u>
→ **This is** the book which cost me a lot.

緊連修飾對象

也就是：就是這本書 花了我不少錢。

例 2 這筆記本是我的。它的封面是紅色的。

第一步 找出兩個簡單句中「相同」的人或物,此即可以簡化之處。

The notebook is mine. Its cover is red.

相同的物

第二步 從「關係子句」來判斷要修飾的是「人」還是「物」,並學會分辨主格、所
有格、受格。

Its cover is red.

★ Its 是「它的」,應該用「物的所有格」: whose

第三步 把整個關係子句緊連第一句要修飾的對象。

The notebook is mine. Its cover is red.
→ The notebook whose cover is red is mine.

緊連修飾對象

也就是:<u>封面紅色的</u> 筆記本是我的。

例 3 這台車子價值不斐。我把它停在我房子的前方。

第一步 找出兩個簡單句中「相同」的人或物,此即可以簡化之處。

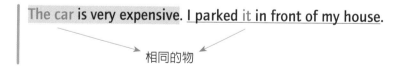

The car is very expensive. I parked it in front of my house.

相同的物

第二步 從「關係子句」來判斷要修飾的是「人」還是「物」,並學會分辨主格、所
有格、受格。

I parked it in front of my house.

★ it 是 park 的受詞,應該用「物的受格」: which

第三步 把整個關係子句緊連第一句要修飾的對象。

The car is very expensive. I parked it in front of my house.

→ The car which I parked in front of my house is very expensive.

緊連修飾對象

也就是：停在我房子前面的 車子價值不斐。

關係代名詞用 that，更簡單

想要更簡單？當我們強調語氣時，無論是人或事物的主格和受格，都可以用 that 作為關係代名詞。

I have many friends who live in America.

→ who 可以改為 that（受格）

I met the beautiful girl whom you talked about yesterday.

→ whom 可以改為 that（受格）

This is the book which cost me a lot.

→ which 可以改為 that（主格）

The car which I park in front of my house is very expensive.

→ which 可以改為 that（受格）

當要修飾的對象是「人 + 物」的時候，因為關係代名詞不論用 who 或 which 都不對，所以當然只能用 that。

The car ran into a boy and his dog that were just crossing the street.
當小男孩和他的狗正在穿越馬路時，一部車撞上他們倆。

The man and his bike that fell into the river were missing.
那個人和他的車掉進河裡後，就不見蹤影。

使用 that 的禁忌

注意，雖然「受格」關係代名詞可以用 that 代替，不過前面卻不可以有介系詞喔！請看下面例子。

I met the girl that you talked <u>about</u> yesterday.

= ☑ I met the girl <u>about</u> whom you talked yesterday.

（介系詞可以移到 whom 前面）

≠ ☒ I met the girl *about that* you talked yesterday.

📑 關係子句讓句子更輕盈

所有代替「受格」的關係代名詞，在句子中都可以省略掉！

（陰影部分為主要子句，<u>畫底線部分</u>為關係子句。）

The car <u>(which) I parked in front of my house</u> is very expensive.

↑

作 park 的「受詞」，所以可以省略

= The car I parked in front of my house is very expensive.

我停在房子前的車非常昂貴。

The book <u>(that) I read last night</u> wasn't interesting.

↑

作 read 的「受詞」，所以可以省略

= The book I read last night wasn't interesting.

我昨晚讀的那本書，不怎麼有趣。

I met the girl <u>(whom) you talked about yesterday</u>.

↑

作介系詞 about 的「受詞」，所以可以省略

= I met the girl you talked about yesterday.

我遇到你昨天說的那個女生。

The young lady <u>(that) I saw</u> was Phoenix.

↑

作 saw 的「受詞」，所以可以省略

= The young lady I saw was Phoenix.

我之前看到的那個年輕女生是 Phoenix。

「關係代名詞 + be 動詞」也可以一起省略！

> **The student (who is) talking to Dr. Kuo is from Japan.**
>
> = The student talking to Dr. Kuo is from Japan.
>
> 正在跟郭教授講話的學生來自日本。

> **The books (that are) in the box are Amy's.**
>
> = The books in the box are Amy's.
>
> 那些箱子裡的書，都是 Amy 的。

> **The children (who are) eating ice cream seem happy.**
>
> = The children eating ice cream seem happy.
>
> 吃著冰淇淋的孩子們，看起來很開心。

> **The boy (who was) hit by a car has stayed in the hospital for several days.**
>
> = The boy hit by a car has stayed in the hospital for several days.
>
> 被車撞傷的小男孩，住院好幾天。

「關係代名詞 + 動詞」可以簡化成只留下動詞的「V-ing」

> **Anyone who wants to join us is welcome.**
>
> = Anyone wanting to join us is welcome.
>
> 我們歡迎任何想要加入我們的人。

> **Everyone who saw him leave was sad.**
>
> = Everyone seeing him leave was sad.
>
> 每一個看到他離開的人都很難過。

> **I like apartments which have a great view.**
>
> = I like apartments having a great view.
>
> 我喜歡有美景的公寓。

where 和 when 是句子的瘦身利器

關係代名詞 (who, whom, which, that) 代替的是一個「名詞」，where 既然表示地方，就應該是副詞，所以它可以在句子中作爲關係副詞。而 when 既然表示時間，也就是副詞，所以它在句子中也作關係副詞用。例如：

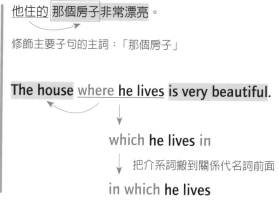

EXERCISE 4-2

請用關係子句，譯出下列句子。

例 工廠是一個 工人生產貨品的 所在地。

我們先找出主要句：

A factory is a place where workers make goods.

> ★ 形容詞子句，形容 "a place"。
> ★ 表示「地方」，用關係副詞 where 一字，即可連接前後兩句。

表示地方，where 也可以還原成 which 跟介系詞。
（「在」工廠是 at，所以把 where 改成 which ... at）

→ A factory is a place which workers make goods at.

也可以把介系詞搬到關係代名詞前，也就是把 which ... at
改為 at which ...

→ A factory is a place at which workers make goods.

現在請自己動筆寫寫看：

① 城市是 大多數人居住的 一個地方。

A city is a place where most people live.

> ★ 形容詞子句，形容 "a place"。
> ★ 表示「地方」，用關係副詞 where 一字，即可連接前後兩句。

= _____.

（表示地方，where 也可以還原成 which 跟介系詞。「在」城市用 in。）

= _____.

（介系詞也可以搬到關係代名詞前面。）

② 農場是 農作物生長的 一個地方。

A farm is a place _____.

= _____.

（表示地方，where 也可以還原成 which 跟介系詞。）

= _____.

（表示地方，where 也可以還原成 which 跟介系詞。）

在做第三題之前，我們先了解以下的用法。假如：

Avery's birthday	1983/07/10
Phoenix's birthday	1984/09/12
Ivan's birthday	1985/09/15

例 1983 年 7 月 10 號是 Avery 誕生 的日子。

July 10, 1983 is the day when Avery was born.

> ★ 形容詞子句，形容時間 "the day"。
> ★ 因為表示「時間」，所以用 when 連接前後兩句。

表示時間，when 也可以還原成 which + 介系詞。

→ July 10, 1983 is the day which Avery was born on.

介系詞也可以搬到關係代名詞前面

→ July 10, 1983 is the day on which Avery was born.

---

③ 1984 年 9 月 12 日是 Phoenix 出生 的日子。

Sept. 12, 1984 is the day when Phoenix was born.

> ★ 形容詞子句，形容時間。
> ★ 表示「時間」，用關係副詞 when 一字即可連接前後兩句。

Sept. 12, 1984 is the day _____.

= _____.
（表示時間 when 也可以還原成 which 跟介系詞。）

= _____.
（介系詞也可以搬到關係代名詞前面。）

④ 1985 年 9 月 15 日是 <u>Ivan 誕生</u> 的日子。

Sept. 15, 1985 is the day _____.

= _____.

（表示時間 when 也可以還原成 which 跟介系詞。）

= _____.

（介系詞也可以搬到關係代名詞前面。）

📖 EXERCISE 4-2 參考答案

① A city is a place which most people live in.

A city is a place in which most people live.

② A farm is a place where crops grow.

A farm is a place which crops grow in.

A farm is a place in which crops grow.

③ Sept. 12, 1984 is the day which Phoenix was born on.

Sept. 12, 1984 is the day on which Phoenix was born.

④ Sept. 15, 1985 is the day when Ivan was born.

Sept. 15, 1985 is the day which Ivan was born on.

Sept. 15, 1985 is the day on which Ivan was born.

關係子句有「限定用法」與「非限定用法」

　　限定和非限定用法其實很簡單，它們的差別就在於，非限定用法在關係子句前後有逗點，而限定用法並沒有。

　　口訣：非限定用法的關係子句，用「逗點隔開」。
　　　　　整個子句等於補充，拿掉不影響句意。

我們看下面的例子：

非限定用法：**Mr. Lee, whom I met yesterday, teaches Chemistry.**
　　　　　　　李先生他是教化學的，我昨天碰巧遇見他。

　　我只認識一個 Mr. Lee，不管昨天有沒有被我遇到，李先生就是教化學。關係子句只是補充說明「我昨天見到他」，即使沒有這個關係子句，語意也很清楚。既沒限定，就要用逗點隔開。

限定用法：**The professor <u>whom I met</u> teaches Chemistry.**
　　　　　 我遇到的那個教授是教化學的。

　　限定用法就是指，修飾對象數量眾多，必須透過這個關係子句來限定出在討論的為何者。以這句為例，世界上教授很多，不是任何一個教授都教化學，而是限定「我所遇到的」那一位教授，才是教化學的，所以不需要逗號。比較下面的句子：

> **The teacher took some students to the library. The students <u>who felt bored</u> fell asleep.**
> 老師帶了一些學生去圖書館。只有覺得無聊的學生才睡著了。
> ★ 有「限定」覺得無聊的學生，所以關係子句前後不用逗點。

> **The teacher took some students to the library. The students, <u>who felt bored</u>, fell asleep.**
> 老師帶了一些學生去圖書館。全部的學生因為覺得無聊都睡著了。
> ★ "who felt bored" 只是補充說明學生的狀況，既是「非限定」所以用逗點。
> ★ 主要句是 The students fell asleep。

EXERCISE 4-3

【一】請用關係子句完成下列句子。

① I'll always remember the person _____.

② Ask Amy. She is the one _____.

③ I put the books _____ on the table.

④ I like flowers _____.

⑤ I'll never forget the day _____.

⑥ Winter is the time of the year _____.

⑦ I know a man _____.

⑧ The car _____ is very expensive.

⑨ In our country, there are many people _____.

⑩ Dr. Kuo is the professor _____.

【二】請運用關係子句合併改寫，簡化以下的句子。

① The jacket is new. He is wearing it.

_____

② The woman called the police for help. Her child was missing.

_____

③ The city is crowded. I grew up in the city.

_____

④ I saw the man. He stole Jane's bike.

_____

⑤ The man was friendly. Tom chatted with him yesterday.

_____

⑥ 10:15 is the time. The movie starts at that time.

_____

【三】請簡化下列各句中的關係子句。

① The girl who is sitting next to me is Amanda.

_____

② The students who studied hard got good grades.

_____

③ There is a man who wants to talk to you.

_____

④ I sold everything which was in my old house.

_____

⑤ That is the dog that bit me on my leg last night.

_____

📖 **EXERCISE 4-3 參考答案**

※ 畫底線的部分為關係子句

【一】

① I'll always remember the person <u>who once helped me</u>.

② She is the one <u>who knows the answer</u>.

③ I put the books <u>that I bought yesterday</u> on the table.

   = I put the books <u>which I bought yesterday</u> on the table.

   = I put the books <u>I bought yesterday</u> on the table.（因為關係代名詞是受格，所以可以省略）

④ I like flowers <u>whose color is red</u>.

⑤ I'll never forget the day <u>when I first met you</u>.

   = I'll never forget the day <u>which I first met you on</u>.（在「哪一天」用 on）

   = I'll never forget the day <u>on which I first met you</u>.

⑥ Winter is the time of the year <u>when the weather is the coldest</u>.

⑦ I know a man <u>who never eats noodles</u>.

⑧ The car <u>which he drives</u> is very expensive.

⑨ In our country, there are many people <u>who ride bikes to work</u>.

⑩ Dr. Kuo is the professor <u>whose course I'm taking this semester</u>.（course 是「課程」，而 semester 是「學期」）

【二】

① The jacket <u>which he is wearing</u> is new.

② The woman <u>whose child was missing</u> called the police for help.

③ The city <u>where I grew up</u> is crowded.

   = The city <u>which I grew up in</u> is crowded.

   = The city <u>in which I grew up</u> is crowded.

④ I saw the man <u>who stole Jane's bike</u>.

⑤ The man <u>whom Tom chatted with yesterday</u> was friendly.

   The man <u>with whom Tom chatted yesterday</u> was friendly.

⑥ 10:15 is the time <u>when the movie starts</u>.

   = 10:15 is the time <u>which the movie starts at</u>.

   = 10:15 is the time <u>at which the movie starts</u>.

【三】

① The girl ~~who is~~ <u>sitting</u> next to me is Amanda.（關係代名詞 + be，可以刪掉）

② The students <u>studying</u> hard got good grades.（主動的用 V-ing 一個字就夠了，所以 studying 一字即可）

③ There is a man <u>wanting</u> to talk to you.（主動的用 V-ing，wanting 一字即可）

④ I sold everything ~~which was~~ in my old house.（關係代名詞 + be，可以刪掉）

⑤ That is the dog <u>biting</u> me on my leg last night.（主動的用 V-ing，biting 一字即可）

把句子寫得更細膩
——創造名詞子句

　　名詞子句其實就是一個「長的名詞」，讓我們可以把「一個完整的句子」轉變成一個名詞，使原來兩個「簡單句」因爲其中一句話已經變成一個名詞，所以兩個簡單句變成一個簡單句，而且意思更清楚。我們現在先看名詞子句多有用。

📄 將兩個簡單句變成一個名詞子句，意思更清楚

前面加一個 that，就成了名詞子句。

原來的句子：

The earth is round. It is a fact.
地球是圓的。這件事是一個事實。

★ It 其實指的就是前面「地球是圓的」這件事情，不要再重複，應該把 it 跟前句合併，如下：

→ <u>That</u> <u>the earth is round</u> is a fact.

　　　　　　名詞子句當主詞

He is a good student. We believe it.

→ We believe <u>that</u> he is a good student.
　我們相信他是一個好學生。

　　　　　　　　名詞子句當 believe 的受詞

Students should study hard. **It** is important.

→ <u>That</u> <u>students should study hard</u> is important.
　學生努力用功是很重要的。

　　　　　　　名詞子句當作主詞

已有疑問詞就不用 that

原來的句子：

<u>What did the teacher say?</u> I don't know <u>it</u>.

老師說什麼呢？我不知道。

★ it 指「老師說了什麼」這件事情，所以同樣可以把它和前一句合併。

→ I don't know <u>what</u> the teacher said.

名詞子句當 know 的受詞

📖 活用虛主詞 it

另外，如果要強調語氣時，前面的英文句子也可以改寫成：it is ... + that 子句，這就是所謂的「虛主詞」的句型。

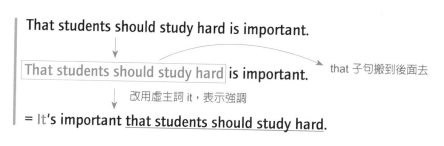

That students should study hard is important.

That students should study hard is important. → that 子句搬到後面去

改用虛主詞 it，表示強調

= It's important <u>that students should study hard</u>.

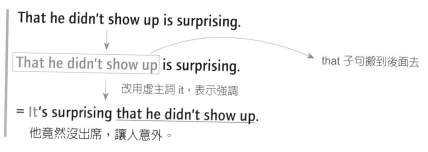

That he didn't show up is surprising.

That he didn't show up is surprising. → that 子句搬到後面去

改用虛主詞 it，表示強調

= It's surprising <u>that he didn't show up</u>.

他竟然沒出席，讓人意外。

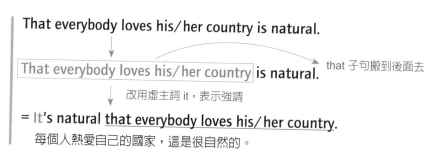

That everybody loves his/her country is natural.

That everybody loves his/her country is natural. → that 子句搬到後面去

改用虛主詞 it，表示強調

= It's natural <u>that everybody loves his/her country</u>.

每個人熱愛自己的國家，這是很自然的。

EXERCISE 5-1

模仿下面的例句，完成虛主詞和 **that** 子句互映的練習。

> 例 It is a fact that living creatures cannot live without water.
>
> = That living creatures cannot live without water is a fact.
>
> 生物沒有水無法存活是一項事實。

① It's true that smoking is bad for one's health.

= That _____

② _____

= That he had a car accident is too bad.

③ It's surprising that _____

= That _____

④ It's strange that _____

= That _____

EXERCISE 5-1 參考答案

① That smoking is bad for one's health is true.
② It's too bad that he had a car accident.
③ It's surprising that he is the murderer.
   = That he is the murderer is surprising.
④ It's strange that he didn't tell you the truth.
   That he didn't tell you the truth is strange.

📄✎ 把問句變成名詞子句，使句子更精鍊

　　問句分成兩種：一種是「疑問詞問句」（含有疑問詞 why, who, how, what, when, where ...），而另一種則是 Yes-No 的「是非問句」，它不含疑問詞。請看以下這兩種問句：

疑問詞問句：

| **What's your name?** ⟶ **My name is Jane.**（回覆「什麼」）
| 你叫什麼名字？　　　　 我叫做 Jane。
| **Where do you live?** ⟶ **I live in Taipei.**（回覆「哪裡」）
| 你住在哪裡？　　　　　 我住在台北。

是非問句：

| **Are you a student?** ⟶ **Yes, I am.**（回覆「是否」）
| 你是一個學生嗎？　　　 是的，我是。
| **Do you like cats?** ⟶ **No, I don't.**（回覆「是否」）
| 你喜歡貓咪嗎？　　　　 不，我不喜歡。

　　不論是疑問詞問句或是是非問句，這兩種問句都可以變成「名詞子句」，成爲一個句子的一部分。

📄✎ 疑問詞問句

　　只要把主詞和動詞改成直述句的順序，就變成「名詞子句」。

疑問詞問句 ↓	What ~~did~~ she say? ↓
主詞和動詞順序調整成直述句，成爲名詞子句，（同時別忘了修改動詞時態）：↓	what she said ↓
修改爲名詞子句之後，可以成爲句子的一部分	I don't know <u>what she said</u>. 我不知道她說了什麼。

★ 由疑問句改成的名詞子句，也叫做「間接問句」。

★ 真正的疑問句則是「直接問句」。

問句：Where ~~does~~ she live?

↓

名詞子句：where she lives（動詞變回現在簡單式）

↓

例句：I don't know <u>where she lives</u>.
　　　我不知道她住在哪裡。

問句：Who is he?

↓

名詞子句：who he is

↓

例句：I don't know <u>who he is</u>.
　　　我不知道他是誰。

問句：Where will he go?

↓

名詞子句：where he will go

↓

例句：I don't know <u>where he will go</u>.
　　　我不知道他將要去哪兒。

問句：Why didn't you see him?

↓

名詞子句：why you didn't see him

↓

例句：Can you tell me <u>why you didn't see him</u>?
　　　你可以跟我說你為什麼沒看到他嗎？

問句：What has he done?

↓

名詞子句：what he has done

↓

例句：I don't know <u>what he has done</u>.
　　　我不知道他做了什麼。

疑問詞當作主詞時，本身就可以成為名詞子句。

如果疑問句沒有主詞，而直接用疑問詞來當主詞，則它本身就可以當成名詞子句。

問句：What happened to him?（what 為主詞）
↓
名詞子句例句：I don't know <u>what happened to him</u>.
我不知道他發生了什麼事情。

問句：Who killed the cat?（who 為主詞）
↓
名詞子句例句：Can you tell me <u>who killed the cat</u>?
你可以跟我說是誰殺了這隻貓嗎？

是非問句也可成為名詞子句

是非問句轉變成名詞子句，需要以下步驟：

是非問句 ↓	Is she Mary? ↓
把主詞和動詞順序調整，成為直述句：↓	She is Mary. ↓
前面加上 whether 或是 if：	I don't know <u>whether</u> she is Mary.

問句：Can she speak English?
↓
直述句：She can speak English.
↓
前面加上 if：I don't know <u>if she can speak English</u>.
我不知道她是否會說英文。

問句：<u>Have</u> you seen this movie before?

直述句：You have **seen the movie before.**

前面加上 whether：**Can you tell me <u>whether you have seen this movie before</u>?**
你可以告訴我，你之前有看過這部電影嗎？

★ 補充：whether ... 或是 if ... 這樣的句型，句尾也可以加上 "or not"，以強調語氣。

- I don't know <u>whether</u> she is Mary <u>or not</u>.
- I don't know <u>if</u> she can speak English <u>or not</u>.
- Can you tell me <u>whether</u> you have seen this movie before <u>or not</u>?

Ch
1

EXERCISE 5-2

請練習把疑問句改成名詞子句。

① How old are you?

Can you tell me _how old you are?_

② Whose book is this?

I don't know _____

③ What did he buy?

Do you know _____

④ Who is coming?

Ask him _____

⑤ Where will she go?

Please tell me _____

⑥ How does he go to school?

I don't know _____

⑦ Is there anybody in the classroom?

Can you tell me _____

⑧ Did he show up?

I don't know _____

⑨ Has he finished his homework?

Ask him _____

② I don't know whose book this is.

③ Do you know what he bought?

④ Ask him who is coming.

⑤ Please tell me where she will go.

⑥ I don't know how he goes to school.

⑦ Can you tell me whether there is anybody in the classroom?

⑧ I don't know if he showed up or not.

⑨ Ask him whether he has finished his homework or not.

📄 「疑問詞 + to V」也是名詞

疑問詞（when, where, who, what, which, how, whether, whose, whom）後面可以加上 to，再加上動詞，一樣變成名詞。

I don't know <u>what</u> I should do.

↓

= I don't know <u>what</u> to do.
我不知道該怎麼做。

Can you tell me <u>how</u> I can get to the nearest bus stop?

↓

= Can you tell me <u>how</u> to get to the nearest bus stop?
你能不能告訴我如何到最近的車站？

My parents can't decide <u>what</u> they should buy.

↓

= My parents can't decide <u>what</u> to buy.
我的父母沒辦法決定該買什麼。

📄 名詞子句就是名詞

既然名詞子句是一個「長的名詞」，用法和位置就完全如同名詞，它們在句子中，都可以扮演「主詞」、「受詞」、「補語」、「同位語」。

① 當作主詞

<u>Where he is hiding the money</u> is still unknown.
錢被他藏去哪仍是一個謎。

<u>That the sun rises in the east</u> is a truth.
太陽打東邊升起是一項定律。

② 當作受詞

I don't know <u>whether they will show up</u>.（當 know 的受詞）

我不知道他們會不會出現。

Please tell me <u>where you found it</u>.

（名詞子句當 tell 的直接受詞，tell 的間接受詞是 me）

請告訴我你在哪找到這東西。

③ 當作補語

The problem is <u>how we can find the money</u>.（主詞補語）

問題是我們該如何找到資金。

The question is <u>why he didn't call you</u>.（主詞補語）

問題是他為什麼沒打給你。

④ 當作同位語

No one wants to face the fact that he is dead.

沒人想要面對他已經過世的事實。

The reason why he suddenly left is unknown.

沒人知道他為何突然離開的原因。

★ 關於「同位語」

所謂同位語，就是兩個人或物，在整個句子中，詞性相同，意義也一樣。

我們看下面例子：

Mr. Smith , our new teacher , is very kind to us.

我們的新老師史密斯先生對我們很好。

our new teacher 和 Mr. Smith 都是名詞／指同一人，所以是同位語。

📝 to V 和 V-ing 也可以作名詞

其實「不定詞」(to V) 和「動名詞」(V-ing) 同樣都具有名詞的功能，因此都可以在句子中當作「主詞」、「受詞」、「補語」。

① 當作主詞

To see is to believe.（To see 作主詞，to believe 作補語）

= **Seeing** is believing.
　眼見為憑。

Eating vegetables and fruits is important.

= **To eat vegetables and fruits** is important.
　多吃蔬菜水果很重要。

② 當作受詞

I want <u>a dog</u>.
　　　↑ 一般名詞作 want 的受詞

I want <u>to buy a dog</u>.
　　　　↑ to V 作 want 的受詞

I like <u>swimming</u>.
　　　↑ V-ing 作 like 的受詞

= I like <u>to swim</u>.
　我喜歡游泳。

③ 當作補語

　　　　　　　　主詞　　　　　　　　　主詞補語

The most important thing for students is <u>to study hard</u>.
對學生最重要的事情就是努力念書。

　　受詞　　受詞補語

Tell him to work harder.
告訴他努力點。

EXERCISE 5-3

【一】 **1.** 按照括號中的提示，選擇一個正確的疑問詞。

2. 先造出疑問句，再把疑問句改寫成名詞子句，作為句子的一部分，並運用想像力寫出一個句子。

例 Sam will go (home).

　　疑問句：<u>Where</u> will Sam go?

　　名詞子句：Please tell me <u>where Sam will go</u>.

① Tom bought (a book).

　　疑問句：_____

　　Do you know _____

② John is (my brother).

　　疑問句：_____

　　Can you tell me _____

③ He left (last night).

　　疑問句：_____

　　I don't know _____

④ His name is (Avery).

　　疑問句：_____

　　Please tell me _____

【二】請活用名詞子句，將下列中文翻譯成英文。

① 我不知道 Tom 是不是生病了。

_____

② 請你告訴我 Mr. Smith 在哪。

_____

③ 你可以告訴我你的電話幾號嗎？

_____

④ 我們不知道怎麼到最近的超市。

_____

⑤ 我相信 Amy 會贏。

_____

⑥ 我認為 Judy 是一個聰明的人。

_____

⑦ 學英文很有趣。

_____

【三】把下面句子錯誤的地方圈起來，並改正。

① Please tell me how old are you.

_____

② I don't know why he not come.

_____

③ I don't know is he a teacher or not.

_____

④ I want to know who is your brother.

_____

⑤ Can you tell me which one do you like.

_____

⑥ Why is he so happy is unknown.

_____

⑦ Can you tell us where find it?

_____

⑧ I don't know why is the computer not working.

_____

📖 EXERCISE 5-3 參考答案

【一】

① What did Tom buy?

Do you know what Tom bought?

② Who is John?

Can you tell me who John is?

③ When did he leave?

I don't know when he left.

④ What is his name?

Please tell me what his name is.

【二】

① I don't know whether Tom is sick or not.

② Please tell me where Mr. Smith is.

③ Can you tell me what your telephone number is?

④ We don't know how to get to the nearest supermarket.

⑤ I believe that Amy will win.

⑥ I think that Judy is a smart person.

⑦ Learning English is fun.

【三】

① Please tell me how old are you.
   → Please tell me how old **you are**.
② I don't know why he not come.
   → I don't know why he **didn't come**.
③ I don't know is he a teacher or not.
   → I don't know **if** he is a teacher **or not**.
④ I want to know who is your brother.
   → I want to know **who your brother is**.
⑤ Can you tell me which one do you like.
   → Can you tell me **which one you like**.
⑥ Why is he so happy is unknown.
   → **Why he is so happy** is unknown.
⑦ Can you tell us where ___ find it?
   → Can you tell us **where to find it**?
⑧ I don't know why is the computer not working.
   → I don't know **why the computer isn't working**.

Chapter 2

寫出好文章

UNIT 06 英文作文有一定的結構

　　英文寫作和中文寫作最大的不同之處在於，中文作文可以奔放，比較不受文章結構的約束，而一篇好的英文作文則必然有嚴謹並具邏輯性的文章結構。一篇英文作文，是由幾個段落依固定的架構完成，而每一個段落的架構，又像是一篇文章架構的縮影。（當然，某些極短篇的文章或是初中級全民英檢的作文測驗，有時候甚至不用分段，整個短文就只是一個段落。）所以我們第一步要先學會寫出一個好的段落，然後再學習好好地運用邏輯性，這樣自然而然就能輕鬆學會如何寫出整篇好文章。

一個段落的結構分成三部分

主題句：一個段落，或是一個不分段的短篇文章，都應該有一句「主題句」來說明段落內容的主旨。主題句常放在文章的第一句，表明作者對於題目的立場，不過有時候，在主題句的前面也可以加上若干文字，目的在於吸引人進入文章主題，這些文字就被稱為「引言」。

支持句：主題句之後有許多的「支持句」，用來強化主題句。支持句在於將主題句中所提的重點，做進一步的演繹。例如，除了可以闡述主題句的理由或細節，也可以用資料、數據以及例子來支持主題句的看法（這種資訊在進階英文作文中，尤其珍貴）。

結論句：最後得為文章下結論。結論可以總結全文、提出建議、或是提出挑戰。只要是有意義、有思想的皆可，但不宜冗長，宜精簡有力。

主題句		支持句		結論句
（段落主旨）	+	（包含理由、解釋、細節、例子、數據資料）	+	（總結、建議、提出解決方法） ★ 結論須呼應主題句，否則就離題了。

我們先試著看一篇短文，題目是「我最喜愛的書」"My Favorite Book"。

（引言 ▶）Have you ever imagined being able to fly in the sky? If you never have and you'd like to have a try, with *Harry Potter* in your hands, you have a chance to get rid of the real world, and dream of doing magic. Reading the novel makes you feel you are one of the characters in the story. You are able to do things that you can't in everyday life like making the dishes do themselves and flying in the sky without taking a plane. If you have a bad day, throwing yourself into the world of *Harry Potter* will make you feel much better, because everything is possible there and you even get to undo the things you did wrong in the real world! *Harry Potter* allows you to forget who you are and get rid of the troubles in your life, and once you open it, it's impossible to put down.

（主題句 / 支持句 / 結論句）

利用這篇短文讓我們回顧一下段落的結構：

引　言：先搭一座橋，讓人進入主題句。透過讀者的想像，引起他們對這篇文章的好奇心。

主題句：點出最喜歡的書是《哈利波特》（回應題目），並且明白地說明這篇文章的主題就是：這本小說可以讓你暫時忘掉現實，想像你擁有魔法。

支持句：「進一步」解釋，例如，讀這個小說可以讓你感覺身歷其境，並提供一些書中的細節來支持主題，包含碗筷可以自動清洗……等。

結論句：總結我為什麼喜歡這本小說？因為在魔法世界，任何不可能之事都化為可能，讓我忘掉煩惱。

引言　→　主題句　→　支持句　→　結論句

這樣就譜成了一個完整的邏輯，文章怎麼會不順暢？

EXERCISE 6-1

閱讀下面的各段落後，試著分析看看哪一句是主題句表明主旨，哪些是支持句，哪一句是結論。

① Talking to a stranger is the most frightening thing for me because I'm a very shy person. I don't feel scared when I see horror movies or listen to ghost stories, but whenever a stranger talks to me, my brain stops working. I don't know what to say. Yesterday there was a man on the street asking me if I knew how to get to the nearest bus stop, but I ran away. I feel terrible. I think I should start to learn how to speak confidently in front of others.

② Water, air and food are believed to be the necessities to keep us alive, but for modern people there is one more thing we cannot live without: the computer. A computer plays an important role in helping us with difficult jobs and maintaining our friendships. With a computer, we can easily write a report without being ashamed of our terrible handwriting. And a computer doesn't help with work alone. Since we all are too busy doing our jobs to have time to meet our friends, a computer allows us to get online to chat with friends. So how can you say "no" to a computer!

③ A place in Taiwan that no tourist should miss is the night market. When you feel bored and want to have a snack at 10:00 p.m., visiting a night market will satisfy your needs. You can find some tasty local food there, such as stinky tofu. And when you are full, you can enjoy the excitement and noise of shopkeepers fighting for your attention. If your feet get sore from walking past one vendor after another, you can also get a foot massage at the night market, so you can have energy to shop again. With such a nice place to go at night, I wonder why you would ever waste your time sleeping!

※ 套色字的部分為主題句，畫底線的部分為結論句，其餘的是支持句。

① Talking to a stranger is the most frightening thing for me because I'm a very shy person. I don't feel scared when I see horror movies or listen to ghost stories, but whenever a stranger talks to me, my brain stops working. I don't know what to say. Yesterday there was a man on the street asking me if I knew how to get to the nearest bus stop, but I ran away. I feel terrible. <u>I think I should start to learn how to speak confidently in front of others.</u>

② Water, air and food are believed to be the necessities to keep us alive, but for modern people there is one more thing we cannot live without: the computer. A computer plays an important role in helping us with difficult jobs and maintaining our friendships. With a computer, we can easily write a report without being ashamed of our terrible handwriting. And a computer doesn't help with work alone. Since we all are too busy doing our jobs to have time to meet our friends, a computer allows us to get online to chat with friends. <u>So how can you say "no" to a computer!</u>

③ A place in Taiwan that no tourist should miss is the night market. When you feel bored and want to have a snack at 10:00 p.m., visiting a night market will satisfy your needs. You can find some tasty local food there, such as stinky tofu. And when you are full, you can enjoy the excitement and noise of shopkeepers fighting for your attention. If your feet get sore from walking past one vendor after another, you can also get a foot massage at the night market, so you can have energy to shop again. <u>With such a nice place to go at night, I wonder why you would ever waste your time sleeping!</u>

Ch
2

主題句太重要了

　　主題句是一個段落的靈魂，寫好主題句就已經替一個好的段落開路。吸引人的主題句有三個重點：

1. 句子中要有「關鍵詞」，提示文章重點。並且字彙要精緻，才能立刻脫穎而出。

2. 主題句內容不能太廣太模糊，需精簡，但也不能太細節，因爲細節屬於支持句。

3. 主題句須預留能夠進一步發揮的空間，而不是一個簡單的事實。現在我們來看下面幾個例子，並做分析。

　　以下有三個主題句，我們比較看看哪個比較好：

題目：「抽菸」"Smoking"

1. I think smoking is bad, because it makes people feel uncomfortable.
2. Smoking can damage your health and relationships so slowly that you hardly notice it until it's too late.
3. My father has had the bad habit of smoking for many years.

　　以上三句，哪一句能讓讀者明白作者接著要寫什麼？也就是說，三句都表示反對抽菸，但哪一句讓我們更清楚知道作者反對的理由爲何（這也正是這篇作文的方向）？我們一起來看看。

1. **I think smoking is bad, because it makes people feel uncomfortable.**

　　　缺點 • 沒有關鍵詞說明作者反對的重點爲何。

　　　　　• people feel uncomfortable 的理由太過模糊，未能點明爲何大家不喜歡 smoking。

　　　　　• 這樣的主題句雖然說出反對的立場，不過讀者並不清楚作者接下來要說什麼，說了等於沒說。

關鍵詞

2. **Smoking can damage your health and relationships so slowly that you hardly notice it until it's too late.**

　　　優點 • 點明抽菸會傷害個人「健康」以及「人際關係」，所以接下來我們知道作者要談論這兩部分。

- 雖然點明了主題，但對於如何傷害健康和人際關係，則留下需要解釋的空間，讓文章得以發揮。
- 不用刻意寫出「我覺得抽菸不好」，因為從詞句中就能清楚明白作者的立場。

3. My father has had the bad habit of smoking for many years.

　　缺點 雖然點出 bad，表示不認同抽菸，不過這個句子只是陳述一個事實，缺乏申論的空間，必然無法發展出精彩的內容，所以讀者也無法清楚明瞭作者為何認為抽菸不好。

我們再繼續比較下面另外三個主題句，看哪一句最好：

題目：我最喜愛的活動 (My Favorite Activity)

1. My favorite activity is outdoor activity, because I like to go out.
2. When I'm free, I like to play table tennis with my best friend Jenny at the school gym, and we always have a lot of fun, so playing table tennis is my favorite activity.
3. Peace and knowledge are the sweet fruit of reading.

【分析】

太廣泛　　　　　理由只在重複前面的 outdoor 而已

1. My favorite activity is <u>outdoor activity</u>, because <u>I like to go out</u>.

　　缺點 • 主題句內容範圍太廣，缺乏焦點，不知道他喜歡的究竟是哪種戶外活動。
　　　　• 喜歡的原因 (I like to go out) 也犯了同樣的錯誤，除了很籠統外，前面早有 outdoor 一字，使得句意仍在原地打轉，所以是贅句。

2. When I'm free, I like to play table tennis with my best friend Jenny at the school gym, and we always have a lot of fun, so playing table tennis is my favorite activity.

　　缺點 • 雖然點出喜歡的活動，不過句子太囉唆、內容太過細節，不應該把「最喜歡跟誰」一起做和「地點」都放在主題句，因為這應該是支持句中舉例的內容。
　　　　• 喜歡的理由竟是因為 we have a lot of fun，理由同樣太過籠統。

3. Peace and wisdom are the sweet fruit of reading.

優點 •「平靜」和「智慧」是開卷讀書所得到的好處，清楚點明作者最喜歡的活動（閱讀）的兩個理由。

•留下伏筆，需要進一步解釋為什麼作者認為閱讀最能帶來平靜和智慧，給予支持句發揮的空間。

EXERCISE 6-2

【一】請分析下面各句，在欠佳的主題句前面打 X。而在良好的主題句中，將可能成為文章發展重點的<u>關鍵字畫底線</u>。

① _____ My first job experience taught me the importance of humbleness.

② _____ I have played on our school baseball team for many years.

③ _____ Last week, I went to the supermarket with my mother.

④ _____ Early to bed and early to rise makes a man healthy, wealthy and wise.

⑤ _____ Industry is the best treasure my parents have ever given to me.

⑥ _____ I found Jerry really funny.

⑦ _____ Listening to the waves at the beach can calm you down.

⑧ _____ People from different countries can have very different ideas about what is polite.

⑨ _____ My favorite snacks are potato chips and chocolate bars.

⑩ _____ I had a nightmare when I took a nap this afternoon.

Ch
2

【二】請練習為下列主題各寫一句精彩的主題句。

① 主題：Junk Food

_____

_____

_____

② 主題：My Summer Vacation

_____

_____

_____

③ 主題：My Dream

_____

_____

_____

④ 主題：The Most Important Thing in My Life

_____

_____

_____

⑤ 主題：My Favorite Season

_____

_____

_____

⑥ 主題：My Parents

_____

_____

_____

📖 **EXERCISE 6-2 參考答案**

【一】

① O My first job experience taught me the importance of humbleness.

② X 只是陳述一個事實，無法吸引讀者繼續閱讀，也沒有可以讓支持句發揮的空間。

③ X 只是描述過去一件事情，缺乏可以進一步闡述的理由。

④ O Early to bed and early to rise makes a man healthy, wealthy and wise.

⑤ O Industry is the best treasure my parents have ever given to me.

⑥ X funny 意義太過廣泛，主題句變的太過模糊，文字也不夠精彩。

⑦ O Listening to the waves at the beach can calm you down.

⑧ O People from different countries can have very different idea about what is polite.

⑨ X 雖然有點出喜愛的東西，不過卻沒有點明喜歡的理由。一方面無法吸引讀者繼續閱讀。另一方面，句子沒有重點。

⑩ X 一樣只是描述一個事實，沒有表達作者對這個事情的態度和感受。讀者無法了解作者的想法和立場，也缺乏繼續發揮下去的空間。

【二】

※ 畫底線的部分是關鍵字，每一個都可以在支持句當中好好發揮。

① Poor concentration and lack of energy are the heavy prices for enjoying junk food.

② The beautiful scenery and the hospitable people in Hualien gave me no choice but to spend my whole summer vacation there, which was lovely.

③ A sweet family of my own with a beautiful wife and cute children is all I want and the only thing that can complete my life.

④ Memories, sweet or sad, are the last things I would ever let go of.

⑤ The smell of flowers and the singing of birds can make you wish to wake up in spring every morning.

⑥ My parents are always the lighthouse in my life to guide me through the downs.

支持句不可離題

　　因為一個題目可以從許多不同的角度切入，我們才需要一個主題句來告訴讀者，文章鎖定的範圍和重點是什麼。主題句確定討論的範圍後，支持句就負責強化主題句中的內容。然而讀者在寫作時最容易犯的錯誤就是，忘了自己當初設定主題句的目標，寫出一些和題目相關，但是跟主題句無關的句子。這樣支持句就失去強化主題句的功能，當然也會使段落或篇章變得沒有重點，不知所云。

　　我們先看看下面這篇文章，請讀者分析，哪裡不大對勁？

題目：音樂 Music

（主題句 ▶）Nothing is better than music to heal a broken heart. My favorite love songs helped me get rid of the pain after I broke up with my boyfriend. Listening to the songs, I was comforted to know that someone understood exactly how I felt. Feeling understood made me feel less alone. The songwriters and singers were just like friends standing by my side, bringing me out of my depression. My favorite singer is A-mei, because she's so talented; in fact, I've collected all of her albums. （結論句 ▶）With their company, I'm not afraid to believe and trust in love again.

── 支持句

　　看完上面的文章，各位可以找出哪裡離題了嗎？也就是說，哪一句不但沒有呼應主題句，而且與前後句格格不入呢？

答案 My favorite singer is A-mei, because she's so talented; in fact, I've collected all of her albums.

原因 作者把最喜愛的歌手加入文章中，雖然跟題目「音樂」似乎相關，卻不符合主題句。在主題句中，作者已經表示，文章主要談論音樂如何幫助她度過失戀的低潮，卻突然插進一個句子表示她很喜愛歌手阿妹，每張專輯都買，這樣不僅離題且失去支持句的功能，破壞文章的整體性和強度。

※ 但是，如果是寫好幾個段落的文章，就可以把 A-mei 另寫成一個段落。

EXERCISE 6-3

【一】下面每一題都有一個主題句和三個支持句，請找出無法呼應主題句的支持句，並在句子前面打 X。

① Dogs are humans' best friends.

_____ Dogs are loyal to their owners.

_____ Dogs are smarter than cats.

_____ Dogs protect their owners.

② Eating fruit and vegetables is very important to our health.

_____ Fruit has a lot of vitamin C, which can protect our skin.

_____ Fruit and vegetables, being lower in fat, can help you stay slim.

_____ You can make fruit juice with a blender.

③ Christmas is a great time for all of our family to get together and have a great time.

_____ Christmas is the day when Jesus was born.

_____ Children love Christmas because they can get presents from their relatives.

_____ It's fun to help your parents decorate the Christmas tree.

④ Online shopping makes our life much easier.

_____ Shopping online can help you save a lot time walking from one store to another.

_____ You can order things from all over the world on the Internet.

_____ Your credit card information might be stolen.

⑤ Learning English can enrich your life.

_____ The most difficult part of learning English is remembering the new words.

_____ Learning English can allow you to read English books, and get to know other cultures.

_____ Knowing how to speak English, you can make friends from other countries.

⑥ Supermarkets offer better quality and more product choices than small grocery stores.

_____ You can find a wide variety of fruit and vegetables in a supermarket.

_____ You can find a label on the food in the supermarket telling you clearly what date to eat it before.

_____ Shopkeepers in grocery stores are usually friendlier.

【二】請針對下面的主題句，給予三個支持的論點。（這三個論點就可促成支持句）

例 Life in the country is more interesting and comfortable than that in the city.
1. Living in a big city doesn't allow you to have enough personal space.
2. Breathing fresh air while taking a walk in a field is refreshing.
3. The sounds made by frogs and insects are your best bedtime song.

① An allowance can help teach children valuable life lessons.

_____

_____

_____

② Too much stress can endanger your mental and physical health.

_____

_____

_____

③ Technology sometimes spoils the quality of life.

_____

_____

_____

④ You can start protecting the Earth by changing your life habits.

_____

_____

_____

⑤ Learning English can broaden your horizons.

_____

_____

_____

【三】請在下面段落中，做到以下三項：

　　1. 先把主題句找出來，並圈起關鍵字。

　　2. 把支持句內任何破壞文章整合性和連貫性的文句刪掉。

　　3. 把結論句畫底線。

① Many believe that online games are too violent, and worry about their bad influence on young players. In fact, most of these games advertize that they provide a space to do what people are not allowed to do in real life, e.g. killing and fighting, to attract young people. Players are encouraged to kill one another in the game in order to score points. Many students spend too much time playing these online games after school and forget about their homework. A lot of people worry that young students will learn that violence is the only way to deal with people who upset them. Some people believe, however, that they can learn the importance of peace this way. Nevertheless, most parents hope that the government can find a way to stop their kids from playing these violent games.

② Cycling seems to have become the number one outdoor activity for Taiwanese people wanting to exercise and relax. On holidays and weekends, you can always see groups of people enjoying a pleasant ride along the riverside. The beautiful scenery along the river always attracts many people. Why is cycling becoming a favorite of local people? It's because there are few better ways to workout and have fun at the same time. More and more people are finding that this activity helps to exercise their leg muscles and burn fat. As people eat too much junk food and fewer vegetables, being overweight is becoming an ever more serious problem. They are also finding that breathing fresh air and seeing the beautiful scenery from the seat of a bike really helps them to forget their troubles and release stress. There is one disadvantage, though: since bikes are now so "cool," you quickly find yourself standing at the end of a very long line if you want to buy a new one.

📖 EXERCISE 6-3 參考答案

【一】

① X　　Dogs are smarter than cats.
　　　　狗與貓的比較，與主題句「狗是人類最好的朋友」並不相關。

② X　　You can make fruit juice with a blender.
　　　　主題句主要是在闡述「吃蔬菜和水果對人健康的益處」，並非討論如何製造果汁。

③ X　　Christmas is the day when Jesus was born.
　　　　主題句要談「聖誕節對家庭的意義」，並非討論聖誕節的由來。

④ X　　Your credit card information might be stolen.
　　　　主題句已經闡明要談「網路購物的好處」，不可以突然改變立場。

⑤ X　　The most difficult part of learning English is remembering the new words.
　　　　談論「學習英文的困難」，和主題句中關鍵字 "enrich your life"（豐富你的人生）立場相左。

⑥ X　　Shopkeepers in grocery stores are usually friendlier.
　　　　主題句中的關鍵字是 "quality" 和 "more choices"，不應該突然離題比較「人員」，也不該突然改變立場，稱讚雜貨店的好處。

【二】

① • An allowance can teach children the value of a dollar.
　 • Having an appropriate amount of money can help children learn money management.
　 • An allowance can help children understand the importance of saving.

② • Too much stress can cause great anxiety and nervousness.
　 • Those who have been under great pressure may experience serious headaches and muscle tension.
　 • A strong feeling of being overwhelmed often strikes those who are stressed out.

③ • The virtual world created by technology can cause people to avoid real interaction with their friends and families, thus jeopardizing interpersonal relationships.
　 • The invention of computers facilitates efficiency but at the same time indirectly forces us to do

more work.

- Over-reliance on high-tech equipment can paralyze our lives once that equipment breaks down.

④ • To be smart green shoppers, we can start by choosing products which are less harmful to the environment or use recycled materials.

- While shopping, you should bring a cloth bag instead of using plastic bags.

- Taking public transportation or bicycling can reduce the waste and pollution resulting from driving.

⑤ • As an international language, English enables you to cross the linguistic boundaries between different cultures.

- English opens the possibility of absorbing knowledge beyond your native language.

- Learning English may enrich your travel experiences.

【三】

① Many believe that most online games are too violent and worry about their bad influence upon the young players. In fact, most of these games advertize that they provide a space to do what people are not allowed to do in real life, e.g. killing and fighting, to attract young people. Players are encouraged to kill one another in the game in order to score points. ~~Many students spend too much time playing these online games after school and forget about their homework.~~（主題句的關鍵字清楚標示，這一段要討論電玩太過暴力，對孩童有負面影響。這句突然討論小孩花了太多時間玩電玩而沒寫功課，雖然也是玩電玩的負面例子，不過不符合主題句的中心思想：「暴力」。）A lot of people worry that young students will learn that violence is the only way to deal with people who upset them. ~~Some people believe, however, that they can learn the importance of peace this way.~~（不可以突然改變立場，忽然覺得電玩似乎也有正面的影響）Nevertheless, most parents hope that the government can find a way to stop their kids from playing these violent games.

② Cycling seems to have become the number one outdoor activity for Taiwanese people wanting to exercise and relax. On holidays and weekends, you can always see groups of people enjoying a pleasant ride along the riverside. ~~The beautiful scenery along the river always attracts many people.~~（主題句所討論的是「人」在騎腳踏車，卻突然冒出「河岸的風景」。雖然看似有關，但是非常突兀。）Why is cycling becoming a favorite of local people? It's because there are few better ways to workout and have fun at the same time. More and more people are finding that this activity helps to exercise their leg muscles and burn fat. ~~As people eat too much junk food and fewer vegetables, being overweight is becoming an ever more serious problem.~~（此句描述人們健康的問題，雖然也有呼應前一句的關鍵字 "fat"，但已經明顯離開「腳踏車」的主題）They are also finding that breathing fresh air and seeing the beautiful scenery from the seat of a bike really helps them to forget their troubles and release stress. There is one disadvantage, though: since bikes are now so "cool," you quickly find yourself standing at the end of a very long line if you want to buy a new one.

創造文章的「整體性」和「連貫性」

　　我們從前個單元了解到,一個篇章或段落的成敗,往往取決於是否有一個精彩的主題句,以及支持句是否能夠呼應主題句。不過一個篇章中的句子,除了要能夠呼應和強化中心主旨外,句與句之間的連貫性也非常重要。如果句子彼此連接不當,文意就不會順暢,讀者也會讀得不痛快。因此,這一課我們得學習,如何讓一個段落和整篇文章除了具有凝聚力外,文句也得以流暢,創造文章的整體性和連貫性。接下來將從以下兩個要點詳細說明:(一)重複「主題句」和前一句的「關鍵字」。(二)「轉折語」使文意圓順地轉彎。

📝 重複「主題句」和前一句的「關鍵字」

　　其實,不論是全篇文章,或是一個段落,只要一個簡單的方法,就可以加強它們的整體性和連貫性,那就是:「重複關鍵字」。也就是說,如果要強化前後句的連貫性,只要重複前一句子中的關鍵字。當然,如果這些第二次出現的關鍵字也可以同時呼應主題句中的關鍵字,就更好了。現在我們看下面例子。

(★ 支持句中與主題句關鍵字重複之處分別以套色、陰影、加框 等相同的標示來表示。)

主題句:Many believe that most online games are too violent and worry about their bad influence upon the young players.

支持句:In fact, most of these games advertize that they provide a space to do what people are not allowed to do in real life, e.g. killing and fighting, to attract young players.

　　事實上,重複的關鍵字,未必要用一模一樣的文字,同義字或涵義相近的詞彙有更好的效果。像前面的例子中 "killing and fighting" 就具有 violent 的意涵。現在我們再繼續看下面的兩個例子,練習如何用相似的文字重複關鍵字:

練習一

主 題 句：Cycling seems to have become the number one outdoor activity for Taiwanese people wanting to exercise and relax.

支持句①：On holidays and weekends, you can always see there are groups of people enjoying a pleasant ride along the riverside.

支持句②：Why is cycling becoming a favorite of local people? It's because there are few better ways to workout and have fun at the same time.

練習二

主 題 句：People all over the world have their own special ways to cure illness.

支持句①：They all believe when the correct foods are eaten together, they can help you get rid of common ailments, such as stomachaches, sore throats and coughs.

支持句②：In America, some believe when you have stomach pain, you should have some cola and crackers together.

支持句③：In England, they might mix some butter and sugar and let kids lick it from a spoon if they have a sore throat.

支持句④：In Taiwan, some people believe if you keep coughing all the time, you should put salt into some soda and drink it.

結 論 句：No one knows whether these foods really have magic powers, but one thing is for sure. If you believe it, it works!

　　由以上範例我們可以清楚地看見關鍵字如何被重提，雖然意思相同，詞彙卻不同。透過重複這些意思相近的詞彙，前後文的意義就立刻連結起來，並建立起段落的邏輯性。

請閱讀下面的段落。

1. 找出主題句，並參考先前的範例將句中的關鍵字分別做不同標示。

2. 在支持句裡找出和主題句的關鍵字意義相似或重複之處並做相同的標示。

3. 找出結論句。

Makeup is a woman's best friend because it not only helps hide any flaws, but also makes them look even prettier. Every woman knows exactly what she needs when she wakes up and finds that she has dark circles around her eyes and looks pale. These problems can easily be solved by just putting on a little foundation and lipstick. But that's not all a woman does before she is ready to go out. If she wants to look really special, some more work needs to be done. Eye shadow can highlight the beauty of her eyes, and some blush can make her look lively. If merely putting on some makeup can change a "Jane Doe" into a beauty, I think every woman will agree that no matter how long it takes to put on the makeup before going out, it's worthwhile.

📖 EXERCISE 7-1 參考答案

主 題 句：Makeup is a woman's best friend because it not only helps hide any flaws, but also makes them look even prettier.

支持句 ①：Every woman knows exactly what she needs when she wakes up and finds that she has dark circles around her eyes and looks pale.

支持句 ②：These problems can easily be solved by just putting on a little foundation and lipstick.

支持句 ③：But that's not all a woman does before she is ready to go out. If she wants to look really special, some more work needs to be done.

支持句 ④：Eye shadow can highlight the beauty of her eyes, and some blush can make her look lively.

結 論 句：If merely putting on some makeup can change a "Jane Doe" into a beauty, I think every woman will agree that no matter how long it takes to put on the makeup before going out, it's worthwhile.

📑 「轉折語」使文意圓順地轉彎

　　轉折語能夠適時告訴讀者文章接下來可能轉彎的動向，讓讀者可以順利地融入作者的思路。通常，在語氣改變之處，運用這些具有連接性的轉折語，就能夠強化文章的連貫性。現在我們就來比較下面兩段文章，看看轉折語的好處。

使用轉折語之前：

For most of people, chocolate is something more than just food. A lot of women believe it has magic powers, because eating chocolate can give them the feeling of falling in love. There is a lot of research showing that chocolate can help clean your blood and protect your heart. The reason why people are crazy for chocolate is not only because of its benefits but also because of its flavor. Many agree the flavor of good chocolate is rich and mysterious. It seems that there is no end to good reasons for you to spend the money in your pocket on chocolate. More and more people are buying it for themselves as candy and also as a gift for their friends. Chocolate is becoming more and more popular—and expensive!

★ 分析：以上沒有轉折語，所以文意不順暢。

使用轉折語之後：

For most people, chocolate is something more than just food. For example, a lot of women believe it has magic powers, because eating chocolate can give them the feeling of falling in love. In addition, there is a lot of research showing that chocolate can help clean your blood and protect your heart. However, the reason why people are crazy for chocolate is not only because of its benefits but also because of its flavor. Many agree the flavor of good chocolate is rich and mysterious. It seems that there is no end to good reasons for you to spend the money in your pocket on chocolate. More and more people are buying it for themselves as candy and also as a gift for their friends. As a result, chocolate is becoming more and more popular—and expensive!

　　比較上面兩篇文章，我們可以清楚地發現，雖然第一篇已有不少句子重複了前一

句或主題句中的關鍵字，但是讀者在閱讀時，仍然須要花點功夫，才能建立句與句之間的邏輯關係。而加入轉折語後，文章就變得更為流暢，閱讀起來也十分輕鬆。現在我們就來認識寫作時一些重要的轉折語，並且看看它們的運用時機。

表示「順序」的轉折語：

（一）	（二）	（三）	（四）
first 第一 in the beginning 一開始 at first 起初 to start with 首先	meanwhile 同時 in the meantime 同時 at the same time 同時	second 第二 next 接下來 then 然後 afterwards 之後 to follow up 接下來	finally 最後 at last 最後 to sum up 總結來說 in conclusion 結論是

★ 上面同組的轉折語，意義相近，可交換使用。

範例

Making fried rice is quite easy. First, you have to boil the rice for 20 minutes. In the meantime, you fry onions with some other vegetables. Next, beat two eggs and pour them into the vegetable mixture. Then, cook them for another 3 minutes. Finally, add the rice and mix everything together. Pour in some soy sauce and serve.

做一道炒飯並不難。首先，你必須先花 20 分鐘把飯煮熟。煮飯的同時，你可以把洋蔥跟一些其他青菜炒熟。接下來，你需要打兩個蛋，並將它們倒入前面所拌炒的青菜中。然後，將所有材料再炒三分鐘。最後，把煮好的飯放入鍋中，混合所有材料。加上一點醬油，就可以上桌了。

「舉例子」用的轉折語：

as an illustration 舉例來說 for example 舉例來說	for instance 舉例來說 to demonstrate 舉例來說

Smoking can jeopardize your health. For example, you can get lung cancer.
抽菸有害於你的身體健康。舉例來說，你可能得到肺癌。

May is such an irresponsible person. For instance, she forgot there was a meeting yesterday and didn't show up.

梅是一個不很負責任的人。例如，她忘了昨天得開會，所以沒有出席。

You can call Jackson a workaholic. As an illustration, he would rather work overtime on weekends than go out with his girlfriend.

傑克森被稱為工作狂一點也不為過。舉例來說，他寧可週末加班工作，也不願意陪女朋友出門。

Drink driving is very dangerous. To demonstrate, one third of car accidents last year were the result of drink driving.

酒駕是非常危險的。舉例來說，去年發生的車禍有三分之一是因為酒駕所引起。

表示「此外」，並稍具有「強調之意」的轉折語：

in addition 此外 besides 此外	moreover 此外 furthermore 此外	more significantly 此外

Jimmy is a very talented person. He is a famous artist and dancer. In addition, he can speak many languages. （In addition 因為單獨使用，所以是副詞）

吉米是一個多才多藝的人。他是一個有名的藝術家和舞者。除此之外，他還會說多國語言。

You shouldn't go out. It's late. Besides, a storm is coming. （Besides 為副詞）

你不應該出門了。現在已經三更半夜。此外，暴風雨就要來了。

He can speak many languages. In addition to his native language, English, he speaks Japanese very well. （In addition to 為介系詞）

= He can speak many languages. Besides his native language, English, he speaks Japanese very well. （besides 為介系詞）

他會說很多語言。除了他的母語英語外，他日語也說得相當好。

Jogging everyday can help you lose weight. Moreover, it can build up your muscles.

= Jogging every day can help you lose weight. Furthermore, it can build up your muscles.

每天慢跑可以幫助你減重。此外，它還可以幫助你的肌肉變得更結實。

表示「與前面相反的情況」的轉折語：

However 然而 Nevertheless 然而 On the contrary 相反地 On the other hand, 另一方面則是……	In contrast 迥然不同地 Instead 反而 Unexpectedly 沒想到 Surprisingly 意外的是

He promised he would come. However, he didn't show up.

= He promised he would come. Nevertheless, he didn't show up.

他答應他會來。然而，他卻沒出現。

I thought it was going to rain. On the contrary, all the dark clouds disappeared in few minutes.

我以為快下雨了。沒想到，所有的烏雲在幾分鐘內全消散了。

Sara doesn't know whether she should break up with her boyfriend. On the one hand, she still has feelings for him. On the other hand, she doesn't think he is the right guy for her.

莎拉不知道該不該跟她男友分手。一方面，她對他仍有感情。另一方面，她卻認為這個男生並不適合她。

Cities are crowded and noisy. In contrast, the countryside is quiet and peaceful.

城市壅擠喧鬧。相較之下，鄉村顯得安靜祥和。

He didn't give up. Instead, he worked even harder.

他不但沒有放棄，反而更加努力。

表示「結果」、「因此」的轉折語：

therefore 因此 consequently 因此	thus 因此 hence 因此	as a result 因此 unsurprisingly 可想而知地

Bicycles are difficult to see in the dark. Therefore, riders should wear reflective clothing.

腳踏車在黑暗中不易被看見。因此，騎士應該穿著能夠反光的服裝。

The Earth's oil reserves will run out in no time. Thus, we need to find some alternative energy resources.

地球上的石油儲量很快就會消失殆盡。因此，我們必須尋找替代能源。

Mary was really tired today. As a result, she fell asleep very quickly once she lay down on the couch.

瑪莉今天實在太累了，所以當她一躺上沙發，就立刻睡著了。

Cats are born with claws; hence, they can climb trees.

貓生來就有爪子。因此，牠們能夠爬樹。

Peter was a very lazy person. Consequently, he got fired by his boss.

彼得是一個很懶惰的人，所以他被他的上司開除了。

EXERCISE 7-2

【一】請根據句意，填入適當的轉折語。

① He did mouth-to-mouth[①] on the girl. _____, she started to breathe on her own again.

② He was unable to sleep. _____, he took some sleeping pills[②].

③ The little boy fell off his bike. _____, he wasn't hurt at all.

④ You shouldn't go out, because it's about to rain. _____, it's very late.

⑤ Living in a big city is very convenient. _____, you can find a store just a few steps from the house.

⑥ If you get lost, first, you should stay calm. _____, you try to call someone for help.

⑦ He didn't study hard enough. _____, he didn't pass the test.

⑧ _____ being sick, he hurt his ankle[③], so he lost the game.

> ① mouth to mouth 口對口人工呼吸
> ② sleeping pill 安眠藥
> ③ ankle 腳踝

【二】請將下列轉折連接語正確地填入空格。

Moreover	For example	First	However	Therefore

① Many people envy a star's glorious[①] life. (1)_____, it may not be as wonderful as you think it is. Being a star has many disadvantages[②]. (2)_____, stars are under a lot of pressure all the time, because fans always expect more from them and think they are perfect. (3)_____, the stars cannot afford to make any mistakes on the stage. (4)_____, if they get a cold and perform badly, the fans will be very disappointed. (5)_____, if the stars are very popular, they could be very busy and have almost no time for their family and

104

themselves, so their life can be very lonely and tiring. If you understand all this, I wonder if you'd really still want to be a star.

① glorious 亮麗的
② disadvantages 缺點

On the contrary   On the other hand   Then   However   For instance

② It's not easy to take care of a baby. Here are some tips for a novice. If a baby keeps crying, there are two things you might need to check first. On the one hand, the diaper^ might be wet; (1)_____, the baby could be hungry. If you try both things and nothing works, you shouldn't worry too much. (2)_____, you should stay calm and see if there is any other reason why the baby is crying. (3)_____, the baby might just have been scared by a loud noise. Holding him/her may calm him/her down. (4)_____, if you can't find the reason, there might be something wrong with the baby. (5)_____, you'd better take him/her to see the doctor as soon as possible.

③ diaper 尿布

【三】地圖下方有一段被打亂的篇章，共有九個句子。請依地圖及句子中轉折語的提示，把這九個句子按正確的語序重組，幫助問路人抵達終點。

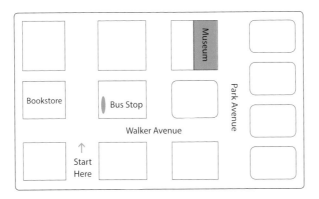

A. The nearest bus stop is on New Street, just across from the bookstore.

B. There are two ways to get to the museum.

C. It only takes you 2 minutes to get there by bus.

D. The bus will stop right in front of the museum.

E. On the one hand, you could walk there.

F. Then, walk two blocks and turn left at the corner of Walker and Park.

G. Walk another two blocks and the museum is on your left.

H. First, go down New Street and turn right onto Walker Avenue.

I. On the other hand, you could consider taking a bus.

正確語序：＿＿＿＿＿＿＿＿＿＿＿＿＿＿＿＿＿＿＿＿＿＿＿

📖 EXERCISE 7-2 參考答案

【一】

① Finally   ② Therefore   ③ Nevertheless 或 Fortunately

④ Besides   ⑤ For instance   ⑥ Next

⑦ As a result / Unsurprisingly   ⑧ In addition to

【二】

① (1) However   (2) First   (3) Therefore   (4) For example   (5) Moreover

② (1) on the other hand   (2) On the contrary   (3) For instance   (4) However   (5) Then

【三】

B → E → H → F → G → I → A → D → C

英文作文入門
一定要會的句型

　　學會了一個文章該有的組織、結構之後，因為句子就是決定文章好壞的關鍵，所以我們也該練習一些寫作時常用的句型。許多人寫文章時最容易出現的毛病就是，整個文章常以「我」的句型開頭，例如：I think ... 或是 I believe ...。文章本來就在表達個人的觀點，所以這樣的句型不但沒有意義，也缺乏變化，非常無趣。請拿出自己曾寫過的文章圈圈看，是不是也有相同的問題呢？學習各種重要的句型，除了能熟悉寫作，讓文句更有節奏，更能吸引讀者閱讀。因此這個單元，將介紹一些我們絕對不能不會的重要基本句型。

「比較性」的句型（一）

① **as ... as ...**（一樣多）

$$as + \begin{cases} 形容詞 \\ 副詞 \\ many / few\ 可數名詞 \\ much / little\ 不可數名詞 \end{cases} + as ...$$

Jim is as tall as **Ted.**（as + 形容詞 + as）
吉姆跟泰德長得一樣高。

Jenny jumps as high as **Sara.**（as + 副詞 + as）
珍妮跟莎拉跳得一樣高。

Bruce has as many / few books as **John.**（as + many / few 可數名詞 + as）
布魯斯跟約翰有一樣多／少的書。

Peter has as much / little money as **Sam.**（as + much / little 不可數名詞 + as）
彼得跟山姆有一樣多／少的錢。

She is as successful as (she is) expected.
她如同大家所期待般地成功。

★ 括弧內的主詞和 be 動詞可一起省略。
★ 句子最後的 expected 是過去分詞當形容詞。

注意！當 as ... as 前面加上 not，成了否定句型，就表示前者比後者「差」。我們看下面的例子：

Jane is not as beautiful as Amy.（not as + 形容詞 + as）
珍不像艾咪那麼漂亮。

Helen is not as slim as Sylvia.（not as + 形容詞 + as）
海倫不像席薇亞那麼苗條。

② as ... as + ┌ **possible**
              │   （盡可能）
              └ **one can**

She is going to run as fast as possible.

= She is going to run as fast as she can.
她會盡可能跑快一點。

Jim ate as many pieces of cake as he could.

= Jim ate as many pieces of cake as possible.
金已經盡可能地吃了不少蛋糕。

EXERCISE 8-1

【一】以下每一組有兩樣東西，請用 **as ... as** 的句型造句。

① a mouse / an elephant

_____

② working / playing

_____

③ a boy / a man

_____

④ a monkey / a child

_____

⑤ honey / sugar

_____

【二】依照括號中的提示改寫。

① My brother gets up early, and my sister gets up early, too. (as ... as)

_____

② Sam has only $35, but Tom has $100. (not as ... as)

_____

③ Jim plays basketball well, and I do too. (as ... as)

_____

④ I did my best to run fast. (as ... as one could)

⑤ He will finish the work quickly. (as ... as possible)

📖 EXERCISE 8-1 參考答案

【一】

① A mouse is not as big as an elephant.

② Playing is as important as working.

③ A boy is not as strong as a man.

④ A monkey is as smart as a child.

⑤ Honey is as sweet as sugar.

【二】

① My brother gets up as early as my sister.

② Sam does not have as much money as Tom.

③ Jim plays basketball as well as I.

④ I ran as fast as I could.

⑤ He will finish the work as quickly as possible.

📄 「比較性」的句型（二）

① 形容詞／副詞比較級 + **than**

我們來看下面的例句：

> **The weather in winter is** cooler than **that in summer.**（形容詞 + than）
> 冬天的天氣比夏天更涼爽。
>
> **Good health is** more important than **money.**（形容詞 + than）
> 身體健康比金錢更重要。
>
> **A scooter goes** faster than **a bike.**（副詞 + than）
> 機車跑得比腳踏車快。

單音節的字比較級習慣字尾加上 er，兩個音節以上的字，因為已經很長了，所以比較級多半習慣在前面加上 more。不過要注意，有些字是不規則變化，例如：

> good → better
> **Her school performance is better than mine.**
> 她在校的表現比我好。

> bad → worse
> **Nothing is worse than death.**
> 沒有什麼事情比死亡更糟。

> far → farther
> **I walked farther than my brother did.**
> 我走的比我弟弟遠。

★ further 跟 farther 的比較：farther 與 further 不論作形容詞或副詞都可以用來指「距離更遠」。但 further 還可以指抽象程度上的更進一步、更詳盡，請特別注意！我們來看下面的例子：

  • **Thailand is farther / further away from Japan than Taiwan is.**
    泰國比台灣距離日本較遠。
    ☑ Do you have any further questions?
       你們有任何額外的問題嗎？
    ☒ Do you have any *farther* questions?

比較級常有以下的困惑，我們看下面的例子：

I gave Mary more than Jane. (這句會造成混淆)

→ Jane 若當主詞

= I gave Mary more than Jane gave Mary.
我給瑪莉比珍給瑪莉還要多。

→ Jane 若當受詞

= I gave Mary more than I gave Jane.
我給瑪莉比我給珍還要多。

如何避免混淆呢？通常這樣的情況我們只要在 Jane 後面加上一個字，Jane 就是「主詞」。

I gave Mary more than Jane did.

另外，比較級的句型，所比較的兩個東西「必須對等」，我們看下面的例子：

⊠ My legs are longer than she.

「我的腿」不應該拿來跟「她的人」相比，所以應該改正為：

☑ My legs are longer than hers.
我的腿比她的還要長。

下面的句子也犯了同樣的錯誤：

⊠ Today's weather is hotter than yesterday.
☑ Today's weather is hotter than yesterday's.
今天的天氣比昨天的天氣熱。

「天氣」和「天氣」比，「今天的天氣」不該拿來跟「昨天」比，而是和「昨天的天氣」比才對。在比較時，可以用 that 來代替前面提過的單數名詞，而 those 代替複數名詞，我們看例子就會明白：

The weather in Taiwan is warmer than that in Japan.
（that 代替單數名詞 the weather）
台灣的氣候比日本的氣候暖和。

The colors of this shirt are brighter than those of yours.
（those 代替複數名詞 the colors）
這件衣服上的色彩比你衣服上的鮮豔多了。

　　在上面的句型，我們學了 more than 是「A 比 B 更……」，當然我們也可以反過來用 less than 來說「B 不如 A……」。請看下面的句型：

② less ＋ ┌ 形容詞
　　　　　│　　　　　　＋ than
　　　　　└ 副詞

Good health is more important than money.
健康比錢財重要。
↓ 反過來說
＝ Money is less important than good health.
　錢財不如健康來的重要。
↓ 等於
＝ Money is not as important as good health.

　　還有一個「比較級」的慣用語，就是「越來越……」，也可以用來增加寫文章時句型的變化：

③ ┌ -er and -er
　 │　　　　　　　（越來越）
　 └ more and more

The weather in May is getting hotter and hotter.
五月的天氣逐漸變得越來越熱。

He walks more and more slowly because he is tired.
他走得越來越慢了，因為他累了。

④ **The + 比較級⋯⋯，the + 比較級 （越⋯⋯，就越⋯⋯）**

The darker **the chocolate (is),** the better **it tastes.**
巧克力顏色越深，嚐起來味道越好。

The closer **I got to the camp fire,** the warmer **I felt.**
越靠近營火，我就覺得越暖和。

★ 寫這個句型時，先別管「越」這個字，然後把去除越字後的兩個簡單句寫出。接著把中文中「越」本來所修飾的對象圈起來。將圈起來的字前面加上 the 並且形成比較級，挪至句子的開頭，最後把後面剩下的內容抄寫完畢。注意！兩句子中間只需要放逗號，無須再加連接詞。

People get old. They get up early.
人們變老，他們早起床。

↓

People get old. **They get up** early.

↓

The older people get, the earlier they get up.
人們變得越老，他們就越早起床。

【一】以下每一組中有兩樣東西，請用比較的句型 **more / -er ... than** 來造句。

① a wolf / a dog

_____

② a mountain / a hill

_____

③ a butterfly / a cockroach（蟑螂）

_____

④ an orange / a lemon

_____

⑤ an adult / a child

_____

⑥ metal（金屬）/ cotton

_____

【二】請將前一題六個已經造好的句子，用 **less ... than** 或 **not as ... as** 的句型改寫。

① _____

② _____

③ _____

④ _____

⑤ _____

⑥ _____

small	hard	thirsty	sleepy
good	heavy	excited	

① If you continue overeating, you'll become *fatter and fatter*.

② Christmas is coming. Everybody is getting _____.

③ Since the weather is so hot, he is getting _____.

④ While the storm was getting closer, it rained _____.

⑤ I felt _____ with each passing minute when I stayed up late last night.

⑥ His health condition has become _____ after he quit smoking.

⑦ Since I've been carrying the box for a while, it seems to have become _____.

⑧ An ice cube (冰塊) gets _____ after it has been taken out of the refrigerator (冰箱).

【四】請將下面的句子改寫成 **The more / -er ..., the more / -er** 的句型。

① If you get old, your hair becomes gray.

The older you get, the grayer your hair becomes.

_____

② If you study hard, you get good grades.

_____

③ When he gets angry, I feel scared.

_____

④ If you walk fast, you'll get there soon.

_____

116

⑤ When you are happy, you laugh loudly.

_____

⑥ If you get excited, your heart beats quickly.

_____

📖 **EXERCISE 8-2 參考答案**

【一】

① A wolf is more dangerous than a dog.

② A mountain is higher than a hill.

③ A butterfly is more beautiful than a cockroach.

④ An orange is sweeter than a lemon.

⑤ An adult is taller than a child.

⑥ Metal is heavier than cotton.

【二】

① A dog is less dangerous than a woof.

② A hill is not as high as a mountain.

③ A cockroach is less beautiful than a butterfly.

④ A lemon is not as sweet as an orange.

⑤ A child is not as tall as an adult.

⑥ Cotton is less heavy than metal.

【三】

② more and more excited　　③ more and more thirsty　　④ harder and harder

⑤ more and more sleepy　　⑥ better and better　　⑦ heavier and heavier

⑧ smaller and smaller

【四】

② The harder you study, the better grades you get.

③ The angrier he gets, the more scared I feel.

④ The faster you walk, the sooner you get there.

⑤ The happier you are, the more loudly you laugh.

⑥ The more excited you get, the more quickly your heart beats.

假設語氣句型使文章活潑

未來假設

法則 **If** 子句要用現在式代替未來式

> If it rains tomorrow, I will stay home.
> 如果明天下雨,我就會待在家裡。
>
> If you are free tonight, we can go to the party together.
> 如果你今晚有空,我們可以一同去參加派對。
>
> If you can't finish the work today, you must do it tomorrow.
> 如果你今天不能做完這項工作,明天你一定得完成。
>
> If Mr. Wang calls, tell him I'm having a meeting.
> 如果王先生打來,就跟他說我正在開會。
>
> If I have enough time, I go to the gym everyday.
> 如果我有空的話,我每天都會上健身房。

現在假設:「與現在事實相反的假設」

法則 **If** 子句的動詞往過去降一級,從現在變成「過去式」。
主要子句用 **would/should/could/might**(助動詞的過去式)+ 動詞

> If I had enough money, I would buy the car.
> 如果我現在有足夠的錢,我就會買下這部車。
>
> If we had wings, we could fly in the sky.
> 如果我們有翅膀,我們就可以在天空中翱翔。
>
> If Jenny weren't sick, she should be here to help you.
> 如果珍妮沒有生病,她就會在這幫忙你。

注意!在假設語氣中,所有 be 動詞的過去式都是用 were !

☒ If I *was* you, I would take the teacher's advice.

☑ If I were you, I would take the teacher's advice.
如果我是你,我會接受老師的建議。

過去假設語氣:「與過去事實相反的假設」

法則 **If** 子句的動詞往過去再降一級,就是「過去完成式」

主要子句用 **would/might/should/could** + **have** + 過去分詞

(因為這些助動詞沒有 P.P.,無法形成過去完成式 (had + P.P.),因此借用現在完成式)

> If Jane had listened to her father's advice, she wouldn't have made the mistake.
> 如果珍當初能夠聽從她父親的建議,她就不會犯錯了。
>
> If I had got up earlier this morning, I could have arrived in time.
> 如果我今天早上再早點起床,我就能夠及時趕到。
>
> If Jimmy had studied harder, he might have got better grades.
> 如果吉米當初認真點讀書,他就有可能得到更好的成績。

強制語氣

法則
- **suggest**
  that + 句子 (任何人稱,包括第三人稱單數也須使用原形動詞)
- **insist**

> The doctor suggested that my father (should) give up smoking.
> (give 用原形動詞)
> 醫生建議我的父親應該要戒菸。
>
> The chairman insisted that Jennifer (should) be present in the meeting.
> (be 用原形動詞)
> 主席堅持珍妮佛得出席會議。

另外,insist 也可以在後面接 on,既然 on 是介系詞,後面必接名詞類,包括「動名詞」或「名詞」:

> The chairman insisted on Jennifer's presence in the meeting.
> The chairman insisted on offering me a present.

EXERCISE 8-3

【一】請運用括號中的動詞，按照句意填入適當時態，完成下列句子。

① If I had worn enough clothes, I _____ (not get) a cold last week.

② If I were in my house now, I _____ (take) a bath now.

③ If it rains tomorrow, we _____ (not go) to the party.

④ If I _____ (be) a teacher in the future, I _____ (be) kind to my students.

⑤ If Sally had had enough money, she _____ (buy) the car last year.

⑥ If the grocery store is open, I _____ (buy) some necessities this afternoon.

⑦ If I had known the truth, I _____ (forgive) Jane.

⑧ If there were no water, every living thing _____ (die).

⑨ If I were ten years older, I _____ (make) a different decision.

⑩ If it were not cold today, I _____ (go) swimming.

【二】請將下列句子翻譯成英文。

① 如果我有足夠的雞蛋跟麵粉，待會我就可以烤個蛋糕。（實情：不知道夠不夠）

_____

② 如果我有足夠的雞蛋跟麵粉，我現在就可以烤個蛋糕。（實情：可惜不夠）

_____

③ 我如果明天有空，我將會探望我的祖父母。

_____

④ 如果你再瘦一點，看起來會更漂亮。

_____

⑤ 如果我當初不是住在台北，我們就不會變成好朋友。

_____

⑥ 如果我今早記得帶傘，我就不會在上班途中淋溼了。

_____

⑦ 氣象員建議我們今天下午出門前應該帶把傘。（氣象員 weatherman）

_____

⑧ 我媽媽堅持我上學之前得吃早餐。

_____

Ch
2

📖 EXERCISE 8-3 參考答案

【一】

① wouldn't have got 過去假設

② could take 現在假設

③ won't go 未來假設

④ am; will be 未來假設

⑤ could have bought 過去假設

⑥ will buy 未來假設

⑦ would have forgiven 過去假設

⑧ would die 現在假設

⑨ would make 現在假設

⑩ would go 現在假設

【二】

① If I have enough eggs and flour, I can bake a cake.

② If I had enough eggs and flour, I could bake a cake. 現在假設

③ If I'm free tomorrow, I'll visit my grandparents.

④ If you were a little thinner, you would look much prettier. 現在假設

⑤ If I hadn't lived in Taipei, we wouldn't have become friends. 過去假設

⑥ If I had remembered to bring an umbrella with me this morning, I wouldn't have got wet on my way to work. 過去假設

⑦ The weatherman suggested that we (should) bring an umbrella with us before leaving home this afternoon.
suggest 後面直接用原形動詞（即使第三人稱單數或過去式動詞，也不用加 "s"）

⑧ My mom insists that I (should) eat my breakfast before going to school.
insists 後面直接用原形動詞（即使第三人稱單數或過去式動詞，也不用加 "s"）

必備的基本句型（一）

之前已經介紹了幾個重要的基本句型，接下來將再進階介紹若干寫作必備的句型。

① ┌ **no matter** + 疑問詞
  │   （不論）
  └ 疑問詞 **-ever**

No matter what **happens, you should never give up on your dream.**

= Whatever **happens, you should never give up on your dream.**
　　不論發生任何事，你都不該放棄你的夢想。

No matter which **one you choose, I'll like it.**

= Whichever **you choose, I'll like it.**
　　不論你選擇哪一個，我都會喜歡。

No matter how **the weather is tomorrow, we'll go to the zoo.**

= However **the weather is tomorrow, we'll go to the zoo.**
　　不論明天天氣如何，我們都會去動物園。

在上面的例子中，no matter 所引導的子句應該爲「直述句」，而不是一個問句，請避免寫出下面的句子：

⊠ **No matter how** long *does it take*, I'll wait for him.

☑ **No matter** how long it takes, **I'll wait for him.**
　　不管花多少的時間，我都會等他。

和 if 子句一樣，即使在談論未來的情況時，由 no matter 所引導的子句也用現在式代替未來式。

⊠ **No matter where you** *will* go, I'll follow you.

☑ **No matter where you** go, I'll follow you.

= Wherever **you go, I'll follow you.**
　　不論你去哪，我都會跟隨你。

現在讓我們來比較另一個意思同樣為「不論……」的好用句型：

② Whether ... or （不論）

> Whether you like Tom or not, you have to get along with him.
> 不論你喜不喜歡湯姆，你都得跟他相處。

當 whether 後面接的句子較長時，也可以直接把 whether or not 放在句首：

> Whether or not you like Tom, you have to get along with him.
>
> Whether you believe it or not, Sam is married and has three kids.
> = Whether or not you believe it, Sam is married and has three kids.
> 不論你信不信，山姆不但已婚還是三個孩子的爸。
> Whether it's sooner or later, you have to accept the fact that he is dead.
> 不論何時，你遲早得接受他已經過世的事實。

更近一步精簡的句子：whether A or B 的句子，可以將 whether 和主詞都省略，只留下 A or B。我們看下面的例子：

> Whether you believe it or not, Sam is married and has three kids.
>   ↓ Whether 和主詞 you 都刪掉
> = Believe it or not, Sam is married and has three kids.
>
> Whether you like it or not, you have to accept the fact that he is dead.
>   ↓ Whether 和 you 一起刪
> = Like it or not, you have to accept the fact that he is dead.

③ When it comes to （談到……）

> When it comes to playing basketball, Jack is second to none in his school.
> 說到打籃球，傑克可是不輸給他學校的任何人。
> ★ when it comes to 的 to 是介系詞，後面接的動詞改為動名詞 playing。
>
> When it comes to love, no one is wise in his own affairs.
> 一談到愛情，人多半皆是當局者迷。
> ★ when it comes to 後面接名詞 love。

④ ┌ **As soon as ...**
│   （一……，就……）
④ └ **The moment ...**

> As soon as **we got home, the phone rang.**
>
> = The moment **we got home, the phone rang.**
>   當我們一到家，電話就響起來。
>
> The moment **she heard the news of Billy's death, she fainted.**
>
> = As soon as **she heard the news of Billy's death, she fainted.**
>   一聽到比利的死訊，她就昏了過去。

要表達「一……，就……」的意思，用下面的句型也很好：

⑤ **Upon V-ing, ...** （一……，就……）

> As soon as he saw the suspect, he called the police.
>
> = Upon seeing **the suspect, he called the police.**
>   他一看到嫌疑犯，就馬上打電話給警方。

注意！用 upon V-ing 的句子，要特別注意兩邊的主詞為同一人，當主詞不同時，就可能不能改寫。我們看下面的示範：

> ☑ As soon as <u>we</u> saw the thief, <u>he</u> ran away.
>   當我們一看見小偷，他拔腿就跑。
>
> ☒ Upon seeing the thief, he ran away. （左半句主詞為 we，右半句主詞為 he）

⑥ **Once ...** （一旦……，就……）

> Once **you get into the habit of smoking, it'll be hard to quit.**
>   你一旦養成抽菸的壞習慣，就很難戒除。
>
> Once **it passes into October, the weather will get really cold.**
>   這裡一旦進入了十月，天氣就會變得很冷。

EXERCISE 8-4

【一】請將下列詞彙，填入最適合的空格中。

No matter what	Once	Whether or not	The moment
Whenever	Upon	When it comes to	

① _____ we got home, it began to rain.

② _____ I see him, he is always working.

③ _____ he will win the game, he is always the best in the eyes of his
parents.

④ _____ music, classical music is my favorite.

⑤ _____ hearing the doorbell ring, the little boy quickly opened the
door.

⑥ _____ happens to him, he always looks on the bright side.

⑦ _____ you get old, you see things differently.

【二】請將下列句子，翻譯成英文。

① 一談到旅遊，山姆就變得很興奮。

_____

② 她不論有多麼忙，總是保持微笑。

_____

③ 不論這是不是一個故事，聽起來都相當真實。

_____

④ 當我第一次看到莎拉，我就知道我戀愛了。

_____

⑤ 你一旦長大了，你就得學會照顧自己。

_____

⑥ 不論你選擇哪一條路，它都會引領你到同樣的地方。

_____

📖 EXERCISE 8-4 參考答案

【一】

① The moment

② Whenever

③ Whether or not

④ When it comes to

⑤ Upon

⑥ No matter what

⑦ Once

【二】

① When it comes to traveling, Sam becomes very excited.

② No matter how busy she is, she always wears a pleasant smile.

③ Whether it's a story or not, it sounds real.

④ The moment I saw Sara for the first time, I knew I was in love.

⑤ Once you are a grown-up, you have to learn to take care of yourself.

⑥ Whichever road you take, it will lead you to the same place.

① It ⎰ **goes without saying**
   ⎱ **is needless to say** + **that** 子句（不言而喻；不用說，當然是……）

> It goes without saying that love is the most valuable thing in the world.
>
> = It's needless to say that love is the most valuable thing in the world.
> 愛是世界上最珍貴的東西，這是不言而喻的事。
>
> It's needless to say that no one can live without friends.
>
> = It goes without saying that no one can live without friends.
> 不用說，人活在世上當然不能沒有朋友。

It's needless to say that ... 的句子，時常也可以省掉 It's 簡化爲 Needless to say, ...。
我們看下面的例子：

> It's needless to say that everyone should obey the law.
>
> = Needless to say, everyone should obey the law.
> 不用說，每個人都應該遵守法律。

② **It is said that** + 句子（據說……）

> It's said that old is gold.
> 人們總說舊的總是比較好。
>
> It's said that the key to success is to have faith in yourself.
> 據說成功的關鍵在於對自己有信心。

這樣的句型也可以有另一種寫法，我們看下面的例子：

> It's said that Mr. Wang won the lottery last week.
>
> = Mr. Wang is said to have won the lottery last week.
> 聽說王先生上個星期中了樂透。

It's said that the company is closing in a few months.

= The company is said to be closing in a few months.

這公司聽說在幾個月內就要結束營運。

③ I've been told that + 句子（有人告訴我，……）

I've been told that old is gold.

有人告訴我，舊的是寶。

I've been told that the key to success is to have faith in yourself.

有人告訴我，成功的關鍵就是對自己要有信心。

④ It occurs to 某人 that + 句子（突然想起……）

It suddenly occurred to Mr. Brown that he should make a call to his boss.

布朗先生突然想到他該撥電話給他的老闆。

Did it ever occur to you that maybe you should tell him the truth?

你是否曾經想過，或許你應該告訴他實情。

⑤ have
- something
- anything
- nothing
- little
- much

to do with ...（與……有／沒有關係）

His strange behaviors have much to do with his brain damage.

他怪異的行為跟他腦部的損傷有很大關聯。

The man said that the car accident had nothing to do with drunk driving.

那個男人表示，車禍跟酒駕毫無關係。

Success has little to do with luck—hard work is key.

成功多半來自努力，鮮少與好運有關。

【一】請依照句意提示，將以下的子句放入恰當的位置。

> A. When it comes to love,
> B. It is said that
> C. Whether he is rich or poor,
> D. It goes without saying that
> E. No matter how tired I may be,
> F. It occurred to him that

① _____ he forgot to call back his wife.

② _____ the moon has the power to influence our moods.

③ _____ everyone should love his/her own country.

④ _____ people have very different ideas about it.

⑤ _____ I must finish the work.

⑥ _____ I will marry him.

【二】請將下列各句，翻譯成英文。

① 據說夢跟一個人的慾望有很大的關聯。

_____

② 地球是圓的，這是無庸置疑之事。

_____

③ 比利突然想到，今天是他女朋友的生日。

_____

④ 據說史密斯先生以前是一個警官。

_____

⑤ 警方認為這個男人與艾咪的失蹤有關聯。

_____

📖 EXERCISE 8-5 參考答案

【一】

① (F) ② (B) ③ (D) ④ (A) ⑤ (E) ⑥ (C)

【二】

① It's said that dreams have much to do with a person's desires.

② It goes without saying that the Earth is round.

③ It suddenly occurred to Billy that today is his girlfriend's birthday.

④ Mr. Smith is said to have been a police officer in the past.

⑤ The police believe that this man has something to do with Amy's disappearance.

① 人 ⎡ be
      ⎣   used to + n / V-ing 子句（習慣於……）
        get

He is used to sleeping late.（受詞為 sleeping late）
他習慣了晚起。

More and more young people get used to staying up nowadays.
（受詞為 staying up）
現今越來越多年輕人漸漸習慣熬夜。

★ get used to 和 be used to 都是「習慣於……」的意思，但是因為 get 比 be 有動態，所以 get used to 有強調「漸漸習慣」的意思。

I'm used to your presence and cannot imagine living without you.
（受詞為 your presence）
我已經習慣你的存在，我沒辦法想像沒有你，該怎麼過日子。

be used to 和 used to 意義不一樣：be used to + n / V-ing 是「習慣於……」，used to + 原形動詞則是「過去曾……」。請看以下例子。

② 人 **used to** + 原形動詞（過去曾……）

I used to be a doctor.（used to + 原形動詞 be）
我以前曾經是一名醫生。

I used to drive to work every day.（used to + 原形動詞 drive）
我過去曾每天開車上班。

used（使用）單獨一個字，是一般動詞，和 be used to 的片語意義完全不一樣。

The camera is used to take pictures.
相機是用來拍照用的。

③ **look forward to** + **n. / V-ing**（期待）
★ look forward to 的 to 是介系詞，故後面必須接名詞或動名詞當受詞。

I look forward to <u>hearing</u> from you soon.（接動名詞當受詞）
我期待很快能聽到你的消息。

I'm looking forward to <u>my birthday party tomorrow.</u>（接名詞當受詞）
我很期待我明天的生日派對。

★「期待」有時候用 look forward to，有時候則用 looking forward to。簡單式 look forward to 突顯正式性，多用於文書上。使用進行式比較親切生動，多用於口語中。

④ ┌ **cannot help + V-ing**
  │   （忍不住；不得不；無可奈何地）
  └ **cannot (help) but + 原形動詞**

Upon hearing the bad news, the woman could not help crying.
一聽到壞消息，這位女士忍不住放聲痛哭。

Because of the heavy rain, they couldn't help but cancel the football game.
因為傾盆大雨，他們不得不取消美式足球賽。

After hearing the joke, all of us could not help but laugh out loud.
聽完了笑話，我們大家都忍不住笑出來。

⑤ **have** ┌ **difficulty**
          │ **trouble**   **(in) V-ing**（有困難⋯⋯）
          └ **problems**

Jane had difficulty finishing the work in time.
珍很難即時做完這份工作。

Peter has trouble remembering who he was after having a car accident.
彼得發生車禍後，就想不起他自己是誰。

⑥ **have** ┌ **a good time**
          │   **(in) V-ing**（很享受⋯⋯）
          └ **fun**

Did you have a good time going out with Jerry last night?
你昨晚跟傑瑞約會好玩嗎？

I had a lot of fun having dinner with Sally.
我很享受昨天跟莎莉共進晚餐。

★ 使用 busy 這個字時，用法也一樣，我們看看這個例子：Sylvia has been busy (in) planning her wedding for a long time.（席薇亞已經有好長一段時間忙著計畫她的婚禮。）

⑦ mind +
┌ V-ing
│   （介意……）
└ if 句子

Most people wouldn't mind yielding their seats to the elderly on a bus.
大部分的人願意在公車上讓座給年長者。

Would you mind if I smoked here?（mind 後的 if 子句常用過去簡單式）

= Would you mind my smoking here?

你介意我在這抽菸嗎？

★「Would you mind if ...」，if 後面的子句比較常用過去簡單式，並非表示過去時態，只是表示一種委婉的語氣。

Ch 2

回答的時候，如果表示不介意，則應該搭配使用否定回答。我們看下面的例子：

A: Would you mind closing the door? 你介意關門嗎？
B: No, I wouldn't. 我不介意關門。
B: Yes, I would. 我介意。

⑧
┌ keep
│ stop ... from + V-ing （防止……去；使……無法）
└ prevent

The storm stopped us from going on a picnic.
暴風雨使我們無法去野餐。

The seatbelt keeps you from getting hurt if you get into an accident.
安全帶防止你在車禍中受傷。

Putting on sunscreen can prevent you from getting sunburned.
擦上防曬乳可以防止你被曬傷。

UNIT 8 133

EXERCISE 8-6

【一】請為以下的空格選擇正確答案。

① (　) Would you mind _____ off the radio?

    (A) to turn   (B) turning   (C) turn   (D) turned

② (　) A raincoat can keep you _____ getting wet in heavy rain.

    (A) in   (B) of   (C) from   (D) on

③ (　) John was really tired. As soon as he lay down on the couch, he couldn't help but _____ asleep.

    (A) to fall   (B) falling   (C) fell   (D) fall

④ (　) My parents used _____ for a walk after dinner.

    (A) to go   (B) going   (C) to going   (D) go

⑤ (　) The police have problems _____ the killer.

    (A) to find   (B) find   (C) of finding   (D) finding

⑥ (　) I really look forward _____ your new book.

    (A) to reading   (B) in reading   (C) to read   (D) reading

⑦ (　) Sam is busy _____ his new novel.

    (A) of writing   (B) to write   (C) in writing   (D) write

【二】請將下列各句，翻譯成英文。

① 大部分的美國人習慣在早上出門前洗個澡。

_____

② 我想琳達不會介意你用她的電腦。

_____

③ 為了避免小孩受傷，家長必須將危險物品收好。

_____

④ 我很享受昨晚和珍在派對上共舞。 (have a good time)

_____

⑤ 我們很期待今年聖誕節的到來。

_____

⑥ 我有困難借你那麼多錢。

_____

Ch
2

📖 EXERCISE 8-6 參考答案

【一】

① (B)　② (C)　③ (D)　④ (A)　⑤ (D)　⑥ (A)　⑦ (C)

【二】

① Most Americans <u>are used to</u> tak<u>ing</u> a shower before going out every morning.

② I don't think Linda would <u>mind</u> <u>if you use her computer</u>.
   I don't think Linda would <u>mind</u> <u>your</u> us<u>ing</u> her computer.

③ In order to <u>prevent</u> the kids <u>from</u> gett<u>ing</u> hurt, parents should put away the dangerous things.

④ I <u>had a good time</u> danc<u>ing</u> with Jane at the party last night.

⑤ We are <u>looking forward to</u> <u>the coming</u> of Christmas this year.
   We <u>look forward to</u> <u>the coming</u> of the Christmas this year.

⑥ I <u>have problems in</u> lend<u>ing</u> you so much money.

必備的基本句型（四）

① the last ...
- that ...
- to V

（最不可能……；最不願意……）

> He is the last person that I would like to make friends with.
>
> 他是我最不想交朋友的人。
>
> ★ the last 本來是指「最後一個」，當順位被排到最後，就引伸出「最不願意」的意思。
>
> Kate is the last person to give up her dreams.
>
> 凱特是最不可能放棄自己夢想的人。
>
> Mr. White is the last person to hurt his wife, for he loves her so much.
>
> 懷特先生是最不可能傷害他老婆的人，因為他非常愛她。

② had better + 原形動詞 （最好……）

> For your own good, you'd better tell the police the truth.
>
> 為了你自己好，你最好跟警方說實話。
>
> Since you have a bad cough, you'd better quit smoking.
>
> 既然你咳嗽得那麼厲害，你最好還是不要抽菸了。

注意！had better 常縮寫成 'd better 的型式，許多人在還原後，常誤認為 would better，要小心避免。

☒ You *would better* put on a jacket, for it's windy out there today.

☑ You had better put on a jacket, for it's windy out there today.

你最好多穿件夾克，因為今天外頭風很大。

很多人也會誤以為 had better 的 had 為「完成式」，而後面動詞使用過去分詞。其實 had better 連用，是助動詞，所以後面用原形動詞。

had better 的否定為 had better not，要避免寫出下面的句子：

☒ You *hadn't better* do it, if you don't want to get into any trouble.

☑ You had better not do it, if you don't want to get into any trouble.
你最好不要做這件事情，如果你不想惹上任何麻煩。

③ **would rather** + 原形動詞 + **than** + 原形動詞 （寧可……也不願……）

> I would rather cook for myself than eat out.
> 我寧可自己煮飯，也不願外出用餐。
>
> I would rather be hungry than eat junk food.
> 我寧可肚子餓，也不願吃垃圾食物。
>
> She would rather be alone than hang out with her friends.
> 她寧可自己獨處，也不願跟她的朋友出去玩。

④ **according to** + 名詞 （根據……；依照……而定）

> According to the timetable, we have to finish the work before July 31.
> 根據行事曆，我們必須在七月三十一日前完成這項工作。
>
> We should divide the cakes according to how many people we have here.
> 我們應該按照在場的人數分配這些蛋糕。　　　　　　↑ 名詞子句
>
> According to our law, youth under 18 cannot buy alcohol.
> 根據我們的法律，十八歲以下的青少年不得買酒。

⑤ **As / So far as** ⎡ 人
　　　　　　　　　be concerned, 句子 （就……而言）
　　　　　　　　⎣ 物

> As far as I'm concerned, friendship is much more important than anything else.
> 就我個人而言，友情遠重要於任何其他事情。
>
> So far as dessert is concerned, pudding is always my favorite.
> 就甜點而言，布丁總是我的最愛。
>
> As far as many modern women are concerned, marriage is no longer a
> necessity.
> 就許多現代女性而言，婚姻不再是必需品。

EXERCISE 8-7

【一】請先了解下列各句文意，再依照括號內的提示語改寫。

① It is better for you to eat less junk food and more fruits and vegetables. (had better)

_____

② John will never do such a dangerous thing. (the last person ...)

_____

③ As far as I'm concerned, swimming is better than jogging on such a hot day.
(I would rather ... than)

_____

【二】請完成下列句子。

① I would rather give up everything than ...

_____

② According to the latest weather report, ...

_____

③ Amanda is the last person ...

_____

④ You'd better not ...

_____

【三】請將下列各句，翻譯成英文。

① 就我個人而言，健康遠比金錢重要。

_____

② 根據醫生的說法，你應該一天吃三次藥。

_____

③ 我寧願原諒，也不願恨一個人。

_____

Ch
2

④ 你上課的時候最好作筆記。

_____

📖 EXERCISE 8-7 參考答案

【一】

① You'd better eat less junk food but more fruits and vegetables.

② John will be the last person to do such a dangerous thing.

③ I would rather swim than jog on such a hot day.

【二】

① I would rather give up everything than lose my love.

② According to the latest weather report, there won't be any rain tomorrow.

③ Amanda is the last person that I would like to work with.

④ You'd better not do something before you think carefully.

【三】

① As far as I'm concerned, health is far more important than money.

② According to the doctor, you should take the medicine three times a day.

③ I would rather forgive than hate someone.

④ You'd better take notes in class.

Chapter 3

讓文章活起來

看圖寫作文

　　一篇文章，除了組織、句型和文法正確外，如果要提升文章的精彩度，就得應用一些「策略」。不同的策略可以讓文章更精彩切題，這些方法包括「講故事」、「用例子」、「說明程序」、「善用比較」等。在接下來的幾個單元，我們將按照技巧分門別類地來看，如何用不同的方式讓作文更豐富。

　　首先是「看圖說故事」，這種題型在大考和初、中級全民英檢常出現。寫這類文章時，最重要的就是「活潑的想像力」、「優美的文字」、「正確的文法」、「流暢的表達」和「有趣的內容」。原則上，內容如果是按照一定的順序推展，大致不會有什麼問題。例如，按照「時間」的前後、「空間」的遠近等等來進行寫作。不過，如果只是呆板地陳述一件事情，自然引不起讀者的興趣，所以製造一點「幽默感」也是提升作文的好方法。另外，遇到記敘文的題目，沒有任何圖片時，想像力就可以大大地揮灑，下筆前先在自己頭腦中勾勒趣味的漫畫，依照前章所討論過的邏輯：主題句＋支持句＋結論句，就可以快速地寫出一篇好文章。

　　提醒大家，即使是看圖寫文章，如果圖畫許可，我們仍然要盡量保持寫作的邏輯：引言（可有可無）＋主題句＋支持句＋結論句。

📝 看圖寫作（一）

　　請根據以下四張圖片，依照「主題句」、「支持句」、「結論句」的結構，寫出一篇作文。

① ② ③ ④

寫寫看

_____

_____

_____

_____

_____

_____

_____

_____

_____

_____

_____

_____

Ch
3

That Was Close!

（圖 **1**，可作為引言▶）Working in a tall apartment building, Steven, a window washer, <u>is responsible for</u>[①] polishing[1] the windows.（圖 **2**，可作為主題句▶）One day, he was repeating[2] his familiar[3] work <u>as usual</u>[②]—washing and wiping[4] the window panes—but didn't know that day he would come so close to death. He cleaned the windows <u>one after another</u>[③] as he always did without noticing[5] that from one of the windows, a piece of glass was missing and an accident was waiting for him.（圖 **3**▶）When he finally came to the specific[6] window, Steven took up the wiper, stepped on the chair, and stretched[7] his left arm toward[8] it. Not knowing the pane of glass had disappeared[9] for some reason, he leaned[10] his body forward. <u>All of a sudden</u>[④], he started to fall out of the window without realizing[11] what was going on. At that moment, his whole life flashed[12] before his eyes like a slideshow.（圖 **4** ▶）He thought he would die, but <u>luckily</u>[⑤] his right hand grabbed the window frame[13] <u>in time</u>[⑥], so he only fell down from the chair with a great shock.（結論句▶）The accident taught him one thing: you can never be too careful.

┐
│ 支持句
┘

好險！

身為一個清潔工，史堤芬在一棟大樓裡負責擦玻璃的工作。有一天，他如同往常重複著他熟悉的工作——刷洗跟擦拭窗戶，他卻料想不到，今天他將與死神擦身而過。如同平常一般，史堤芬清理一塊接著一塊的玻璃，並沒有注意到所有玻璃之中，有一塊不見了，而一場意外正伺機而動。當他最後來到那一塊玻璃不見的窗戶，史堤芬拿起了他的抹布，踏上椅子，並將左手伸向玻璃。因為不知道玻璃為何消失不見，他把整個身子向前傾。在他意會發生什麼事之前，突然他開始跌出窗外。在那一瞬間，他人生像幻燈片般閃過他的眼前。他想他死定了，但還好他的右手即時抓住窗檔，所以他只是跌落椅子，受到極大的驚嚇。這個意外教他學會一件事：你永遠可以更小心。

※ 請對照範文中藍色數字所標示的字詞。

1. **polish** (*v.*) 磨光；擦亮

   His glasses were dirty, so he <u>polished</u> them with his handkerchief.
   他的眼鏡髒了，所以他用手帕把它擦乾淨。

★ polish 也可以用來指讓某技巧更精煉，我們看下面的例子：He loves chatting with native speakers, because it helps to polish his English speaking skills.（他喜歡跟英語人士聊天，因為這樣有助於磨鍊他的英語口說技巧。）

2. **repeat** (*v.*) 重複

Tom was asked to <u>repeat</u> what the teacher had just said.
湯姆被要求重複老師所說的話。

3. **familiar** (*adj.*) 熟悉的

The lost boy started to cry when he finally saw someone <u>familiar</u>.
走丟的小男孩忍不住哭了起來，當他終於見到熟悉的面孔。

4. **wipe** (*v.*) 擦拭

The housekeeper <u>wipes</u> the dining table with a dry cloth every day.
女管家每天都會用乾抹布擦拭餐桌。

5. **notice** (*v.*) 注意到

Sophia didn't <u>notice</u> that her boyfriend was holding a blue rose in his hand.
蘇菲亞沒注意到她男朋友的手上正握著一朵藍色玫瑰。

6. **specific** (*adj.*) 特定的

There is no <u>specific</u> answer to this question. All answers are acceptable.
這個問題沒有特定的答案，所有答案都可以被接受。

7. **stretch** (*v.*) 伸出；伸展

I <u>stretched</u> out my arms, but I still couldn't reach the leaves on the tree.
我伸出我的雙臂，但仍然搆不到樹上的葉子。

8. **toward** (*prep.*) 朝向

The taxi driver drove <u>toward</u> the airport at high speed.
計程車司機以高速駛向機場。

9. **disappear** (*v.*) 消失

Who stole my teddy bear? It couldn't have just <u>disappeared</u> for no reason!
誰偷走了我的泰迪熊？它不可能就這樣憑空消失！

10. **lean** (*v.*) 把……靠向……

Judy <u>leans</u> her head against the wall.
茱蒂把頭靠在牆壁。

11. **realize** (*v.*) 意識到；了解到

Sharon finally <u>realized</u> how terrible her ex-boyfriend was.

雪倫終於意識到她的前男友有多麼糟糕。

★ realize 後面常接 that 再加句子，來表示對一件事情的了解。

12. **flash** (*v.*) 掠過

A bolt of lighting <u>flashed</u> across the sky.

一道閃電從天空中掠過。

13. **frame** (*n.*) 框架

Michelle likes to put her photos in picture <u>frames</u>.

蜜雪兒喜歡把她的照片擺進相框裡。

英文檢定常考句型與改寫

※ 請對照範文中圈起數字所標示的片語和句型。

① **be responsible for** 負責⋯⋯

Jennifer ⎡ is responsible for
⎢ has taken charge of ⎤ planning the whole project.
⎣ is in charge of

珍妮佛負責籌畫整個計畫案。

② **as usual** 一如往常

As usual, ⎤
⎢ Larry is late for class again.
As always, ⎦

一如往常，賴瑞上學又遲到了。

③ **one after another** 一個接著一個

The students walked in the classroom ⎡ one after another.
⎢ one by one.
⎣ one after the other.

學生們一個接著一個走進教室。

★「一個接著一個」有許多不同的英文表達方式。

★ 上面的用法雖然意思都一樣，但是 one after the other 更強調每個動作相隔的時間很短，有一個緊接著另一個的意味。

④ **all of a sudden** 突然地

「突然」有很多不同的表達方法，除了 suddenly 之外，我們看下面還有哪些類似的替換用法。

All of a sudden,
Unexpectedly, ⎤ the car crashed into a big tree.
All at once, ⎦

〔突然之間／出乎意料之外／一瞬間〕，那部車撞上了一棵大樹。

⑤ **luckily** 幸運地

Luckily,
⎤ nobody was hurt in the car accident.
Fortunately, ⎦

很幸運地，在這場車禍中無人受傷。

⑥ **in time** 及時

He finished the work ⎡ in time.
⎢ on time.
⎣ in no time.

他〔及時／準時／很快〕就完成了工作。

★ in time 表示在「時間期限內完成」；而 on time 則是「時間到了、而準時完成」；至於 in no time 則是「很快速、立即」的意思。

📝 看圖寫作（二）

　　請根據以下四張圖片，依照「主題句」、「支持句」、「結論句」的結構，寫出一篇作文。

寫寫看

_____

_____

_____

_____

_____

_____

_____

_____

_____

_____

_____

_____

_____

_____

A Blind Date

（圖1，可作為引言▶）As far as Mr. Handsome[1] is concerned, making friends online has almost become his second career[2]. He works during the day, but flirts with[3] girls on the Internet at night <u>in hopes of</u>① "falling" in love. （主題句 ▶）However, his passion for love drove[4] him to lose sight of reason and forget the warning[5] of an old saying: "LOOK" before you "LEAP[6]."Of all the girls he <u>is fond of</u>② chatting with, he has a special crush on[7] a girl named Angel. The conversations between them promised Handsome a wonderful relationship, so one day he finally thought <u>it was time to</u>③ ask her out. Angel seemed more than happy and made a promise to meet him immediately[8] without <u>a second thought</u>④. They <u>agreed to</u>⑤ meet the next day, carrying a rose as a token[9] of love to identify[10] themselves. （圖2 ▶）That night Handsome was <u>too</u> excited <u>to</u>⑥ fall asleep, and couldn't help but wonder how lovely, mature[11] or sexy Angel would be. （圖3 ▶）Sleepless, he got up right after the sun rose[12] and dressed himself nicely, hoping that Angel would love him at first sight[13]. （圖4 ▶）Finally, they met. A girl biting a rose was walking toward him. That had to be his Angel, but she was far from[14] looking like an angel. Standing there in total shock, a thought suddenly crossed Handsome's mind: （結論句▶）"nothing is greater than imagination[15]."

— 支持句

Ch
3

盲目的約會

對韓森來說，網路交友幾乎快要變成他第二個正職。他白天工作，晚上則忙著在網路上跟女生談情說愛，希望因此可以「墜入」愛河。然而，愛情的熱忱使他喪失了理智，也忘記了一個諺語的忠告：「三思而後行。」在所有他喜歡聊天的對象中，他對一個叫安琪的女孩情有獨鍾。他們相談甚歡，因此韓森認為他們一定能夠譜出一段浪漫的戀情。所以，有一天，他終於覺得是時候約她出來見面。安琪似乎喜出望外，不加思索便立刻答應了。他們說好隔天見面，並以一朵玫瑰作為愛的信物來辨識彼此。那天晚上，韓森太興奮以至於無法入睡，他忍不住開始幻想到底安琪看起來會是可愛、成熟或是性感呢？整夜失眠後，隔天太陽一升起，他就立刻起床好好的打扮一番，希望安琪會對他一見鍾情。最後，他們終於碰面了。一個女子嘴裡叼著玫瑰走向他。那一定是他的安琪（天使）沒錯，只是她完全不像一個天使。他全傻了，頭腦裡只閃過一個念頭：「想像力真是不可思議。」

1. **handsome** (*adj.*) 英俊的

   Every girl dreams of getting married to a <u>handsome</u> guy someday.

   每個女孩都夢想有一天可以跟一個英俊的男生結婚。

   ★ Handsome 亦可當作人名，在文章裡，名字「韓森」與帥哥一語雙關。

2. **career** (*n.*) 職業

   Jason's <u>career</u> as a dancer started in 2002.

   傑森是從 2002 年開始從事舞者一職。

3. **flirt with** (*v.*) 調情

   Paul is a ladies' man; you can always see him <u>flirting with</u> girls.

   保羅可以說是情場高手，你總是可以看到他跟不同的女孩在調情。

4. **drive** (*v.*) 驅使

   The noise coming from the party <u>drove</u> the neighbor to call the police.

   派對傳出的噪音迫使鄰居報警處理。

5. **warning** (*n.*) 警告

   Fever is a <u>warning</u> sign of a cold.

   發燒可以視為生病的警訊。

6. **leap** (*v.*) 跳躍

   The fugitive <u>leapt</u> from the bridge into the river after he was surrounded by the police.

   當他被警方包圍後，逃犯從橋上縱身躍入河裡。

7. **have a crush on** 迷戀

   Jill <u>had a crush on</u> Brad Pitt after she saw his movie.

   姬兒看完布萊德‧彼特的電影後，就瘋狂地迷戀上他。

8. **immediately** (*adv.*) 立刻；立即

   Laura <u>immediately</u> apologized to the man after she stepped on his foot.

   羅拉不小心踩到那個男生的腳後，立刻向他道歉。

9. **token** (*n.*) 象徵

   Betty gave Julie a bracelet as a <u>token</u> of their friendship.

   蓓蒂給了茱莉一條手鍊，當作他們友誼的象徵。

10. **identify** (*v.*) 辨識

Twins sometimes look too similar to <u>identify</u> one from the other.

雙胞胎有時候看起來長得太像，以至於旁人難以分辨兩者。

11. **mature** (*adj.*) 成熟的

I think I am <u>mature</u> enough to make decisions for myself.

我想我已經夠成熟，可以自己做決定了。

12. **rise** (*v.*) 升起；上升

Like the Sun, the Moon <u>rises</u> and sets everyday.

如同太陽一樣，月亮每天都會升起和落下。

★「日出」是 sunrise；「日落」是 sunset。

13. **at first sight** 第一眼

Joe and Polly said they had fallen in love <u>at first sight</u>.

喬和波莉說他們彼此一見鍾情。

14. **far from** 差很多；完全不……

My writing ability is <u>far from</u> good.

我的寫作能力一點都不好。

15. **imagination** (*n.*) 想像力

<u>Imagination</u> is the source of invention.

想像力是發明之始。

英文檢定常考句型與改寫

① **in the hope of** 抱著……希望

Sally looked everywhere in the house,
- in the hope of finding
- in hopes of finding
- wishing to find
- hoping that she could find

the missing earring.

莎莉在家裡翻箱倒櫃，希望能夠找到那只不見的耳環。

② **be fond of** 喜愛

Jenny
- is fond of
- enjoys
- loves

listening to music.

珍妮很喜愛聽音樂。

③ **it's time ...** 是……的時間了

It' time
- for him to go to bed.
- that he went to bed.
- for bed.

是他該上床的時間了。／他早該上床睡覺了。／上床睡覺的時間到了。

★ it's time that 後面句子用過去式，是一種與現在相反的假設語氣，表示「早該……，卻還沒。」

④ **a second thought** 仔細思考

Paul signed the contract without
- a second thought.
- thinking twice.
- careful consideration.

保羅〔不加思索／沒有多想／沒有仔細思考〕，就簽了合約。

⑤ **agree to** 同意

Peter and Jerry cannot agree
- to give up the new project.
- with each other.
- on the new contract.
- that Kate is smarter than everyone else.

彼得和傑利無法〔放棄新的計畫案。／彼此認同。／對新合約意見一致。／同意凱特比起其他人都還要聰明。〕

★ agree 表示對人或事物的認同，用法如下：

agree
- to V
- with 人 (*n.*)
- on 事、物 (*n.*)
- that 句子

⑥ **too ... to** 太……以至於不能……

Bill is
- too young to
- not old enough to
- so young that he cannot

understand.

比爾〔太年輕以至於／年紀不夠大以至於／年紀還如此之小，所以他〕還不了解。

★ 上面三種句型 too ... to、enough ... to、so ... that 常常交替使用，是全民英檢和大考出現多次的改寫題型，要特別注意！

📄✏ 看圖寫作（三）

　　請根據以下四張圖片，依照「主題句」、「支持句」、「結論句」的結構，寫出一篇作文。

寫寫看

_____

_____

_____

_____

_____

_____

_____

_____

_____

_____

_____

_____

_____

A Bad Habit

（圖1，可作為主題句▶）Many people think having a bad habit[1] is not a big deal and ignore the potential dangers it might cause. Ted happened to^① be one of these people. He was in the habit of^② dropping cigarette[2] butts after smoking. What' worse, he never put them out[3]. Warned by many people as he had been^③, he never took the warning to heart[4].（圖2▶）One morning, Ted was walking down the street, smoking as usual. When he had finished smoking, he carelessly tossed the lit cigarette butt down as usual.（圖3▶）But this time, Ted didn't know a fateful[5] gust of wind would roll[6] it over to a wooden[7] house. Not aware of^④ the wisp[8] of smoke that started to wriggle[9] its way up like a snake behind his back, Ted just walked away.（圖4▶）A spark[10] at the corner of the wooden house soon turned into tongues of flame that devoured[11] half the house in a blink. Luckily, no one was injured in the accident. The news of the accident soon spread throughout town. Learning about it, Ted felt deeply regretful[12] that his bad habit had almost led to^⑤ a tragedy[13].（結論句▶）So guilty[14] was Ted that he swore[15] to quit smoking for good[16]^⑥, to avoid^⑦ anything like this happening again.

支持句

壞習慣

很多人認為壞習慣無傷大雅，也因此忽略了壞習慣可能潛在的危險性。泰德就是一個這樣的人。他習慣亂丟菸蒂，更糟的是，他從不將它們熄掉。許多人早就警告過他，但他從沒放在心上。一天早上，泰德走在街上，如同往常一邊吸著菸。當他抽完的時候，仍如同平時一樣順手將燃燒中的菸蒂丟棄。但這次，泰德萬萬沒想到，一陣致命的風竟會將菸蒂吹向木製的房屋。沒有注意到一股白煙，像一條蛇般在他的背後慢慢的竄起，泰德逕自走開了。一個在木屋角落的小星火瞬間就變成了數條火舌，一眨眼之間，就吞沒了大半的房子。所幸，沒有人在這次意外中受傷。這個意外的消息很快就在小鎮中傳了開來。知道了這件事情，泰德感覺到愧疚萬分，因為他的壞習慣差點釀成了一椿悲劇。他十分內疚，發誓一定要戒菸，以避免類似的事件重演。

1. **habit** (*n.*) 習慣

   Smoking and drinking are bad habits that are difficult to quit.
   抽菸和喝酒都是很難戒掉的壞習慣。

2. **cigarette** (*n.*) 香菸

   <u>Cigarettes</u> are becoming more and more expensive.

   香菸變得越來越貴了。

3. **put out** 熄滅

   All people in this building need to know how to <u>put out</u> fires.

   這棟大樓裡的每個人都必須知道該如何滅火。

4. **take ... to heart** 留心；在意

   Jenny always <u>takes</u> others' advice <u>to heart</u>.

   珍妮總是將他人的建議牢記在心。

5. **fateful** (*adj.*) 災難性的

   His <u>fateful</u> decision resulted in his own tragedy.

   他致命的決定造就了他自己的悲劇。

6. **roll** (*v.*) 滾動

   They <u>rolled</u> the dice to decide the winner.

   他們擲了骰子來決定誰是贏家。

7. **wooden** (*a.*) 木製的

   I think I'm too heavy to sit on this small <u>wooden</u> chair.

   我想我太胖了，不能坐在這張小小的木椅上。

8. **wisp** (*n.*) 一縷；一束

   A <u>wisp</u> of smoke rose from the chimney.

   一縷輕煙自煙囪升起。

9. **wriggle** (*v.*) 蠕動

   Earthworms <u>wriggled</u> out of the wet soil for air after the rain.

   下雨後，蚯蚓鑽出濕潤的土壤來呼吸空氣。

10. **spark** (*n.*) 火花

    Sometimes you can see a blue <u>spark</u> when two rocks are hit together.

    當兩塊石頭碰撞時，有時候你可以看到藍色的火光。

11. **devour** (*v.*) 吞噬

    The hungry beggar <u>devoured</u> the bread in one bite.

    飢餓的乞丐一口就吞掉了吐司。

12. regretful (*adj.*) 懊悔的

Sandy is <u>regretful</u> that she didn't study hard when she was a student.

珊蒂對於自己當學生時沒有努力讀書而感到懊悔。

13. tragedy (*n.*) 悲劇

Some people love <u>tragedies</u>, whereas some prefer comedies.

有些人喜歡悲劇，而另一些人則偏好喜劇。

14. guilty (*adj.*) 有罪惡感的；內疚的

Flora felt <u>guilty</u> about lying to her boss.

芙蘿拉對於跟老闆說謊的事感到內疚。

15. swear (*v.*) 發誓

Helena <u>swore</u> not to talk to Harry again.

海蓮娜發誓再也不要和海利說話。

16. for good 永遠地

Gary often beats his wife. I hope she will leave him <u>for good</u>.

蓋瑞常常痛打他的妻子。我希望她可以永遠地離開他。

★ for good 意思等同於 forever。

英文檢定常考句型與改寫

① **happen to** 碰巧

I ┌ <u>happened to</u> meet a movie star ┐ yesterday.
　└ <u>met</u> a movie star <u>by chance</u> ┘

我昨天碰巧遇到一個電影明星。

★ 注意：happen to 後面接「動詞」的時候，才有「碰巧」的意思。如果後面接「名詞」（也就是受詞），意思則是「發生到……」，我們看下面的例子。

• **I happen to <u>know</u> him.**（happen to 後面接「動詞」）
我碰巧認識他。

• **This kind of accident could happen to <u>anyone</u>.**（happen to 後面接「名詞」）
這樣的意外可能發生在任何人身上。

② **in the habit of** 習慣

Larry ┌ is used to ┐
　　　│ is in the habit of │ drinking a glass of warm water in the morning.
　　　└ is getting into the habit of ┘

賴瑞〔一直以來習慣／習慣／漸漸養成習慣〕早上喝一杯溫開水。

③ **... as/though ...,** 句子　**雖然……，但是**

這樣的句型其實是由 though 所引導的句子轉變而成的倒裝句，我們看下面的例子：

Slowly as / though he works, he always makes every window clean and shiny.

= Though he works slowly, he always makes every window clean and shiny.

★ 許多字都可以移至句首形成倒裝，在變成倒裝句後，though 也可以用 as 來代替。但要注意，名詞移到句首時，前面的冠詞 a、an、the 都要取消。

<u>Excellent student</u> as he is,
（名詞；an 取消）

<u>Hard</u> though he studied,　┤　he didn't pass the exam.
（副詞）

<u>Smart</u> as he is,
（形容詞）

〔雖然他是一個優秀的學生／雖然他很努力讀書／雖然他很聰明〕，他並沒有通過考試。

④ **be aware of**　**察覺到；意識到**

Ivy was not　┤　aware of getting on the wrong bus.

conscious of getting on the wrong bus.

aware that she had got on the wrong bus.

艾葳沒有察覺她上錯了公車。

⑤ **lead to**　**導致；引起**

The heavy rain　┤　led to

resulted in　├　a flood.

brought about

豪雨引起了洪水。

⑥ **So +**　┌ 形容詞
　　　　　　　　　　如此……以至於
　　　　　　└ 副詞

→ **變成倒裝句，目的在於「強調語氣」**

這樣的句型其實是由 "so ... that" 所產生的倒裝句，把「形容詞」、「副詞」移至前面來強化語氣。

這樣的句子要注意動詞和主詞的位置，我們來看下面的例句：

■ She was so shy that she couldn't look at the man.

倒裝：**So shy** was she that she couldn't look at the man.（be 動詞與主詞倒裝）

■ She felt so tired that she couldn't help but fall asleep.

倒裝：So tired did she feel that she couldn't help but fall asleep.（加上助動詞，而且將 so 倒裝到句首，主詞放到後面去。）

⑦ **to avoid** 以免；以避免

Don't forget to set your alarm clock ⎧ in case you sleep late.
                                      ⎩ to avoid sleeping late.

不要忘了設你的鬧鐘，以避免你睡太晚。

★ in case 可以當作「從屬連接詞」使用，後面接一個子句。

★ 如果是 in case of，後面要加上一個「名詞」。

★ avoid 後面接 V-ing。

UNIT
10

例子賦予文章說服力

　　例子放在文章中，最能夠增加文章的說服力。我們可以使用一個「長而仔細的例子」，也可以同時用「兩三個短的例子」來增加文章的可信度。例子可以是我們「個人或他人的經驗」、「假設的情況」、「事實」，當然如果能夠含有「數據」，就更顯專業了。不過，我們使用一個以上的例子時，要注意這些例子之間是否有強烈的關連？例子所使用的文字是否連貫性良好？例子選擇是否恰當？在這個單元我們一起透過幾個範例來學習如何用例子寫文章。

用例子寫文章（一）

The Importance of Playing

（引言▶）For most parents, their children's grades could always be better. As a result, seeing their sons and daughters immersed[1] in books seems to please[2] these parents most. However, having some extracurricular[3] activities might be more important than parents think for their children. （主題句▶）Whether it is a quiet activity <u>such as</u>① playing cards or chess or an active one like playing basketball, these games <u>in fact</u>② help to develop a child's brain and body. （例子一：靜態運動的好處▶）A game like cards or chess trains a player to develop[4] a better sense of logic[5], which is something difficult to learn from books. （例子二：動態運動的好處▶）On the other hand, doing some active exercise like playing basketball can not only strengthen[6] a child's muscles but also forces[7] blood to deliver more oxygen and nutrients[8] to the brain. Therefore, the brain is refreshed[9], and the body becomes strong and healthy enough to confront[10] any challenge[11]. （結論：玩樂反而讓孩童有更好的潛力▶）<u>It turns out that</u>③ children who <u>spend a lot of time playing</u>④ have much more potential[12] than those who don't. And this piece of wisdom[13] in fact is nothing new. <u>Just as the old saying goes</u>⑤, "All work and no play makes Jack a dull[14] boy."

── 支持句

玩樂的重要

對大部分的家長而言，小孩的成績總是可以更好。因此，沒有什麼比看到他們小孩埋首苦讀更讓他們心滿意足。然而，課外活動對小孩來說，遠比家長想的更為重要。不論是進行一個靜態的遊戲，例如：玩撲克牌、下棋或是從事動態活動，像是打籃球，實際上都有助於小孩身心上的成熟。進行像是玩撲克牌和下棋這類活動，可以幫助玩家培養良好的邏輯觀念，這是很難在課本中習得的。另一方面，打籃球這類的動態活動，不只能夠強化小孩的肌肉，還能夠使血液攜帶更多氧氣和養分至大腦，因此，大腦得以活化，而身體變得更為強壯、健康，足以面對各種挑戰。結果，花許多時間玩樂的小孩到頭來，比死讀書的孩子有更多的潛力。事實上，這道理早就不是什麼新聞，就如同這句古老諺語所言：「只工作不玩樂，會讓一個人變的乏味。」

1. **immerse in** (*v.*) 埋首於

   No matter when you see Bonnie, she is always <u>immersed in</u> her work.
   不論你何時看到邦妮，她總是埋首於工作。

2. **please** (*v.*) 討人喜歡

   The best thing to <u>please</u> a girl is a bouquet of flowers.
   沒有什麼比一束鮮花更能討女孩子的歡心。

3. **extracurricular** (*adj.*) 課外的

   Many Taiwanese students are not willing to do any <u>extracurricular</u> reading.
   許多台灣學生不願意做任何課外閱讀。

4. **develop** (*v.*) 逐漸養成；發展

   Working out <u>develops</u> muscles.
   健身可以使肌肉發達。

   ★ develop 同時也有照片沖洗的意思，所以洗照片叫做 develop photos.

5. **sense of logic** 邏輯概念

   ★ sense 是感知的意思，sense of ... 代表對什麼東西的感察能力，例如：He has no sense of direction.（他方向感很差。）

6. **strengthen** (*v.*) 強化

   Reading the Bible can <u>strengthen</u> your faith in God.
   閱讀《聖經》可以強化你對上帝的信仰。

7. **force** (*v.*) 迫使

The warden uses punishments to <u>force</u> the prisoners to behave themselves.

管理人員利用處罰來迫使囚犯遵守規矩。

8. **nutrient** (*n.*) 養分

Milk contains lots of <u>nutrients</u> that can help children grow up strong and healthy.

牛奶含有許多養分，能夠幫助孩子健康成長。

9. **refresh** (*v.*) 使得到補充；使重新振作

A lot of people take a shower before going to bed to <u>refresh</u> themselves.

許多人睡覺前會沖個澡，讓自己好好放鬆。

10. **confront** (*v.*) 迎面對抗

It takes courage to <u>confront</u> one's own weakness.

面對自身的弱點是需要勇氣的。

11. **challenge** (*n.*) 挑戰

Avery is a person willing to accept any unknown <u>challenge</u>.

艾佛瑞是一個樂於接受任何未知挑戰的人。

Ch
3

12. **potential** (*n.*) 潛質；潛力

It's unfortunate that many people do not achieve their <u>potential</u>.

許多人沒有發揮他們的潛力，實在是一件很可惜的事情。

13. **wisdom** (*n.*) 智慧

The police showed great <u>wisdom</u> in dealing with the bank robber.

警方在與銀行搶匪周旋時，展現高度的智慧。

14. **dull** (*adj.*) 令人生厭的；無趣的

Because I can't dance, I often feel <u>dull</u> and awkward at parties.

我因為不會跳舞，在派對上總是感覺無聊又尷尬。

① **such as** 例如

I like sweet fruits ┬ such as ┬
　　　　　　　　　├ like　　├ apples, litchi and grapes.
　　　　　　　　　└ e.g. ┘

我喜歡甜的水果，例如：蘋果、荔枝和葡萄。

★ 上面三個都是介系詞，所以其後都一定得接「名詞」。

★ e.g. 為拉丁文的縮寫，意思是同 for example。許多人常會將其與 ex. 混淆，而 ex. 是 example 單一字的縮寫，較常用在數學上，表示例題。在寫作中舉例的時候，常使用 e.g.。

② **in fact** 實際上

As a matter of fact, ┐
In fact, 　　　　　　├ everybody needs love.
Actually, 　　　　　┘

實際上，人人都需要愛。

③ **It turns out that** + 句子　結果竟然是……。

It turns out that ┬ he is a murderer.
　　　　　　　　├ medicine used incorrectly can be harmful to the body.
　　　　　　　　└ love can sometimes hurt.

結果竟然〔他是一個殺人兇手。／錯誤的用藥可能會傷害身體。／愛有時候很傷人。〕

④ **spend** 時間 + **V-ing** 花了多久的時間，去……。

They spent ┬ three months tour**ing** Taiwan.
　　　　　　├ one week prepar**ing** for the final exams.
　　　　　　└ their whole life help**ing** the poor.

他們花了〔三個月的時間在台灣旅遊。／一個星期的時間準備期末考。／一輩子在幫助窮困的人。〕

⑤ **As the old saying goes, ...** 正如一句諺語所言，……。

As the old saying goes, ┬ "Honesty is the best policy."
　　　　　　　　　　　├ "Beauty is in the eye of the beholder."
　　　　　　　　　　　└ "Actions speak louder than words."

正如諺語所言：〔「誠實為上策」。／「情人眼裡出西施」。／「行動勝於空談」。〕

My Best Teacher Ever

（ 引 言 ▶ ）Teachers <u>play an important role</u>[①] in helping us to acquire[1] knowledge. Some of them teach us how to appreciate[2] the beauty of literature, <u>whereas</u>[②] others clarify[3] the mystery[4] of science. However, I have a lifelong[5] teacher who teaches me much more other than just knowledge—his name is Failure[6]. （主 題 句 ▶ ）Failure always gives me a pang[7] of frustration[8] but then guides[9] me from pain and sorrow to enlightenment[10]. （本文的支持句使用一個長的例子：上學期所發生的事▶）What he taught me last semester, for example, purged[11] my mind of arrogance[12]. As one of the top students in my class, I was proud of my intelligence[13]. Studying after school, in my opinion, was the last thing I needed to do. When it was time for final exams and the examination[14] papers were put on my desk, those questions however, harder than I expected, landed me in total shock. They all seemed familiar, but none of them seemed promising[15]. When the result of the tests was posted, my rank had fallen below the top ten in my class. （結論：學習到的智慧▶）I finally realized that <u>instead of</u>[③] talent and potential, hard work is <u>the real key to</u>[④] success. <u>I am grateful for</u>[⑤] what Failure has taught me. Now, every time I fail[16], I know that there must <u>be</u> something <u>worth</u>[⑥] learning.

━ 支持句

範文翻譯

我最棒的老師

老師總是扮演幫助我們學習知識的重要角色。有些老師教導我們欣賞文學之美，而有些則幫助我們解惑科學之謎。然而，我有一個陪伴我一輩子的老師，教導我比知識更為重要的東西，他的名字叫做：「失敗」。失敗總會讓我陷入一陣挫折感中，但是接著引領我走出痛苦和難過，並給予我啓發。例如，上學期他教會我如何掃除心中的自大。身為班上前幾名，我對自己的聰明才智感到很自豪，當時的我總認為，課後學習根本就是沒必要的事情。當期末考來臨，考題放在我的桌上時，我整個人愣住了，因為題目比我想像中的要難得多。每一題看起來都有印象，但是沒有一題有把握。考試結果出來，我的排名在班上掉到十名之外。我終於了解到，最重要的不是天分和潛力，努力才是成功的關鍵。我很感謝失敗所教導我的一切，現在每一次我失敗，我都明白，一定有什麼值得我學習的東西。

1. **acquire** (*v.*) 獲得;學到

   A part-time job can help students <u>acquire</u> both social and job skills.

   兼職工作可以幫助學生習得社交以及工作技巧。

2. **appreciate** (*v.*) 珍惜;欣賞

   Her advice was not <u>appreciated</u>.

   她的建議並沒有受到重視。

   ★ appreciate 後面常加動名詞或名詞,表示珍惜某件事情。例如:I really appreciate being given this chance to say something.(我真的很感謝有這個機會可以跟大家說說話。)

3. **clarify** (*v.*) 變得清晰;闡明

   The speaker was asked to <u>clarify</u> some confusing points in his talk.

   演講者被要求解釋其演講中令人困惑的一些重點。

4. **mystery** (*n.*) 神祕事物;謎

   How the pyramids were built is one of the greatest <u>mysteries</u> on Earth.

   金字塔到底如何建造的,仍然是世界上最難解的謎團之一。

5. **lifelong** (*a.*) 一輩子的

   Knowledge is a <u>lifelong</u> possession.

   知識是一輩子的資產。

6. **failure** (*n.*) 失敗

   The new project was proven to be a complete <u>failure</u> and was thus shut down.

   這項新的計畫被證實為一大失敗,也因此被終止。

7. **pang** (*n.*) 一陣痛苦

   Jennifer felt a <u>pang</u> of guilt when she lied to her best friend.

   當珍妮佛向她最好的朋友撒謊時,感到一陣罪惡感。

8. **frustration** (*n.*) 挫折

   When children are asked to become more independent, they may experience some <u>frustration</u>.

   當小孩被要求變得更加獨立時,有時候他們會感到相當挫折。

9. **guide** (*v.*) 引導

   He took the arm of the blind man and <u>guided</u> him across the road.

   他挽著那個盲人的手臂,引導他過馬路。

10. **enlightenment** (*n.*) 啓蒙

The Bible has brought <u>enlightenment</u> to many people.

《聖經》啓發了許多人。

11. **purge** (*v.*) 淨化；清除

A rainstorm usually <u>purges</u> the air of pollutants.

一陣豪雨通常可以清除空氣中的汙染物。

12. **arrogance** (*n.*) 自負；傲慢

<u>Arrogance</u> prevents us from progressing.

自負會阻礙一個人的進步。

13. **intelligence** (*n.*) 才智

Everyone admires people of high <u>intelligence</u>.

每個人都會尊敬才智甚高的人。

14. **examination** (*n.*) 考試

The teacher gave us an <u>examination</u> in English.

老師對我們進行英文測驗。

15. **promising** (*adj.*) 有希望的

Michael was considered the most <u>promising</u> new player in the league.

麥克被認為是聯盟中最被看好的新選手。

16. **fail** (*v.*) 失敗

Sam <u>failed</u> to win a place in the finals.

山姆沒辦法在決賽中贏得名次。

英文檢定常考句型與改寫

① **play an important role** 扮演重要的角色

A teacher always plays an important role in
- taking care of the students.
- teaching lessons.
- monitoring bad behavior.

一個老師扮演著〔照顧學生／教導課業／糾正學生錯誤行為〕的重要角色。

② **..., whereas ...** 而

Different people like different drinks; some love coffee, whereas others might

- favor tea.
- be fond of juice.
- prefer soda.

不同的人喜歡不同的飲料。有些人喜歡咖啡，而另一些可能
〔偏愛茶。／喜歡喝果汁。／偏好汽水。〕

③ **instead of** ＋受詞 不……，而；取代……

Since his knee is injured, he'd better swim instead of

- jogg**ing**.
- hik**ing**.
- mountain climb**ing**.

既然他的腳受傷，如果要運動的話，他最好游泳，而不要〔慢跑。／健行。／爬山。〕

④ **the key to** ＋受詞 ……的關鍵

Patience is the key to

- becom**ing** a good teacher.
- victory.
- success fully losing weight.

耐心是〔成為一個好老師／勝利／成功減重〕的關鍵。

⑤ **be grateful**

- **to** 人（這個 to 是介詞）
- **for** 事情　　　　　　　　**對……表示感激**
- **to** 動作（這個 to 是不定詞，所以加原形動詞）

I'm grateful

- to my teacher.（人）
- for what you have done.（事情）
- to have your help.（動作）

我很感激〔我的老師。／你所做的一切。／能夠有你幫忙。〕

⑥ **be worth** ＋受詞 值得……；價值……

This novel is worth

- US$20.00.
- read**ing** carefully.
- add**ing** to your collection.

這本書〔價值美金 20 元。／值得仔細閱讀。／值得加入你的收藏。〕

Pets

（引言▶）More and more people choose[1] to live alone nowadays[2]. But living alone does not necessarily mean being lonely and miserable[3]. Some people find a great partner to spend their time with, <u>that is</u>①, a pet. （主題句 ▶）A pet for most pet owners is not only great company[4] but seems to have magic power to <u>drive away</u>② sorrow and trouble. （例一：金魚解除焦慮▶）The little tricks they do and their cute movements[5] can cheer[6] you up when you are <u>in a bad mood</u>③. Watching goldfish peacefully weave[7] their way through the water plants is always the best medicine to cure anxiety[8]. （例二：狗兒幫你改變心情▶）Moreover, every time when you feel frustrated[9] or small, your dog will remind[10] you how important you are by bringing back every ball and smile you throw to him or her. （例三：貓咪等門的貼心舉動▶）And nothing is more touching[11] than seeing your cat welcome you at the doorstep when you drag[12] your weary[13] body home after an exhausting day. （結論句：重申人們喜歡寵物的主因和寵物對人的正向助益▶）The reason why most people cannot help but love their pets so much is that they make you feel needed, and your devotion[14] to them is never <u>taken for granted</u>④. The feeling of being needed and appreciated reaffirms[15] your own value. Therefore, more and more people agree that with a pet around, a lover is <u>no longer</u>⑤ the only choice.

支持句

範文翻譯

寵物

這個年頭，越來越多人選擇獨居。但是一個人住，並不一定就與孤單和痛苦劃上等號。有些人找到一個可以陪伴他們的更佳伴侶，那就是：寵物。對許多飼主來說，寵物不僅是一個好夥伴，還似乎有某種神奇的力量能夠消除他們的困擾和哀愁。當你處在低潮時，牠們耍的一些把戲和可愛的舉動總能夠轉變你的心情。看著金魚靜謐地穿梭於水草之間，總是治癒你焦慮的最佳良藥。除此之外，當你感到沮喪，對自己失去信心，看著你的狗兒把每一顆你丟出的球啣回腳邊，你就會知道你對牠們有多重要，進而重拾笑顏。還有，當你累了一整天，拖著沉重的身體回到家門前，沒有什麼比看到你家的貓在門廊歡迎你，更讓人覺得感動。人們之所以無法抗拒熱愛寵物，就在於牠們讓你感覺被需要。而你對牠們的付出也從來不會被視作理所當然。這種被需要和珍惜的感受，再次強化了你個人的價值。因此，越來越多的人同意，當你身邊有個寵物，情人不再是唯一的選擇。

1. **choose** (*v.*) 選擇

   Even though he hurt my feelings, I <u>chose</u> to forgive him.
   即使他傷了我的感情，我還是選擇原諒他。

   ★ 很多人常會把「動詞」choose，與「名詞」choice 混淆。「做選擇」我們常用 make a choice 這個片語，我們看下面的例子：There are too many sightseeing spots that Avery would like to go to, so he has to <u>make a choice</u> among them.（有太多觀光景點艾佛瑞想要去，所以他得在這麼多之中做一個選擇。）

2. **nowadays** (*adv.*) 現今；時下

   More and more people prefer organic food <u>nowadays</u>.
   現今社會，越來越多人喜好有機食物

3. **miserable** (*adj.*) 悲慘的

   Many children in the third world lead a <u>miserable</u> life.
   許多第三世界的孩童過著悲慘生活。

4. **company** (*n.*) 陪伴；伴侶

   I bought a puppy for Lily to keep her <u>company</u> when I'm not with her.
   我買了一隻狗給莉莉，當我不在她身邊時，可以陪伴她。

   ★ 英文常用 keep ... company 的片語，用來表示「與……作伴」。

5. **movement** (*n.*) 動作；行動

   The U.S. government is carefully watching the <u>movements</u> of so called terrorists.
   美國政府正密切注意所謂的「恐怖分子」的行動。

6. **cheer up** 使高興

   A good friend always <u>cheers</u> you <u>up</u> when bad things happen.
   一個好朋友總是能夠在壞事情發生時，讓你開心。

7. **weave** (*v.*) 穿梭；交織

   The biker <u>weaved</u> expertly through the traffic.
   那個騎士俐落地在車陣中穿梭。

   His grandma <u>weaves</u> a new scarf for him every winter vacation.
   他的奶奶每年寒假都會織一條新的圍巾給他。

8. **anxiety** (*n.*) 焦慮

   Working under a lot of pressure can cause great <u>anxiety</u>.
   在極大壓力下工作，可能會導致強烈的焦慮。

9. **frustrated** (*adj.*) 沮喪

Children easily feel <u>frustrated</u> if they cannot receive positive feedback from their parents or teachers.

當孩子無法從父母或師長那裡得到正面的肯定時，他們很容易喪失信心。

10. **remind** (*v.*) 提醒

The secretary <u>reminded</u> her boss that he was going to have a meeting this afternoon.

祕書提醒她的老闆，他今天下午有一個會議要開。

★ remind 習慣加上受詞後，用 that 來引導一個「子句」。但也可以用 remind ... of 來連接一個「名詞」。我們看下面的句子：Jenny's beautiful eyes always remind me of her mother.（珍妮美麗的眼睛總讓我想起她媽媽。）

11. **touching** (*adj.*) 感人的

Mary's <u>touching</u> story moved everyone to tears.

瑪莉感人的故事讓每一個人都潸然淚下。

12. **drag** (*v.*) 拖著行進

The little boy <u>dragged</u> a chair across the room to sit beside his mother.

小男孩拖著一張椅子穿過房間，想要坐在他的母親身旁。

13. **weary** (*adj.*) 疲倦的

To achieve one's goal in life can sometimes be a long, <u>weary</u> journey.

要達到人生的目標，有時候是一條漫長且累人的旅程。

14. **devotion** (*n.*) 奉獻；投入

Parents' <u>devotion</u> to their children is selfless.

父母對孩子的奉獻是無私的。

15. **reaffirm** (*v.*) 再次肯定

When Lisa blushed her cheek as she explained what happened <u>reaffirmed</u> my guess that she was lying.

當莉莎在解釋發生的事情時，她臉上的紅暈使我更確定她在說謊。

① **that is, ...** 也就是說；那即是

No pain, no gain; that is, ⎰ success never comes easily.
⎱ only labor can lead you to achieving.

不勞則無獲；那也就是說，〔成功絕非偶然。／只有你的辛勞能帶給你成就。〕
★ that is 是轉折語，因此，如果前面有句子時，that is 的前面要用「分號」。

② **drive away** 驅離

Listening to soft music
Having a spa treatment ⎱ helps to drive away fatigue.
Soaking in a hot spring

〔聽柔和的音樂／接受 SPA 療程／泡溫泉〕有益消除疲勞。

③ **in ... mood** 處在……的心情

I'm not in the mood **to** argue（動詞）.
Since the night is so beautiful, ⎱ Jenny is in the mood **for** love（名詞）.
we are all in a good mood.

因為今天晚上實在太美好，
〔我實在沒心情跟你吵架。／珍妮有一種戀愛的心情。／我們全都有好心情。〕

④ **take ... for granted** 視……為理所當然

others' help for granted.
You shouldn't take ⎱ for granted what your friends do for you.
it for granted that you will win the game.

你不應該把〔別人的幫助／朋友為你的付出／贏得比賽〕視為理所當然。

⑤ **no longer** 不再

no longer believes in Santa Claus.
Patrick is a grown-up now, so he ⎱ no longer asks for an allowance from his parents.
is no longer forbidden to drink alcohol.

派翠克已經長大成人了，所以他
〔不再相信聖誕老人的存在。／不再跟父母要零用錢。／不再不能喝酒。〕

用「比較法」
創造深度

　　「比較」是一個可以廣泛運用到各式文章的技巧。意即用不同的角度或層次來比較兩件事情的異同，讓讀者認知我們的看法，並進一步認同我們的觀點。「比較」可用兩種方式進行，一種是「點的比較法」，另一種則是「面的比較法」。「點的比較法」是一點一點的進行，然後比較兩者同一個點上的差異；而「面的比較法」則是先全面性的分析一個事件的各個點，然後再進行到另一個事件上的各個點，我們看以下例子：

主題：A 書與 B 書的比較

❑ 點的比較法

一、先就「劇情」做比較
* A 書的劇情
* B 書的劇情

二、再做「角色」的比較
* A 書的角色分析
* B 書的角色分析

❑ 面的比較法

一、先一口氣討論 A 書的劇情和角色
二、再討論 B 書的劇情和角色

　　如果我們用「面的比較法」，因為範圍較大，所以不要忘記在分析第二個事件的各點時，仍然要稍微為讀者複習前面所言。另外，這技巧容易犯的錯誤就是，很多人只是單純的比較兩個事情的差異，卻沒有結論，讓人讀完之後不禁納悶：「那又怎樣？」。別忘了，用「比較法」寫作時，差異如果只是 "what"，作文尚未完成，另外還要有 "why"（為什麼要比較？），才有邏輯。文章是思考的產物，沒有邏輯，就兵敗如山倒！

Shopping at Stores vs. Shopping Online

（引言 ▶）<u>Due to</u>① its convenience¹, shopping online has become a fad². With a single click, an order is done, and your products will be in your hand in just one or two days. However, <u>quite a few</u>② people still <u>insist on</u>③ shopping on foot, walking in and out of one store after another and carrying³ bags and bags of products they have bought. It seems that the convenience of online shopping does not dispel⁴ the doubts⁵ of some traditional⁶ consumers⁷. （主題句 ▶）The efficiency of online shopping appears quite satisfying, but the potential risks of buying unsuitable things and revealing⁸ personal information send many skeptical⁹ shoppers into real stores. （點一：網路購物的優點；逛街購物的缺點 ▶）On the one hand, shopping online helps eliminate the effort of traveling to stores. In addition, without physical shop fronts, online stores can offer lower prices than real stores because of savings in rent. （點二：實體店面購物的優點；網路購物的缺點 ▶）On the other hand, you lose the ability to try out the things you buy. For instance, the size and color of the shirts you receive by mail may not live up to your expectations¹⁰, but this doesn't happen when you shop at a real store. Moreover, in a real store, your payment can be made by cash, debit card, or check¹¹. Unfortunately, credit cards are usually the only option¹² when you shop online. As a result, your credit card number and personal information may be at the <u>risk</u>④ of being stolen by hackers¹³ during the transaction. （結論：提供解決兩者缺點的建議 ▶）If you are worried about anything like this happening to you, choose an online store with a good reputation¹⁴ and make sure it has a good return policy¹⁵ and protects your privacy.¹⁶ Otherwise, get yourself up and shop on foot. Besides, doing so is also good exercise.

支持句

範文翻譯

店裡購物 vs. 網路購物

網路的便利性使上網購物變成了一股風潮。只要滑鼠輕輕一點，一筆交易就完成，而且只要一到兩天的時間，商品就會送到你的手上。然而，不少的民眾仍然堅持逛街購物，穿梭在一間一間的店面，提著大包小包買來的東西。這樣看起來，網路購物的便利性，似乎並沒有消弭一些傳統消

費者的疑慮。網路的便利性固然令人滿意，但是買到不適用的東西抑或是洩漏個人資料的危機，仍然讓一些有疑慮的消費者寧可在實體店面消費。一方面，網路確實可以省下買東西的舟車勞頓。而因為沒有實體店面所省下的租金，也讓網路業者可以提供比起在實體店面更低廉的價格。但另一方面，你卻喪失了直接試用商品的機會。舉例來說，你收到的郵寄襯衫，顏色或是尺寸可能跟你預期的有落差。這種情況就不會發生在實體店面。此外，在實體店面，你可以選擇以現金、金融信用卡或是支票付帳，但網路購物，信用卡通常是唯一選擇，因此在網路交易過程中，你的信用卡卡號和你個人資料就有可能被駭客盜取。如果你擔心類似的事情發生在你身上，最好選擇一個具有良好商譽的網路賣家，並確定他們會提供比較好的退貨機制和個人隱私的保護。否則，就快快起身，走路逛街去。此外，逛街購物也是一項不錯的運動。

重點字詞

1. **convenience** (*n.*) 便利　　**convenient** (*adj.*) 方便的
   7-Eleven is a well-known <u>convenience</u> stores in Taiwan.
   7-Eleven 是台灣著名的便利商店之一。
   Discussing homework with friends on LINE is very <u>convenient</u>.
   透過 LINE 跟朋友討論功課很方便。

2. **fad** (*n.*) 一時的流行
   Wearing big fancy hats was once quite a <u>fad</u>.
   在過去，頂著華麗的大帽子一度蔚為時尚。

3. **carry** (*v.*) 攜帶；提
   I have a habit of <u>carrying</u> a small bag with me wherever I go.
   不論我到哪裡，我都習慣提個小包包。

4. **dispel** (*v.*) 驅散；消除
   His explanation <u>dispelled</u> everyone's doubts.
   他的解釋消除了大家的疑慮。

5. **doubt** (*n.*) 疑惑
   There is no <u>doubt</u> about my faith in God.
   我對上帝的信仰是無庸置疑的。

6. **traditional** (*adj.*) 傳統的
   The older generation still has rather <u>traditional</u> views about sex.
   老一輩的人們仍然對性持有相當傳統的觀念。

7. **consumer** (*n.*) 消費者

The prices of goods fluctuate according to <u>consumer</u> demands.
物價是根據消費者的需求而變動。

8. **reveal** (*v.*) 使揭露

A spy cannot <u>reveal</u> his true identity.
一個間諜不可以透露其真實身分。

9. **skeptical** (*adj.*) 懷疑的

Many people are <u>skeptical</u> about the existence of God.
許多人對於上帝的存在存疑。

10. **expectation** (*n.*) 期待

There is sometimes a huge gap between your <u>expectations</u> and reality.
有時候，你所期待的與現實之間有極大的落差。

11. **check** (*n.*) 支票

I don't think I'll make it to the dinner tonight. Can I take a rain <u>check</u>?
我想我今天晚上無法跟你們一起共餐了。可以改天再一起吃飯嗎？
★ check 指支票，但是 rain check 則有延期的意思。英式英文拼為 cheque。

12. **option** (*n.*) 選項

A working mother usually has no <u>options</u> but hire a babysitter to take care of her child.
一個職業婦女經常沒有任何選擇的餘地，只能花錢請保母照顧她的小孩。

13. **hacker** (*n.*) 駭客

Most large companies try to find ways to stop <u>hackers</u> from stealing their business secrets.
大部分的大公司都努力設法阻止駭客竊取他們的商業機密。

14. **reputation** (*n.*) 名聲

The brand has won a lot of loyal customers because of its excellent <u>reputation</u>.
這個品牌因為它極佳的聲譽而贏得了許多忠實顧客。

15. **policy** (*n.*) 政策；方針

One of our school <u>policies</u> is to instill in students a love of reading.
我們學校有一項方針，就是教導學生熱愛閱讀。
★ instill in 指「滲透」

16. **privacy** (*n.*) 隱私

Everyone has to learn to respect others' privacy.

每一個人都必須學會尊重他人的隱私。

英文檢定常考句型與改寫

① **due to** 由於

His absence
- was due to
- resulted from
- was because of

illness.

他會缺席是因為他生病了。

★ due to 的 to 為介系詞，所以後面不可以接動詞或是句子，只能接名詞。

② **quite a few** 不少的

The club has
- quite a few
- a lot of
- plenty of

members.

這個社團有很多的成員。

★ 許多人常常分不清楚 quite a few、a few、few 三者的分別：few 是用來指「很少、幾乎沒有」；
a few 則是指「有一些」；quite a few 卻是指「數量蠻多」的意思。我們看下面的比較：
- Jason has a few friends. 傑森有一些朋友。
- Jason has few friends. 傑森沒什麼朋友。
- I have quite a few ideas. 我有不少主意。

③ **insist on** (*v.*) 堅持

★ insist 後面也可以加上 "that" 來銜接一個「子句」。

The defendant kept
- insisting on his innocence（受詞）.
- insisting that he was innocent（子句）.

被告一再堅稱他是無辜的。

④ **risk** (*v.*) 冒著風險

★ risk 可以當作「名詞」，也可以當作「動詞」用。當動詞時，其後要接 V-ing，我們看下面的用法。

The brave firefighter
- risked los**ing** his life to save the child
- saved the child at the risk of losing his life

in the burning house.

這勇敢的消防員在火場中冒著自己的生命危險救出了小孩。

Handwritten Cards vs. Email Cards

（引言 ▶）Down through the ages, words have never lost their power to bridge[1] the distance between people. They communicate[2] our emotions to others and show our concerns①. （主題句▶）However, hand-written cards and letters are being gradually[3] replaced② by email due to its convenience and faster delivery time. （點一：手寫卡片比 email 麻煩 ▶）Writing Christmas cards was the nightmare[4] of many in the past. A healthy wrist was everyone's wish, for you had to write every single word on every single card for each of your friends and family members. Even if some greetings were exactly the same, you had to repeat[5] the procedure[6] on every single card. If you happened to misspell[7] one word, you had to start all over again. However, email allows you to copy and paste. Corrections[8] can be done as many times as you want without leaving unsightly[9] marks. （點二：email 比郵局寄送更省時 ▶）Besides, with a click, all of your friends can receive[10] your electronic Christmas cards in no time③. You are excused from the toil[11] of rushing[12] to a post office to send the cards a week ahead of time. （結論：email 對人類彼此關係上正面的影響 ▶）Thanks to this new technology[13], the distance between people has been reduced[14], and relationships are easier to maintain.

— 支持句

範文翻譯

手寫卡片 vs. Email 卡片

雖然時代變遷，但文字從未失去弭除人和人之間距離的力量。文字幫我們彼此溝通，也維繫了我們的情感。然而，手寫卡片和信件卻逐漸的被 email 所取代，因為 email 既省事又省時。寫聖誕卡在過去可以說是所有人的夢魘。每個人都希望自己手腕夠健康，因為要給每一個朋友和每一個家庭成員的卡片，你都得一字一句的寫。即使有些道賀詞大同小異，每張卡片你還是得重複一次同樣的程序；如果你碰巧寫錯了一個字，你又得全部重來一遍。然而，email 俱備了複製、貼上的功能。不論你想要修改多少次，也絕對不會留下醜陋的痕跡。除此之外，只要輕輕一點，你所有的朋友都能夠一瞬間收到你的電子聖誕卡，你再也不用辛苦的衝去郵局，趕著在過節前寄出你的卡片。拜這項新科技所賜，人與人之間的距離變得更近，而感情也更容易維持。

1. **bridge** (*v.*) 使……連結

   ★ bridge 當「名詞」是橋梁的意思。當「動詞」時，則是像橋梁一樣，讓兩個東西產生連繫。

   English, as an international language, <u>bridges</u> communication barriers between different countries.

   英文作為國際通用語言，彌合了不同國家之間的溝通障礙。

2. **communicate** (*v.*) 溝通

   Some parents have difficulty <u>communicating</u> with their children.

   有些家長無法跟自己的子女溝通。

3. **gradually** (*adv.*) 逐漸地

   Many rare species on Earth have been <u>gradually</u> disappearing.

   許多稀有的物種已逐漸從地球上消失。

4. **nightmare** (*n.*) 夢魘；噩夢

   The little girl saw a big monster in her <u>nightmare</u>.

   小女孩在她的噩夢裡，看到一隻大怪獸。

5. **repeat** (*v.*) 重複

   A copycat <u>repeats</u> what others have already done.

   模仿者總重複別人做過的事情。

6. **procedure** (*n.*) 程序；步驟

   There are several complex <u>procedures</u> involved in making good wine.

   製造好酒需要經過許多複雜的步驟。

7. **misspell** (*v.*) 拼錯

   People tend to <u>misspell</u> a word if it is too long.

   如果一個字太長，人們就容易拼錯。

8. **correction** (*n.*) 改正；校正

   A book has gone through many <u>corrections</u> before it is published.

   一本書得歷經過很多次校正，才能夠出版。

9. **unsightly** (*adj.*) 醜陋的

   Behind Quasimodo's <u>unsightly</u> appearance is a kind heart.

   在鐘樓怪人醜陋的外表之下，有一顆善良的心。

10. **receive** (*v.*) 收到

You <u>receive</u> a bill after using a credit card to purchase something.
你用了信用卡購買東西後，才會收到帳單。

11. **toil** (*n.*) 辛苦；勞累

The working class can save enough money to buy a house in the city only after years of <u>toil</u>.
只有經過多年的辛苦勞動，勞工階層的民眾才可能擁有足夠的資金在都市中買一間房子。

12. **rush** (*v.*) 衝；趕忙的行動

Many office workers <u>rush</u> into MRT stations after 6 p.m.
下午六點一到，許多上班族一股腦湧進捷運站。

13. **technology** (*n.*) 科技

Many hope that future <u>technology</u> will enable human beings to live in space.
許多人期盼，未來的科技可以使人類在外太空生活。

14. **reduce** (*v.*) 減少

More and more people are starting to recycle in order to <u>reduce</u> waste.
越來越多人開始進行資源回收，以減少廢棄物。

英文檢定常考句型與改寫

① **concern** 使關心；使掛心

★ 注意：concern 既可以當「名詞」，又可以當作「動詞」使用。用下面三句類似的句子，我們來了解 concern 的用法。

■ Peter's parents showed their concern（名詞）for his health problems.
彼得的父母對他的健康表示關心。

■ Peter's health problems concerned his parents.
彼得的健康問題使他的父母很掛心。

■ Peter's parents were concerned about his health problems.
彼得的父母很掛心他的健康問題。

② **replace** 取代

Scientists are trying to find new energy resources to
- replace
- substitute
- take the place of

petroleum.

許多科學家正努力尋找新能源來取代石油。

③ **in no time** 在很短的時間之內

The thief disappeared around the corner
- in no time.
- in the blink of an eye.
- in a flash.

小偷〔一瞬間／一眨眼／突然之間〕就消失在街角。

To Live or Not to Live with Parents

（引言 ▶）Western and Eastern parents hold very different <u>points of view</u>[①] toward raising children. While Western children are expected to be economically independent[1] and leave the nest at 18, Asian parents <u>regard</u>[②] it as a virtue for their children stay at home and share in the household earnings[2]. These two contrary versions of the family show very different ethnic[3] values and result in two different cultures. （主題句 ▶）The development of independence emphasized[4] by Western parents in young children results in mature youngsters but sometimes poor family bonding, while in Asia the emphasis[5] on family love creates a great support system within the family though it sometimes also becomes an accomplice[6] in spoiling[7] children. （面一：西方家庭的優點和缺點，一口氣寫出來 ▶）Most juveniles[8] in the West travel around the country and work part time to pay their tuition[9]. Working facilitates[10] their mastering of interpersonal communication and social skills. However, leaving home so early possibly dilutes[11] the emotional attachment to their parents. When they get old, some parents end up lonely in nursing homes with their children seldom[12] visiting. （面二：東方家庭的優點和缺點，一口氣寫出來 ▶）On the contrary, most Asian parents provide shelter[13] for their children and devote[14] almost all their money and energy to them until they graduate from college and find a job. In this way, their children are <u>liberated from</u>[③] the burden of earning their daily bread and get a chance to explore[15] their interests and <u>focus on</u>[④] their studies. In return, these children feel it's their obligation[16] to <u>look after</u>[⑤] their parents. Nevertheless, in some cases, these carefree children may refuse[17] to grow up, take on proper responsibilities, and ultimately become a parasite[18] on the family. （結論：給予兩種家庭建議 ▶）In fact, neither of these family models is perfect, and each can be a good mirror for the other to reflect upon the shortcomings. Frequent attending to children's emotional needs can make up[19] for the physical distance between Western parents and their children, whereas imposing[20] more duties[21] upon Asian children may increase their confidence and sense of responsibility.

支持句

與父母同住或是不與父母同住

西方和東方的家長對於如何養育孩子，秉持相當不同的看法。西方小孩通常被期許在十八歲之後，能夠經濟獨立並且離開家庭；而東方家長則認為，小孩留在家庭中共享家庭收入，才是一種美德。這兩種相反的家庭原型，顯示了很不相同的種族價值觀，也造就了兩種不同的文化。西方家長重視培養小孩的獨立性，使得這些年輕人變得更成熟，但卻有時候使得家庭凝聚力不足。而在亞洲，重視親情的觀念，在家庭裡創造了一個良好的互助系統，可是有時卻也變成了寵壞小孩的幫凶。在西方，很多青少年都是在國家內不同地方搬遷，並且打工付自己的學費。工作促進了他們人際溝通和社會技巧的成熟。然而，太早離家似乎沖淡了他們對父母情感上的依賴。有些父母晚年時，最終淪落至安養院，小孩也很少前往探望。而亞洲父母卻與前者相當不一樣，他們提供小孩居住的地方，並且投入所有金錢和精力來照顧小孩，直到他們大學畢業自己找到工作為止。藉由這種方式，亞洲小孩不用擔心生計問題，也得以探索自己的興趣並專注在學業上。為了報答父母，這些孩子覺得他們有義務得照顧自己年邁的雙親。然而，有些情況，這些無憂無慮的小孩拒絕長大並承擔責任，最終變成家裡的米蟲。事實上，這兩種家庭似乎都並不是完美典範，可是其中一者可以當作另一者的借鏡，來反思其不足。經常關心小孩的心理需求，或許就可以彌補西方父母與孩子空間上的距離；而讓亞洲小孩從小學會承擔義務或許能夠增加他們的自信心和責任感。

Ch
3

1. **independent** (*adj.*) 獨立自主的

   Teachers should encourage students to have <u>independent</u> thought.

   老師應該鼓勵學生有獨立思考的能力。

2. **earnings** (*n.*) 收入

   Women's <u>earnings</u> used to be lower than men's in the past.

   在過去，女人的收入比起男人低。

3. **ethnic** (*adj.*) 種族的；民族的

   It is common to see <u>ethnic</u> conflicts within a country featuring different races.

   一個國家如果包含許多不同種族，就不難見到種族間的衝突。

4. **emphasize** (*v.*) 強調

   The writer used boldface to <u>emphasize</u> the key words in the article.

   作者用粗體來強調文章中的關鍵字。

5. **emphasis** (*n.*) 強調；重視

   The teacher put <u>emphasis</u> on the key words when he was making a speech.

   這位老師在演講的時候，會特別強調關鍵的字詞。

★ "emphasis" 的動詞為 "emphasize"，不要混淆。我們看下面作「動詞」時的例句：The teacher emphasized what he was saying by using some hand gestures.（這位老師用手勢來強調他說話的內容。）

6. **accomplice** (*n.*) 共犯

The police are trying to find the whereabouts of the murder's <u>accomplice</u>.
警方正試圖找出殺人凶手的共犯。

7. **spoil** (*v.*) 寵壞；破壞

Giving everything to a child will only <u>spoil</u> him or her.
任小孩予取予求只會寵壞他／她。

Let's not <u>spoil</u> the wonderful feeling tonight.
我們別破壞今晚美好的氣氛。

8. **juvenile** (*n.*) 青少年

In most countries, <u>juveniles</u> are not allowed to drink alcohol.
在許多國家，青少年不得飲酒。

9. **tuition** (*n.*) 學費

The <u>tuition</u> at a private school is usually much higher than that of a public one.
私立學校的學費通常較公立學校高出許多。

10. **facilitate** (*v.*) 促進

Wasting energy <u>facilitates</u> global warming.
能源浪費促使了全球暖化。

11. **dilute** (*v.*) 沖淡；稀釋

Brian <u>diluted</u> the concentrated fruit juice with water.
布萊恩加水稀釋了濃縮果汁。

12. **seldom** (*adv.*) 稀少；鮮少

It <u>seldom</u> rains in deserts.（頻率副詞）
沙漠中鮮少降雨。

13. **shelter** (*n.*) 避難所

Home is a <u>shelter</u> from danger.
家是讓我們遠離危險的避難所。

14. **devote** (*v.*) 奉獻於；致力於

He <u>devoted</u> himself to charity.

他全心全意投身於公益。

15. **explore** (*v.*) 探索

The ocean is so huge that there are still a lot of places waiting for us to <u>explore</u>.

海洋是如此浩瀚，仍有許多地方等著我們去探索。

16. **obligation** (*n.*) 義務

Everybody is under an <u>obligation</u> to protect the Earth.

每一個人都有義務來保護地球。

17. **refuse** (*v.*) 拒絕

The police <u>refused</u> to comment on the killing.

警方拒絕對命案發表任何言論。

18. **parasite** (*n.*) 寄生蟲

It's easy to find <u>parasites</u> on wild animals.

在野生動物身上，很容易發現寄生蟲。

19. **make up** (*v.*) 彌補

The manager gave some coupons to <u>make up</u> for the customer's loss.

經理給了這個顧客一些折價券，以彌補他的損失。

20. **impose** (*v.*) 加諸

I don't want to <u>impose</u> on you by staying too long.

我不想耽擱太久而打擾你。

21. **duty** (*n.*) 責任；義務

One of a secretary's <u>duties</u> is to schedule her / his boss's meetings.

祕書的職責之一，就是替她的老闆規劃會議時間。

英文檢定常考句型與改寫

① point of view 觀點

Everybody has to learn to see things from a different
- point of view.
- viewpoint.
- perspective.
- angle.

每一個人需要學會以不同的〔觀點／角度〕來看事情。

② regard (v.) 認為

Virginia Woolf is
- regarded as
- considered
- held as

one of the greatest female writers.

吳爾芙被認為是最偉大的女作家之一。

③ liberate ... from 解放；釋放

The government
- liberated
- freed
- released

all the petty criminals from jail.

政府釋放了所有輕罪犯。

④ focus on 專注於

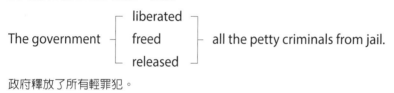

Everybody was trying to
- focus on
- concentrate on

what the speaker was talking about.

每一個人都試圖專心聆聽演講者正在討論的內容。

⑤ look after 照顧

Being a big brother, he needs to
- look after
- take care of
- give attention to

his baby sister all the time.

身為大哥，他必須隨時〔照顧／照料／注意〕年幼的妹妹。

Chapter 4

進階高級寫作

UNIT 12   用字遣詞是化妝師

　　以下是英文作文中常見到的基本用語，我們就用它們來做例子，讓各位讀者一眼就知道如何立刻提升英文寫作的用字遣詞。

📝 寫作的常用語（一）

　　為了突顯這些用語的技巧，我們暫時使用十分口語且淺顯的文字和句子做例子。本書隨後會有嚴格而正式的訓練。

常用語 1　表達「我認為」、「認同」

初級英文	**I think** 例 **I think** she is right.

⇓

高級英文	**I'm convinced**（因為事實證明，而使人相信） 例 **I'm convinced** that she is right. 　我完全相信她是對的。

初級英文	**I regard** 例 **I regard** it as my responsibility.

⇓

高級英文	**I deem**（視為） 例 **I deem** it my responsibility. 　我認為這是我的責任。

初級 英文	**sb. believe** 例 **He believes** that she'll marry him.

⇃⇂

高級 英文	**sb. hold**（堅信） 例 **He holds** that she'll marry him. 他相信她一定會嫁給他。

初級 英文	**all consider** 例 We **all consider** her as a good student.

⇃⇂

高級 英文	**Undeniably**（無可否認地） 例 **Undeniably**, she is a good student. 我們絕對相信她是個好學生。

初級 英文	**believe** 例 It's out of the question that we **believe** this message cannot be wrong.

⇃⇂

高級 英文	**Indisputably**（無可置喙地） 例 This message is **indisputably** true. 這個訊息絕對錯不了。

常用語 2　表達「我不認為」、「不認同」

初級 英文	**I don't think** 例 **I don't think** he is successful.

⇃⇂

高級 英文	**It's challengeable**（可信度不高） 例 His success is **challengeable**. 我不認為他是成功的。

初級 英文	**I disagree** 例 **I disagree of** his attitude.

⇊

高級 英文	**It's disputable**（引人爭論的） 例 His attitude is **disputable**. 我不贊同他的態度。

初級 英文	**I don't believe** 例 **I still don't believe** that he'll marry her.

⇊

高級 英文	**It remains doubtful**（仍不可信） 例 **It remains doubtful** that he'll marry her. 我不相信他會娶她。

常用語 3 表達「可是」、「但是」

初級 英文	**but / however / nonetheless / yet**

⇊

高級 英文	有「比較」的意味：**whereas** 例 He is extroverted, **whereas** she is introverted. 他外向，可是她內向。

有「沒想到」的意味：surprisingly

例 **Surprisingly**, she won!

　但是她居然贏了！

有「遺憾」的意味：unfortunately

例 **Unfortunately**, this was only a dream.

　可是，這只是一場夢。

有「事情不僅於此」的意味：accompanied by the fact

例1 He got married, **but** none of us expected that he would marry Jenny!

　　↓ 改為

　He got married, **accompanied by the fact that** he married Jenny instead!

　他結婚了，不過他娶的是 Jenny！

例2 Mary is an English major, and she is an outstanding student.

　　↓ 改為

　Mary is an English major, **accompanied by the fact that** she is an outstanding student.

　瑪麗是英文系的學生，而且十分優秀。

高級英文

Ch
4

常用語4 　説明「例如」

初級英文	for example / for instance

⇊

高級英文	A supporting fact is（有事實根據的例子） 例 He is happy—**a supporting fact is that** he smiles all the time. 　他很快樂，例如，他臉上常掛著微笑。 A sad fact is（令人難過的例子） 例 He is merciless—**a sad fact is that** he tortures animals. 　他很無情，例如，他會折磨動物。

A pleasant fact is（令人愉快的例子）

例 His efforts are rewarded—**a pleasant fact is that** he is graduating summa cum laude.

他的努力得到回報。例如，他即將以優異的成績畢業。

※ summa cum laude [ˈsʊmə kʌm lɔd] (adv.) 以優異的成績……

A significant reason is（重要的例子）

例 Traveling is beneficial. **A significant reason is that** it enriches our lives and broadens our horizons.

旅行對人有益。例如，它豐富了我們的人生、擴展了我們的視野。

A vivid example is（活生生的例子）

例 He babies her. **A vivid example is** he cooks for her everyday.

他寵愛她。例如，他每天為她下廚。

An example comes to mind（我這就有一個現成的例子……）

例 The National Palace Museum has an unprecedented advantage in capturing ancient Chinese culture. **An example**, the jadeite cabbage, **comes to mind**.

國立故宮博物院在保存古老的中國文化方面得天獨厚。翠玉白菜就是一個現成的例子。

高級英文

常用語 5 説明「另一個例子是」

初級英文	Another example is / There's another example

⇃⇃

高級英文

This example doesn't stand alone（還有例子……）

例 第一個例子 + **This example doesn't stand alone.** + 第二個例子

例 Children can learn to respect animals under parental guidance. **A supporting fact is** that a child who is gentle with animals usually has parents who do the same. **This example doesn't stand alone.** A child who…

孩子經由父母引導而學習如何善待動物。例如，父母如果溫柔地對待動物，孩子通常也會這樣做。又例如，如果……

	This fact is supported by another example. （還有例子……） ※ 不過這些都屬「正面的」例子 例 第一個正面的例子 + **This fact is supported by another example.** + 第二個正面的例子
高級 英文	
	A more insightful example is（還有例子……） ※ 不過例子「更深入」、「更有意義」 例 第一個例子 + **A more insightful example is that** + 第二個更深入的例子

常用語 6　**表達「我永遠不會忘記」**

初級 英文	I'll never forget / I'll always remember

⇩⇩

	An image that never slips from my mind is ...（畫面永遠不會流逝） 例 **An image that never slips from my mind is** + 敘 述：the first time I saw a painting by Van Gogh in person.
高級 英文	A memory that will never fade away is ...（記憶永遠不會淡掉） 例 **A memory that will never fade away is** + 敘 述：the wonderful trip I took to Hokkaido with my family in 2008.
	A scene that shall always remain fresh is ...（此景常新） 例 **A scene that shall always remain fresh is** + 敘 述：the day my best friend got married.

Ch
4

用字遣詞練習：請嘗試用高級英文作文的用字遣詞，改寫以下句子。

① I really think that he will succeed.

改為：＿＿＿＿＿＿＿＿＿＿＿＿＿＿＿＿＿＿＿＿＿＿＿＿＿＿＿＿＿＿＿

② We all believe that he loves her.

改為：＿＿＿＿＿＿＿＿＿＿＿＿＿＿＿＿＿＿＿＿＿＿＿＿＿＿＿＿＿＿＿

③ I don't think boys are lazier than girls.

改為：＿＿＿＿＿＿＿＿＿＿＿＿＿＿＿＿＿＿＿＿＿＿＿＿＿＿＿＿＿＿＿

④ I love pets. For example, I have a cat and two dogs.

改為：＿＿＿＿＿＿＿＿＿＿＿＿＿＿＿＿＿＿＿＿＿＿＿＿＿＿＿＿＿＿＿

⑤ I love you, and I would die for you!

改為：＿＿＿＿＿＿＿＿＿＿＿＿＿＿＿＿＿＿＿＿＿＿＿＿＿＿＿＿＿＿＿

EXERCISE 12-1 參考答案

（以下答案只是參考，讀者可由本書中找出更多的進階用法）

① I'm highly convinced that he will succeed.

② Undeniably, he loves her.

③ It's disputable that boys are lazier than girls.

④ I love pets. A supporting fact is I have a cat and two dogs.

⑤ I love you, accompanied by the fact that I would die for you.

寫作的常用語（二）

常用語 1 表達「更何況」

初級英文	in addition, / moreover, / furthermore, / besides,

⬇⬇

高級英文	**..., let alone** 例 ... because I love her; **besides**, she is my only child. ↓ 改為 ... because I lover her, **let alone** that she is my only child. 我……是因為我愛她，更何況她是我的獨生女。
	still less, 例 I don't mind assisting my students; **besides**, it's my responsibility. ↓ 改為 I don't mind assisting my students; **still less**, I'm fulfilling my responsibility. 我不介意幫助學生，更何況這是我的職責。

常用語 2 說明「現在；目前」

初級英文	now / today / so far / yet

⬇⬇

高級英文	**to date** 例 This work is not finished **yet**. ↓ 改為 This work is not completed **to date**. 這個工作至今尚未完成。

Ch
4

at present

例 **So far** 30 people have already come.

↓ 改為

Thirty people have arrived at present. 目前來了三十人。

※ 在寫作中，0-9 須拼英文字，10 以上則使用阿拉伯數字。

※ 任何數字在句首都須拼出英文。

高級
英文

at the present stage

例 Let's wait and not reveal the crisis **yet**.

↓ 改為

Let's not reveal the crisis **at the present stage**.
我們目前暫時不要揭露危機。

Currently

例 They are doing really well **now**.

↓ 改為

They are **currently** performing marvelously.
他們目前表現得真好。

常用語 3 　我的結論是……

初級 英文	**my conclusion is ... / to sum up,**

⇓⇓

高級
英文

In conclusion,

例 **In conclusion,** + 句子

結論是，……

To summarize,

例 **To summarize,** + 句子

結論是，……

To state succinctly [sək'sɪŋktlɪ],

例 **To state succinctly,** + 句子

結論是，……

初級英文	because / for

⇩⇩

高級英文	**is ascribed to** 例 He is successful **because** he has worked hard. 　　↓ 改為 　　His success can **be ascribed to** hard work. 　　他因努力而成功。 **due to the fact (that)** 例 He failed **because** he never tried his best. 　　↓ 改為 　　He failed **due to the fact** he never tried his best. 　　他因未盡全力而失敗。

常用語 **5**   表達「停止」

初級英文	**stop ... / quit** 例 He is trying to **quit** smoking.

⇩⇩

高級英文	abstain from 例 He is trying to **abstain from** smoking. 　　他正在努力戒菸。

常用語 **6**   說明「習慣於」

初級英文	**be used to** 例 He **is used to** tolerating her.

⇩⇩

高級英文	**habitually** 例 He is **habitually** tolerant of her. 　他已習慣於容忍她。

初級英文	**get used to** 例 Students should learn to **get used to** working quickly and assuming great responsibilities.

⇓

高級英文	**adapt (oneself) to** 例 Students must **adapt themselves to** working efficiently and taking responsibility. 　學生應該習慣有效率地做事情和承擔責任。

常用語 7 　說明「在……方面特別」

初級英文	**especially ...** 例 He is **especially** strong with numbers.

⇓

高級英文	**specialize in** 例 He **specializes in** numbers. 　他對數字很在行。

常用語 8 　說明「比……好」或「不比……好」

初級英文	**better than** 例 His memory **is better than** mine.

⇓

高級英文	**superior to** 例 His memory **is superior to** mine. 　他的記憶力比我強。

| 初級英文 | **worse than / not better than**
例 My performance **is worse than** yours. |

⇓⇓

| 高級英文 | inferior to
例 My performance **is inferior to** yours.
我的表現比你差。 |

常用語9 表達「理當、應該」之意

| 初級英文 | **... should ...**
例 Students **should be** carefree. |

⇓⇓

| 高級英文 | supposedly
例 Students are **supposedly** carefree.
學生應該無憂無慮。 |

| 初級英文 | **... should ...**
例 Boys **should be** taller than girls. |

⇓⇓

| 高級英文 | theoretically
例 Boys are **theoretically** taller than girls.
男生應該比女生高。 |

常用語10 根據（報導）

| 初級英文 | **according to ...**
例 **According to** the newspaper, the birth rate is going down. |

高級英文	allegedly, 例 **Allegedly**, the birth rate is declining. 根據報導，出生率在下降。

常用語 11 真令人驚訝

初級英文	**What a surprise** 例 He didn't come. **What a surprise!**

↓↓

高級英文	surprisingly, 例 **Surprisingly**, he didn't show up. 他居然沒來，真令人驚訝！

常用語 12 我沒想到、真沒想到

初級英文	**I didn't know that** 例 **I didn't know that** I could pass!

↓↓

高級英文	unexpectedly, 例 **Unexpectedly**, I passed! 真沒想到，我居然過關了！

初級英文	**I never knew sth. would happen** 例 **I never knew** we would fall in love.

↓↓

高級英文	had never expected (would happen) 例 We fell in love, which **I had never expected**! 我從沒想到，我們居然戀愛了！

用字遣詞練習：請嘗試用高級英文作文的用字遣詞，改寫以下句子。

① You should forgive people; besides, she is your best friend.

改為：_____

② So far we have 35 applicants.

改為：_____

③ We are trying to get used to this new rule.

改為：_____

④ She is especially good at TESOL.

改為：_____

⑤ Her performance is better than mine.

改為：_____

⑥ My English is no better than yours.

改為：_____

⑦ According to the newspaper, <u>the ruling party</u>[1] won the election.

改為：_____

⑧ To my surprise, <u>the opposition party</u>[2] won the election.

改為：_____

⑨ I didn't know that you were going to marry Tom.

改為：（已舉行婚禮）_____

改為：（尚未舉行婚禮）_____

⑩ If there are 10 <u>purchase orders</u>[3], we should be able to break the record!

改為：_____

1. the ruling party 執政黨
2. the opposition part 反對黨
3. purchase orders 訂單

📖 EXERCISE 12-2 參考答案

（以下答案只是參考，讀者可由本書中找出更多的進階用法）

① You should forgive her, let alone that she is your best friend.
② We have 35 applicants at the present stage.
③ We are adapting ourselves with this new rule.
④ She specializes in TESOL.
⑤ Her performance is superior to mine.
⑥ My English is inferior to yours.
⑦ Allegedly, the ruling party won.
⑧ Surprisingly, the opposition party won.
⑨ A: Unexpectedly, you married Tom!
　 B: I never expected you would marry Tom.
⑩ Ten purchase orders would supposedly break the record.

📖 寫作的常用語（三）

常用語 1 用極大的力量

初級英文	**with great strength** 例 He lifts heavy objects **with great strength**.

⇊

高級英文	with the strength of several people 例 He lifts heavy objects **with the strength of several people**. 他用極大的力量抬重物。

常用語 2 在背後說人壞話

初級英文	**talk behind someone's back** 例 Don't **talk behind my back**.

⇊

高級英文	smear [smɪr] 例 Don't **smear** me. 不要在背後中傷我。

Ch
4

初級英文	**say bad things behind someone's back** 例 Don't **say bad things behind his back**. He is a very good person.

⇊

高級英文	malign [mə'laɪn] 例 Don't **malign** him—he's a good person. 他是一個有品格的人，不要說他壞話。

初級英文	**say bad things about someone** 例 They often **say bad things about her** because they are jealous.

↓↓

高級英文	vilify ['vɪləˌfaɪ] 例 They **vilify** her out of jealousy. 他們說她壞話是因為嫉妒。

常用語 3 百分百地保密

初級英文	**don't tell anyone** 例 He **didn't tell anyone** about it.

↓↓

高級英文	keep sth. strictly confidential 例 He **kept it strictly confidential**. 他沒告訴任何人。

初級英文	**promise not to let anyone know** 例 Please **promise not to let anyone know**.

↓↓

高級英文	maintain absolute secrecy 例 Please **maintain absolute secrecy**. 拜託完完全全保密！

常用語 4 任性而為

初級英文	**do whatever one wants to do** 例 Parents should not spoil their children by letting them **do whatever they want to do**.

↓↓

高級英文	capricious [kəˈprɪʃəs] 例 Children should not be allowed to be **capricious**. 孩子不該被寵而任性。

形容「活潑的」、「有活力的」

初級英文	active

⇩⇩

高級英文	vibrant（活潑的、容光煥發的） 例 You look **vibrant** today. 　　你今天看起來容光煥發！
	animated（生動活潑的） 例 This story is quite **animated**. 　　這個故事很生動。
	lively（生命盎然的） 例 We had a **lively** discussion. 　　我們進行了熱烈的討論。
	vivacious [vaɪˈveʃəs]（有活力的） 例 This old woman is **vivacious**. 　　這位老太太充滿活力。

📄 **較長的寫作常用語**

常用語 1 說明「事實上，並不……」

初級英文	**in fact** + 否定句 / **as a matter of fact** + 否定句 例 **In fact**, this saying isn't true.

⇩⇩

高級英文	there's no factual basis for ... 例 **There's no factual basis for** this. 　　這一方面的觀點並沒有事實根據。

Ch
4

常用語 2 表達「我們都知……有害」

初級英文	**We all know it's harmful to ...** 例 **We all know it's harmful to** eat too much.

⇩⇩

高級英文	poses known hazards to ... 例 Overeating **poses known hazards to** our health. 我們都知暴飲暴食對健康有害。

常用語 3 事實證明，……

初級英文	**The fact proves (that) ...** 例 **The fact proved** the prediction was correct.

⇩⇩

高級英文	the evidence suggests (that) 例 **The evidence suggested that** the prediction was correct. 事實證明，這個預測是正確的。

常用語 4 事實強烈地證明……；無庸置疑的

初級英文	**The fact strongly proves** 例 **The fact strongly proves** that teaching is learning.

⇩⇩

高級英文	an undeniable fact can be found 例 **An undeniable fact can be found** in the expression, "teaching is learning." 教即是學，這是無庸置疑的。

常用語 5 必須決定輕重緩急

初級英文	**must decide what the most important thing to do first is** 例 We **must** learn to **decide what the most important thing to do first is**.

↓↓

高級 英文	prioritize ... 例 We must learn to **prioritize**. 我們必須學會事有先後。

常用語 6 和別人一起（進行社交活動）的時候

初級 英文	while we're (eating) with people for social contact.

↓↓

高級 英文	in social (V-ing) 例1 **While we're talking with people for the purpose of social contact, we** .... ↓ 改為 **In social communicating**, we ... 當我們和別人進行社交方面的交談時，我們…… 例2 **While we eat with people for the purpose of social contact**, we ... ↓ 改為 **In social dining**, we .... 當我們和別人進行吃飯社交時，我們……

Ch 4

常用語 7 我們必須尊重別人，所以我們……

初級 英文	We must respect people, so we ... 例 **We must respect people, so we** should wear suitable clothes.

↓↓

高級 英文	We ... in due respect for others. 例 **We** are properly dressed **in due respect for others**. 為了尊重別人，我們的穿著需合宜。

如果我們……，就會……

初級英文	If we ..., we will ...

⇩

高級英文	... can be ... 例1 **If we** work hard, **we will** succeed. ↓ 改為 Hard work **can be** rewarding. 我們如果有努力，就會成功！ 例2 **If we** have faith, **we will** make it. ↓ 改為 Faith **can be** winning. 我們如果有信心，就會成功！

常用語 9 **如果我們從……的角度來看**

初級英文	If we look at it from the angle of ...

⇩

高級英文	from a ... perspective, ... 例1 **If we look at it from the angle of technology**, iPods are a great technological invention. ↓ 改為 **From a technical perspective**, iPods are a great technological invention. 從技術的角度來看，iPod 是一項很棒的科技發明。 例2 **If we look at it from the angle of money**, he is successful. ↓ 改為 **From a financial perspective**, he is successful. 如果我們以金錢的角度來看，他是成功的。

初級英文	on the basis of ...

⇓

高級英文	on a foundation grown from ... 例1 **On the basis of** love, marriage can succeed. 　　↓ 改為 　　Marriage is optimal **on a foundation grown from** love. 　　婚姻如果以愛為基礎，就會成功。 例2 Friendship grows strong **on the basis of** mutual trust. 　　↓ 改為 　　Friendship strengthens **on a foundation grown from** mutual trust. 　　以互信為基礎的友誼是堅固的。

EXERCISE 12-3

用字遣詞練習：請嘗試用高級英文作文的用字遣詞，改寫以下句子。

① She rushed to rescue the child with great power.

改為：＿＿＿＿＿＿＿＿＿＿＿＿＿＿＿＿＿＿＿＿＿＿＿＿＿＿

② She speaks with an active voice.

改為：＿＿＿＿＿＿＿＿＿＿＿＿＿＿＿＿＿＿＿＿＿＿＿＿＿＿

③ As a matter of fact, I don't think the estimate is reliable.

改為：＿＿＿＿＿＿＿＿＿＿＿＿＿＿＿＿＿＿＿＿＿＿＿＿＿＿

④ We all know that it's harmful to take drugs.

改為：＿＿＿＿＿＿＿＿＿＿＿＿＿＿＿＿＿＿＿＿＿＿＿＿＿＿

⑤ The fact proves that their hypothesis is absolutely correct.

改為：＿＿＿＿＿＿＿＿＿＿＿＿＿＿＿＿＿＿＿＿＿＿＿＿＿＿

⑥ We must respect others while we are talking to people for social contact.

改為：＿＿＿＿＿＿＿＿＿＿＿＿＿＿＿＿＿＿＿＿＿＿＿＿＿＿

⑦ We should care about students, so we should often talk to them.

改為：＿＿＿＿＿＿＿＿＿＿＿＿＿＿＿＿＿＿＿＿＿＿＿＿＿＿

⑧ Since parents should respect their children, we should listen carefully to them.

改為：＿＿＿＿＿＿＿＿＿＿＿＿＿＿＿＿＿＿＿＿＿＿＿＿＿＿

⑨ If you try to be happy, you'll get many things.

改為：＿＿＿＿＿＿＿＿＿＿＿＿＿＿＿＿＿＿＿＿＿＿＿＿

⑩ If we look at it from the angle of money, it's worthwhile.

改為：＿＿＿＿＿＿＿＿＿＿＿＿＿＿＿＿＿＿＿＿＿＿＿＿

EXERCISE 12-3 參考答案

（以下答案只是參考，讀者可由本書中找出更多的進階用法）

① She rushed to rescue the child with the momentum of an avalanche.

② She sounds animated.

③ There's no factual basis for this estimate.

④ Drugs pose known hazard to health.

⑤ An undiminished fact can be found in their hypothesis.

⑥ We must be respectful in social communicating.

⑦ Teachers constantly communicate with students in due concern for them.

⑧ Parents should listen attentively to children in due respect for them.

⑨ Cheerfulness can be rewarding.

⑩ It pays off from a financial perspective.

Ch
4

UNIT 13 句型強烈展現你的英文實力

相信許多人在寫作時都有相同的問題，那就是英文句子一直擺脫不了中式英文。即使擺脫了，也並不順遂，因為難以自在地寫出俐落而精湛的句子。正因為這種桎梏，很多人所寫的英文句子常顯累贅和軟弱，乏論美、力量，當然更缺乏吸引力。

何謂好句子？

1. 文法正確
2. 文字細膩
3. 語意清晰
4. 句子精簡並有力
5. 充滿魅力

當然，英文的句型若要真正脫胎換骨，還是需要藉助大量的造句練習。而在這個單元，我們將示範幾個初級英文及高級英文的句子供大家做對照參考。

例 1	他們不再活潑，而且變得很僵硬。
基礎英文	They are not active anymore, and they have become stiff.
高級英文	**Rigidity replaces animation.**

例 2	他們失去了信心，並且變得很畏怯。
基礎英文	They have lost their confidence, and they have become timid.
高級英文	**Timidity replaces confidence.**

例 3	他們不再精明，而且變得猶豫不決。
基礎英文 ▼	They are no longer sure, and they have become very hesitant.
高級英文	**Hesitation replaces shrewdness.**

例 4	這一堂課，我們能用的語言，僅有英語。
基礎英文 ▼	In this class, English is the only language we can use.
高級英文	**This class is conducted exclusively in English.**

例 5	這個孩子不聽大人的話，而且目無尊長。
基礎英文 ▼	This child neither listens to nor respects adults.
高級英文	**This child acts disobediently and disrespectfully.**

例 6	從 2000 年到 2010 年，因為中國大陸的經濟愈來愈繁榮，人民幣升值了 25%。
基礎英文 ▼	From 2000 to 2010, because of China's increasing prosperity, the RMB has appreciated 25%.
高級英文	**The RMB had appreciated 25% from 2000 to 2010 due to China's unprecedented economic growth.**

例 7	如果你今日夠努力的話，明日必有成功的果實。
基礎英文 ▼	If you work hard enough today, you'll reap the fruit of success tomorrow.
高級英文	**Your efforts today shall be abundantly rewarded.**

例 8	他再三地背叛她，這表示他們的婚姻大有問題。
基礎英文 ▼	He has betrayed her over and over again, which shows they have serious marital problems.
高級英文	**His repetitive betrayals of her have revealed their marital crisis.**

例 9	在八八水災時，洪水和土石流滾滾而來，南台灣許多人死了，財產也喪失了。
基礎英文 ▼	During the "August Eighth" disaster in southern Taiwan, floods and mudslides killed many people. Property was also lost!
高級英文	**Lives and property were taken by the floods and mudslides of the "August Eighth" catastrophe in southern Taiwan.**

例 10	無論你有多累，都不該那麼做！
基礎英文 ▼	No matter how tired you were, you shouldn't have done that!
高級英文	**Fatigue can't justify your behavior.**

例 11	台灣四季分明，而且各有各的美。
基礎英文 ▼	The four seasons are all different from one another, yet each has its own beauty.
高級英文	**Distinctive beauty is found in each of the four seasons in Taiwan.**

例 12	台灣的春天花團錦簇、夏天艷陽高照、秋天秋高氣爽、冬天寒風凜凜，這四個季節也正好述說了大自然的生命。
基礎英文 ▼	In Taiwan, different flowers bloom in spring; the sun shines bright in summer; the air is comfortable in autumn; and the winds are cold in winter. These four seasons describe the life of nature.
高級英文	**In Taiwan, the flowery springs, scorching summers, crisp autumns and freezing winters sound out the rhythm of nature.**

EXERCISE 13

請重新寫以下的句子，使其變成高級英文句：

① If we stay honest, we will be trusted by people.

改為：＿＿＿＿＿＿＿＿＿＿＿＿＿＿＿＿＿＿＿＿＿＿＿＿＿＿

② Even though you are angry, you can't just run away!

改為：＿＿＿＿＿＿＿＿＿＿＿＿＿＿＿＿＿＿＿＿＿＿＿＿＿＿

③ It's pathetic for a man/woman to forgive a wife/husband who has had a love affair.

改為：＿＿＿＿＿＿＿＿＿＿＿＿＿＿＿＿＿＿＿＿＿＿＿＿＿＿

④ They fought all the time, and they finally divorced.

改為：＿＿＿＿＿＿＿＿＿＿＿＿＿＿＿＿＿＿＿＿＿＿＿＿＿＿

⑤ They are deeply in love, very considerate to each other, and enjoy a very happy marriage.

改為：＿＿＿＿＿＿＿＿＿＿＿＿＿＿＿＿＿＿＿＿＿＿＿＿＿＿

⑥ After this accident, he is no longer confident in himself.

改為：＿＿＿＿＿＿＿＿＿＿＿＿＿＿＿＿＿＿＿＿＿＿＿＿＿＿

⑦ There's no reason for you to fail.

改為：＿＿＿＿＿＿＿＿＿＿＿＿＿＿＿＿＿＿＿＿＿＿＿＿＿＿

⑧ Without hope, life is fragile.

改為：＿＿＿＿＿＿＿＿＿＿＿＿＿＿＿＿＿＿＿＿＿＿＿＿＿＿

Ch
4

⑨ I don't mind if you are poor or not — I like you anyway!

改為：＿＿＿＿＿＿＿＿＿＿＿＿＿＿＿＿＿＿＿＿＿＿＿＿＿＿

⑩ It was so hot that many children went to the swimming pool to swim.

改為：＿＿＿＿＿＿＿＿＿＿＿＿＿＿＿＿＿＿＿＿＿＿＿＿＿＿

📖 EXERCISE 13 參考答案

（以下答案只是參考，讀者可由書本中找出更多的進階用法）

① Honesty wins people's trust.

② Anger can't justify your escape.

③ Forgiven extramarital relations still heartbreak the spouse.

④ Frequent conflicts finally led to their divorce.

⑤ Their profound mutual love and consideration are blessed with a happy marriage.

⑥ This accident has deprived him of his self-confidence.

⑦ Your failure is inexcusable.

⑧ Hope strengthens life.

⑨ Your financial status is not an issue to me.

⑩ The high temperatures drove children to the swimming pool.

UNIT 14

使文思如泉湧——邏輯力量大！

曾經在國際新聞中看到一個北歐壯漢拉著一架飛機往前走嗎？就英文作文而言，邏輯的力量正是如此！邏輯的力量是如此之大，它在英文作文中，到底扮演什麼角色呢？邏輯就是腦袋，我們的文章以何為主軸？源自何方？走向何方？如何走去？結果如何？力量如何？這一長串就譜成了文章的 flow。

因此，我們思緒的開展方向必須十分穩定而清楚，這也正是寫作中不可缺少的起、承、轉、合。這四項能幫助我們建構出完整的邏輯，有了邏輯，寫作就能自然發揮；不但能使文意流暢，甚至讓我們寫作的思緒「一發不可收拾」，進而「水到渠成」，整個寫作過程十分輕鬆。

提醒各位讀者，所有的好文章無論屬何種型態，都必具有以下所列出的起承轉合，也就是一個清晰的思維所必掌握的邏輯性。（以下只是列表，讓各位先清晰地勾勒出文章的邏輯。至於如何執行，我們之後再討論。）

📝 **文章的結構**

使文思如泉湧的簡表

起 Initiation	角色	用 thesis statement 寫出文章的 theme（主題），也就是第一段。
	目的	點出文章的主軸、立「起」整篇文章的方向。
	方法	用字遣詞必須引「起」讀者欲窺究竟的興趣。

承 Linkage	角色	文章的第二段，一直到結論之前的最後一段。
	目的	「承」起第一段的重點。
	方法	為了寫出深度與內涵，不能自說自話。可以用事實、資料、訪談、數據來支撐第一段的重點。

轉 **Transitions**	角色	如同蓋房子，磚頭不會一路砌上天，而需轉個彎，才會進入另一個房間，走入另一個境地。也如同畫畫，不會一筆拉個不停，而需轉個彎，才可畫出美麗的圖形。寫文章也完全一樣，在告一段落之後、如果還要續筆，之間也需要轉一下，才可圓順地走入下文。
	目的	使文章自然而優美地「轉接」。
	方法	善用轉折語或過渡語。

合 **Conclusion**	角色	為全文做一個「合」數。
	目的	再次強調第一段的重點，使文章的論點從頭到尾，完全一致。
	方法	順著主文 (body) 的氛圍，將文章的第一段主旨 (theme) 重新強調一次。 它和主題句 (thesis statement) 一樣，用字遣詞字字珠璣、不可隨意，需嚴格注意修辭與意境，氣勢要磅礴！

起承轉合（一）
要「起」得巧

📝 文章之「起」── The Thesis Statement

英文寫作可真是名符其實的「萬事起頭難」。不過學習首重方法，如果方法不對，即使搔破白頭寫出長篇大論，也不會是令人著迷的文章；反之，如果用對了方法，則可在數分鐘之內，輕鬆地下筆，並快速地完成，無論文章長短，均屬佳作。

理由很簡單，只要下筆得法，隨後而來的文思會因為「起」、「承」、「轉」、「合」的連鎖反應，而似泉湧，有若萬馬奔騰，勢不可遏。

換句話說，短短的 thesis statement 已幾乎決定這篇英文作文的成敗。

一個好的 thesis statement，必具備以下特色：

1. 清楚地點出全文的主軸：重點清楚、絕不含糊。
2. 奠定文章將走的方向：方向確定了，可令人一下筆就有如神助、思緒不斷、一氣呵成。
3. 雖然簡潔、清晰，卻不失完整：如果文章有三個重點，在 thesis statement 就必有三個關鍵字，一個不多、一個不少。
4. 生動活潑，引發讀者的興趣，有一窺究竟的慾望。
5. 用字遣詞成熟精湛。
6. 句型精簡有力。

以上是英文作文第一段的重點，我們在下筆練習前，必須再進一步討論它的細節：

1. Thesis Statement 清楚地點出全文主軸。
① Thesis statement 像一棵大樹的種子，也像一個工廠的發電機，它是全文的生命源。
② Thesis statement 也就是全文的 theme，它帶著讀者直窺全文的核心與精神。

Ch
4

③ 每一個題目都可以因人而異而有不同的切入點，因而同一個題目會因為不同的作者而有不同的主題，寫作時一定要守住自己文章的主軸。我們以 "Chinese Cuisine" 為例，它的主題可以是中國菜的歷史、中國菜的烹飪特色、外國人如何看待中國菜，或中國菜和義大利菜之異同……等等。所以，我們的主軸要抓住、思緒要過濾，不能把想到的全寫出來，因為腦筋裝的東西太多了，天馬行空會擾亂文章的中心思想，讓全文摸不清方向和重點。

2. Thesis Statement 不拘泥於固定的文體。

首先，如果 thesis statement 沒抓好，任何的文體都不具意義。

絕對不要將自己綑綁於某種固定的文體，因為 thesis statement 是一個活潑、有力的生命體，我們可以用任何的文體來呈現它。例如，我們可以用「論說性」的文體，卻加上一首詩，就顯得剛柔並濟；也可以用「比較性」的文體加上充分的資料，就顯得嚴謹而客觀；當然也可以用「直述性」的文體，外加一則「新聞性」的報導，就顯得活潑且具深度。

3. Thesis Statement 可以「明示」，也可以「暗示」。

無論是「明示」或「暗示」，均須「確切」而「清楚」地指出全文的主軸。所謂「暗示」，即是指縱使它的內涵或關鍵字不那麼直接，卻能讓讀者心中極自然地期待讀到這篇文章所將闡釋的某些意旨。

4. Thesis Statement 必替下一段穩穩地鋪路。

只要腦中有料，我們的思緒是不會無緣無故斷掉的，所以，只要第一段（也就是 thesis statement）有重點，就已替下一段鋪好了路；換句話說，對作者而言，全文的走勢 (flow) 早已成竹在胸，完全掌控。第二段當然水到渠成、自然而然地延續下來，使全文順暢若流水。

5. Thesis Statement 雖然不長，卻具完整性。

雖然成熟的句子需精簡幹練、切忌冗長，但是 thesis statement 所發出的訊息仍必完完整整，缺一不可。在 thesis statement 之後的段落（也就是 body）之中，任何突發的重點，都將破壞文章的 flow；當然，會「突發」的原因即在於 thesis statement 有缺口、欠完整。

6. Thesis Statement 令讀者欲讀之而後快。

① 膚淺幼稚的字彙難以展現文字之美與巧。短短的 thesis statement 就像一顆鑲在皇冠上的鑽石，必須發光發亮：它的用字遣詞不但優美，而且有力；它不但呈現全文的主軸，而且精緻、讓讀者著迷。

② Thesis statement 也是一把鑰匙，將讀者引進一個神祕而美麗的花園。所以 thesis statement 不是空泛的、沒頭緒的，而是紮紮實實，並替文章孕育了豐富的靈魂和生命。

7. Thesis Statement 的句型成熟精湛。

Thesis statement 既然是全文最主要的部分，句型豈可不慎？磨磨蹭蹭的句子必然堆出一個冗長、鬆散、甚至沒有重心的段落，不但不具吸引力，而且令人愈看愈累。所以，thesis statement 的句型必是精湛而有力的。

8. Thesis Statement 之前亦可加一個 **lead**。

Lead 是什麼？作用何在？怎麼才寫得好？這一方面的細節和練習，我們將隨後再討論。

📝 我們一起提筆來「起」

　　文章如何下筆，一點都不可怕，因為寫作就像畫畫、捏黏土、堆積木一樣，屬於一種創作，應該是一件有趣的事情。一個活潑的題目固然較易寫出生動有趣的文章，但是，對於一個優秀的作者而言，若能就一個沉悶嚴肅的題目寫出一篇活潑生動的作品，就如同木雕藝術家把一塊再平淡不過的木頭雕成一個靈巧迷人的藝術品般，等於完成一個快樂的挑戰。

　　我們該這麼想：文章是人寫出來的，我們的頭腦本來就不該受制於題目，而是題目被我們活化。再枯燥、通俗的題目，碰到活潑的頭腦，都可以寫作出令人印象深刻的作品。

　　其實，初級英文寫作和高級英文寫作的文章結構和邏輯都是一樣的，只是高級作文因為文字、句型、思緒都更靈巧而且更具彈性，所以文章必然更活潑、充實且更具深度。接下來，為了帶領各位清楚地由初級英文寫作進階到高級英文寫作，特意找出平時極常見的、亦即十分平凡的作文題目來分別作示範和解說。初級作文和高級作文

即使寫同樣的題目，甚至寫同樣的內容，兩者的 thesis statement 卻不盡相同。我們一起來試試看。

作文題目 1 My Best Friend

如果 thesis statement 這麼寫：
Everyone has good friends, and so do I! My best friend is ...

缺點 1. 乏味（只是複誦題目而已，不具意義）
2. 陳腔濫調（缺乏主見）
3. 沒有重點（太廣泛了，流於空洞），浪費篇幅！
4. 找不到關鍵字。
5. 沒有指出文章的方向。
6. 用字膚淺。
7. 句子鬆散。

↓ 這樣較好

初級英文作文的 thesis statement 這麼寫：
My best friend is Tina, who is very humorous and is very nice to me.

優點 1. 指出了全文發展的方向：我最好的朋友是幽默而友好的。
2. 有關鍵字：humorous, nice
缺點 1. 用字幼稚。
2. 太呆板、完全不生動。
3. 未能塑造意境。

↓ 表達的內容一模一樣，
但這樣寫就會進化成高級英文作文

高級英文作文的 thesis statement：
Humor and friendliness exemplify my best friend, Tina.

優點 1. 關鍵字清楚：humor, friendliness, Tina。
2. 因此文章的主軸穩定明朗。
3. 字彙成熟有力。
4. 句型精湛俐落。
5. 動詞使用 "exemplify"，使文章活起來。

作文題目 2　My Mother

如果 thesis statement 這麼寫：

I have a great mother, who loves us so much that she works very hard all the time.

缺點 1. 陳腔濫調（絕大多數的母親皆如此）。
　　 2. 沒有重點（太廣泛了，流於空洞）。
　　 3. 找不到關鍵字。
　　 4. 用字膚淺。
　　 5. 句型鬆散無力。
　　 6. 沒有指出文章的方向。

↓　　這樣較好

初級英文作文的 thesis statement 這麼寫：

My mother is a housewife. She is very smart and not only loves us, but other children as well.

優點 1. 有關鍵字：housewife, smart, love(s) other children。
　　 2. 指出全文發展的方向：幼吾幼以及人之幼。
缺點 1. 用字幼稚。
　　 2. 意境未能深入人心。
　　 3. 句型鬆散。

↓　表達的內容一模一樣，
↓　但這樣寫就會進化成高級英文作文

高級英文作文的 thesis statement：

The intelligence and altruistic maternal love of my mother compliment her role as a housewife.

優點 1. 關鍵字清楚：intelligence, altruistic, maternal, housewife。
　　 2. 因此文章的主軸已穩固、明朗。
　　 3. 字彙成熟有力：intelligence 代替 smart；
　　　　　　　　　　 altruistic 代替 loves other children；
　　　　　　　　　　 maternal love 代替 she loves us。
　　 4. 句型精緻俐落。
　　 5. "compliment her role as …" 使文章活潑起來。
　　 6. 「刻畫母親」的意境呈現。

Ch
4

如果 thesis statement 這麼寫：

There are different kinds of beauty. For example, many young people are beautiful, but some old people are also very beautiful. Therefore, age is not a factor of beauty.

優點 點出了文章的方向：美不受年齡的限制。
缺點 1. 字彙淺薄。
2. 句型鬆散。

↓ 這樣較好

初級英文作文的 thesis statement 這麼寫：

Young or old, a person can be beautiful. It's true that children are lovely, but old people are also beautiful, especially if they have a kind heart.

優點 更精確地指出全文的方向：老年人的慈愛之美。
缺點 1. 字彙淺薄，沒有分量。
2. 句型軟弱，沒有力量。

↓ 表達的內容一模一樣，
這樣寫就會進化成高級英文作文

高級英文作文的 thesis statement：

Genuine generosity, true mercifulness and unchallengeable wisdom accent the charisma of old age—the image of real beauty.

優點 1. 關鍵字清楚：generosity, mercifulness, wisdom, old age。
2. 因此確切地點出全文將發展的方向：① 大方 ② 慈愛 ③ 有智慧是老年之美，也是真正的美。
3. 字彙成熟有力。
4. 句子精簡。
5. "accent the charisma of old age" 為文章加入生命，動詞使用 "accent"，句子立刻活潑起來。
6. 意境呈現。

我們接下來跳過失敗的例子，直接進入初級英文作文與高級英文作文的比較。

初級英文作文的 thesis statement 這麼寫：

"I want to eat dumplings!" versus. "I want to eat beefsteak!" Or "Let's visit my parents today!" versus. "Why? You are married and should be independent from your parents!" These conflicts may frequently happen in mixed-cultural marriages.

優點 1. 有關鍵字：cultural conflicts。

2. 鎖定主題：異國婚姻時有衝突。

3. 指出文章發展的方向：異國婚姻常在飲食和家庭方面有歧見。

缺點 1. 用字較幼稚。

2. 關鍵字太少。

3. 那兩句對話放在 thesis statement 太浪費篇幅；應該放在 body，用來支撐 theme。

> 表達的內容一模一樣，
> 但這樣寫就會進化成高級英文作文

高級英文作文的 thesis statement：

Mixed-cultural marriages face unavoidable conflicts, ranging from cuisine to family values.

優點 1. 關鍵字清楚：conflicts, cuisine, family values。

2. 因此全文的主軸已穩固、明朗。

3. 字彙成熟。

4. 句型俐落。

5. "face unavoidable conflicts" 使文章活潑起來。

6. 意境呈現。

Ch
4

假設在一個題目之下文章的方向和內容都完全一樣，只是 thesis statement 寫得好與不好而已。試比較：

● 哪一個 thesis statement 最好？請依優劣排名 1、2、3。

● 排名的原因為何？

Topic 1: My Favorite Song

排名	Thesis Statement
	My favorite song is *Beauty and the Beast* because it has a beautiful melody, and the singer has a deep, attractive voice. 原因：
	I believe my favorite song is *Beauty and the Beast*. The first time I heard it in the movie theater, I was immediately attracted to it. 原因：
	An enchanting melody and romantic lyrics sung with a characterize voice compose my favorite song: *Beauty and the Beast*. 原因：

Topic 2: The Definition of Success

排名	Thesis Statement
	Is a man successful when he is rich? Is a man successful when he is famous? Are we successful when we have a high degree? Are we successful when we have a god job? 原因：

	What is real success? In our society, many people pursue money, careers and degrees so hard that I really doubt they are truly happy. 原因：
	Wealth, fame or high education are not equivalent to success when they are not accompanied by happiness. 原因：

Topic 3: The Value of Forgiveness

排名	Thesis Statement
	No one is perfect, which makes it human and reasonable to forgive people's mistakes. 原因：
	Even an honest person may tell a white lie and even a merciful person may accidentally hurt people. Shouldn't people be forgiven when they make mistakes? 原因：
	Forgiveness can be as virtuous as honesty and mercifulness. 原因：

Ch
4

Topic 1: My Favorite Song

排名	Thesis Statement
2	My favorite song is *Beauty and the Beast* because it has a beautiful melody, and the singer has a deep, attractive voice. 優點 有關鍵字（可以鎖定主題）： *Beauty and the Beast*; beautiful melody; voice 所以知道全文的發展方向將是這首歌的美麗旋律和動人聲音。 缺點 1. 用字遣詞不夠優美。 2. 句型還須加油。
3	I believe my favorite song is *Beauty and the Beast*. The first time I heard it in the movie theater, I was immediately attracted to it. 缺點 1. 沒有主題：只知道是 Beauty and the Beast 這一首歌，但是全無重點，文章將走向何方？沒有鎖定。 2. 文字須加油。 3. 句型須再努力。
1	An enchanting melody and romantic lyrics sung with a characterize voice compose my favorite song: *Beauty and the Beast*. 優點 1. 有關鍵字（所以主題已鎖定）： melody; lyrics; voice; *Beauty and the Beast* 2. 用字遣詞較成熟。 3. 句型簡潔有力：全段只需一個句子，意義就十分完整，而且充滿生命力。

Topic 2: The Definition of Success

排名	Thesis Statement
3	Is a man successful when he is rich? Is a man successful when he is famous? Are we successful when we have a high degree? Are we successful when we have a god job? 優點 主題清楚：「有金錢」、「有名」、「高學位」、「好工作」，不見得就是成功！ 缺點 1. 用字隨便。 2. 句子太囉唆。

2	What is real success? In our society, many people pursue money, careers and degrees so hard that I really doubt they are truly happy. 優點 主題鎖定得更清楚：如果不快樂，一切的金錢和成就都枉然。 缺點 1. 句子鬆散。 　　　2. 用字須再努力
1	Wealth, fame or high education are not equivalent to success when they are not accompanied by happiness. 優點 主題和上一個一樣，清楚地鎖定方向，但是： 　　　1. 用字遣詞較成熟。 　　　2. 句型簡單俐落，句意更清楚。

Topic 3: The Value of Forgiveness

排名	Thesis Statement
3	No one is perfect, which makes it human and reasonable to forgive people's mistakes. 缺點 雖已鎖定主題，但仍不夠精準 (precise)，不知文章將走的方向為何？
2	Even an honest person may tell a white lie and even a merciful person may accidentally hurt people. Shouldn't people be forgiven when they make mistakes? 優點 主題清楚地鎖定：連誠實、慈善的人都會犯錯，我們怎能不原諒人呢？ 缺點 1. 文字不夠成熟。 　　　2. 句型須再努力。
1	Forgiveness can be as virtuous as honesty and mercifulness. 優點 1. 主題清楚：「誠實」、「慈悲」是美德，「寬恕」的這種情操和兩種美德比起來毫不遜色。 　　　2. 字彙成熟。 　　　3. 句型俐落有力。

UNIT 16

起承轉合（二）要「承」得準

文章之「承」—— The Body

　　寫完第一段 (thesis statement) 之後，立即接著寫主文 (body)。所謂「承」，即文章的 body「承擔」上一段所提及的所有重點。這真的很簡單，因為在 thesis statement 中的每一個關鍵字，都至少可寫出一段文章，而這全部的段落加起來，就是全文的 body。

　　請看以下各圖表，即可了解英文作文當中的「起」和「承」之間的關係。

英文作文如果只寫 1~2 頁

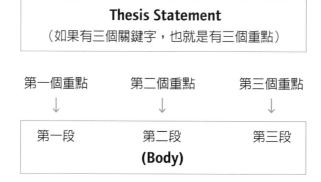

算算段落：

```
        1 段（Thesis Statement）
        3 段（Body）
    ＋  1 段（Conclusion）
      ─────────────────
        5 段（全文）
```

英文作文如果寫 2~4 頁

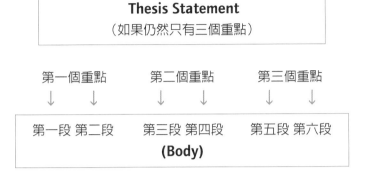

算算段落：

1 段（Thesis Statement）
6 段（Body）
+ 1 段（Conclusion）
8 段（全文）

英文作文如果寫 4~6 頁

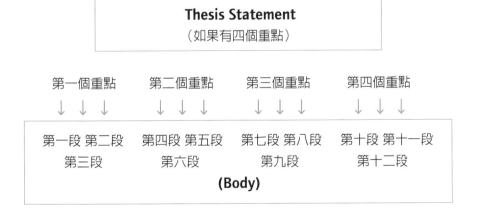

算算段落：

```
        1 段（Thesis Statement）
       12 段（Body）
 +      1 段（Conclusion）
 ─────────────────────────
       14 段（全文）
```

英文作文的長短其實伸展自如。在 thesis statement 當中，關鍵字（也就是重點）可以增減，而在主文 (body) 當中，每一個重點所發揮出來的段落數目也可以增減。如此類推，再多的字數均可輕鬆搞定。

寫作時依照以上的邏輯，就可以在 body 中，活潑地操控 thesis statement 所寫到的每一個重點。例如，一個重點（關鍵字）就可揮灑出一個至多個段落。

我們以 thesis statement 有兩個重點為例：

Thesis Statement ▼	第一個重點 ▼	第二個重點 ▼
Body	第一段：例子 + 第二段：另一個例子 + 第三段：訪談	第一段：例子 + 第二段：另一個例子 + 第三段：訪談

如上，一個重點就可寫出三個段落；如果 thesis statement 只有兩個重點，主文就已經有六段了，再加上 thesis statement 和 conclusion，全文就一共有八段了。

文章既是活的，body 當然也可這樣寫：

Thesis Statement ▼	第一個重點 ▼	第二個重點 ▼
Body	第一段：例子 + 第二段：例子 + 第三段：自己的判斷	第一段：例子 + 第二段：例子 + 第三段：自己的判斷

作文如果還要再長，則可正面和反面均加以討論，亦即：

Thesis Statement	第一個重點	第二個重點
Body	第一段：正面的例子 + 第二段：正面的數據 + 第三段：正面的訪談 + 第四段：反面的例子 + 第五段：反面的數據 + 第六段：反面的訪談	比照左邊寫，這裡又有六段，如此，body 就有十二段了。

又如，我們假設 thesis statement 中有三個重點：

Thesis Statement	第一個重點	第二個重點	第三個重點
Body	第一段：例子 + 第二段：另一個例子 + 第三段：數據	第四段：例子 + 第五段：另一個例子 + 第六段：數據	第七段：例子 + 第八段：另一個例子 + 第九段：數據

↓ 如果作文需要更長

Thesis Statement	第一個重點	第二個重點	第三個重點
Body	第一段：例子 + 第二段：另一個例子 + 第三段：集合別人的觀點（或是文獻資料、訪談） + 第四段：數據	第五段：例子 + 第六段：另一個例子 + 第七段：集合別人的觀點（或是文獻資料、訪談） + 第八段：數據	第九段：例子 + 第十段：另一個例子 + 第十一段：集合別人的觀點（或是文獻資料、訪談） + 第十二段：數據

Ch
4

如果還要繼續加長，還可在 thesis statement 增加重點，使文章更有內涵。

Thesis Statement	第一個重點	第二個重點	第三個重點	第四個重點
Body	第一段：例子 + 第二段：另一個例子 + 第三段：集合別人的觀點（或文獻資料、訪談） + 第四段：數據	第五段：例子 + 第六段：另一個例子 + 第七段：集合別人的觀點（或文獻資料、訪談） + 第八段：數據	第九段：例子 + 第十段：另一個例子 + 第十一段：集合別人的觀點（或文獻資料、訪談） + 第十二段：數據	第十三段：例子 + 第十四段：另一個例子 + 第十五段：集合別人的觀點（或文獻資料、訪談） + 第十六段：數據

如果繼續加長

Thesis Statement	第一個重點	第二個重點	第三個重點	第四個重點
Body	第一段：例子 + 第二段：文獻或訪談 + 第三段：數據 + 第四段：另一個例子 + 第五段：文獻或訪談 + 第六段：數據	第七段：例子 + 第八段：文獻或訪談 + 第九段：數據 + 第十段：另一個例子 + 第十一段：文獻或訪談 + 第十二段 數據	第十三段：例子 + 第十四段：文獻或訪談 + 第十五段：數據 + 第十六段：另一個例子 + 第十七段：文獻或訪談 + 第十八段：數據	第十九段：例子 + 第二十段：文獻或訪談 + 第二十一段：數據 + 第二十二段：另一個例子 + 第二十三段：文獻或訪談 + 第二十四段：數據

　　所以，只要增加 thesis statement 的關鍵字，就可增加段落。而只要言之有物，文

章應該愈長愈有內涵。同時，每一段也可自行調整內涵。例如：

用**正面**的例子來支持我們的觀點。

用**反面而失敗**的例子來支持我們的觀點。

用**現代**的例子來支持我們的觀點。

用**歷史**的例子來支持我們的觀點。

用**名人的看法**來支持我們的觀點（interview 或看書、上網查資料）。

如果找到**數據支持**（以及數據的來源），我們的**論點會更專業**。

也可用**幻想或假設**另立文章的立足點。

然後用**事實**來肯定以上這個立足點。

以上輕輕鬆鬆，不用絞盡腦汁，文章就可以順著發展，而且作品不但絕對不會偏離主題、又具內涵、合邏輯，當然也具有可信度。

如果文章還要長而不失邏輯，以上的例子、數據、訪談均可再使用不同的資料，各加一段，即每個重點都為 body 再帶來一倍的長度；如果還要再長，可以在綜合各種資料和別人的觀點之後，每一個部分都再加上一段自己的討論，就又多了好幾段；如果還要再長，我們也可以繪製表格，使文章更具科學與專業價值，亦即走往論文的領域。

文章的長度可短自數十字，長至數十萬字。但是，無論長短，均需字字珠璣、鎖定主軸、不可偏離。文章只要「起」得好，「承」得準，愈長的文章只有更加細膩深邃。反之，文章如果「起」得不好，或「承」得不準，則勢必天馬行空、愈長愈空洞，輕則令人讀後感到索然無味，重則令人感覺不知所云。

我們在前面已經討論了 body 的任務和內容，現在我們來看看它所涵蓋的段落當中，每一段內容的結構（長相）如何。

主文 (Body) 的架構

首先，body 應順勢出現在 thesis statement 之後，因為 thesis statement 早已替它鋪好了一條順暢之路。

Thesis Statement → 文章的第一段

+

Body → 1. 從文章的第二段開始。
2. 段落數目可多可少。

Body 既然「承」起了 thesis statement，也就是要承接 (bolster) 第一段「主題」的各項重點，所以它的結構必然穩健而紮實，否則這個 body 東倒西歪的，如何承擔重任？

英文作文中，思路清晰、邏輯通順的 body，必有以下的結構：

Body 中的每一個段落均包含三個部分	**topic sentence**：它在這一段的地位，就如同 thesis statement 在全文的地位。因此，它就是這一段的主題。
	小 **body**：它在這一段的地位，就如同主文 (body) 在全文的地位。為了方便討論，我在本書中將把全篇文章的主文稱為大 body，一段當中的主文則稱為小 body。
	main point：它在這一段的地位，就如同 conclusion 在全文的地位。因此，它就是這一段的結論。

就以上的簡表，我們來討論大 body 中的每一個段落的細節：

第一部分：Topic Sentence

一篇作文的 body 中，每一個段落都是一個迷你而完整的世界，正如同上面所列出的簡表，每一段都像一篇小作文，各有自己完整而獨立的意念。

因此，它有自己的 thesis statement，只是名稱改了，被稱為 topic sentence（主題句），顧名思義，它指的就是這一段的 topic，必須展現這一段的主題 (theme)。它既是主題，必也有關鍵字，而且關鍵字必須清晰而有力，才能替隨之而來的小 body 鋪路。

第二部分：小 Body

這一段的開頭既然已有 topic sentence，接著就要用小 body 來承擔 topic sentence 中所提的重點，它的作用和全篇作文的大 body 完全一樣。在這一段當中，也有清晰

的邏輯：topic sentence 為「起」、小 body 為「承」，也因為有邏輯，這個段落亦自然擁有圓順的 flow。

和大 body 的功能一樣，這個小 body 可用例子、數據、理論來支持 topic sentence。當然，再次提醒，例子要活潑生動，文章才有生命。

第三部分：Main Point

大 body 的每一個段落，因為自有其完整性，所以在每一段當中除了主題 (topic sentence)、小主文 (body) 之外，也必須有結論。不過，全篇作文的結論叫做 conclusion，一個段落中的結論則改稱為 main point。

Main point 在段落中的作用和 conclusion 在全文中的作用一模一樣：文章自 theme 開始，經由 body 所呈現的種種細節之後，在這裡又再回到 theme 的重點。這個結論就好像說：看吧！我的立場「自始至終」都完全一致，沒有偏離，也沒有自相矛盾；甚至在每一段之中，邏輯也都是「前後一致」、「思路穩健」！

因此，在大 body 之中，每一個段落之內的邏輯，和全文的邏輯完全相符，我們看以下就會更清楚了：

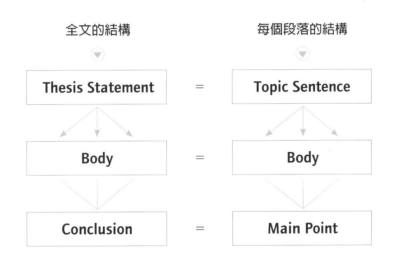

全文的結構　　　　　每個段落的結構

| Thesis Statement | = | Topic Sentence |

| Body | = | Body |

| Conclusion | = | Main Point |

📑 Body 怎麼寫？

文章在 thesis statement 之後即是主文。我們延用 Unit 15 中的作文題目和 thesis statement 來示範如何繼續寫下去，如何將 body 寫得又快又好。

My Best Friend

Thesis Statement
Like how a beautiful melody and classic lyrics interweave to create an intoxicating song, a great sense of humor and loyal friendship exemplify my best friend, Tina. 關鍵字 humor, friendship, Tina

↓ 進入主文

大 **Body** 的第一段 (Humor Part 1)		
使用 例子	**topic sentence**	It's never hard to locate Tina among a group of people. 關鍵字 locate、Tina
	小 **body**	舉例來支撐並刻劃這一段的 topic sentence： 1. Tina 爽朗的笑聲 2. Tina 在人群中的光環 3. Tina 開朗的行為
	main point	It's a true blessing that someone can be so filled with genuine **happiness** like Tina.

解析
1. 因為小 body 中已有快樂的例子，所以它助使結論 (main point) 水到渠成，自然引向 happiness。
2. Main point 中的 "happiness" 回應 topic sentence 的主題：
   她如此開朗快樂，在人群中很難找不到她。

+

大 **Body** 的第二段 (Humor Part 2)		
使用 資料	**topic sentence**	The Bible says, "**A cheerful heart** is good medicine," and Tina **vividly** displays this trait.
	小 **body**	從書本、研究、媒體、網路查出開心對健康有益的資料或數據，使文章更專業。
	main point	The figures have explicitly explained why Tina is always so **dynamic**.

1. 小 body 中提供的資料解釋了 topic sentence 中的 a cheerful heart 的確讓 Tina 神采飛揚；之後，結論 (main point) 水到渠成，邏輯順暢、flow 自然就圓潤了。
2. 結論中的 dynamic 和 vividly 是氣勢相合，也回應 topic sentence 的主題：喜樂的心乃是良藥！喜樂勝於一切！

+

大 Body 的第三段 (Friendship Part 1)		
使用資料	topic sentence	既然上一段用古老的語錄開啓 (A cheerful heart is good medicine)，如果這一段也用同樣的意境和格式，文章即展現文字的平衡之美。這種機會不是每次都有，但是只要可能，就不要放過。 "A hedge between keeps friendship green," realistically illustrates my friendship with Tina.
	小 body	舉例來支撐並刻劃這一段的 topic sentence「君子之交淡如水、水長流」。這一方面的例子很多，所以很好發揮。例如可描述「我和 Tina 雖不是如影相隨，但是我們的友誼長存」。
	main point	Indeed, our friendship stands up to the challenges of both time and space.

1. Main point 的意義是「我們的友誼禁得起時間和空間的考驗」，正完全呼應這一段的 topic sentence（君子之交淡如水、水長流）。
2. 因為小 body 描述我和 Tina 友誼長存，所以結論自然水到渠成，而且邏輯順暢、flow 圓潤。

+

大 Body 的第四段 (Friendship Part 2)		
使用資料	topic sentence	The friendship between Damon and Pythias has been eulogized for ages, and is echoed among similar friendships today.
	小 body	從媒體、書本、網路查詢在現今社會中，堅強友誼的資料或數據。
	main point	The striking figures have extolled the value of true friendship.

Ch
4

1. 小 body 所提供的資料使結論自然水到渠成。

2. Main point 的意涵是「令人領悟真友誼的價值」，也完全呼應這一段的 topic sentence：「Damon and Pythias 之間的真友誼，至今仍有」。

在初級英文寫作中，因爲寫作的經驗不足，所以 body 的結構須完全遵守、十分嚴謹。另外，像全民英檢或托福等任何的英文能力鑑定考試的作文評分標準也都完全鎖定這個格式，提醒各位讀者不可離開這個架構。

不過，在高級英文或專業的英文寫作（例如新聞英文或是 feature story）中，則「邏輯依舊，架構卻更靈活」！其細節及方法，等我們做完這個單元的練習之後，在下一個單元「轉」的部分再作討論。

EXERCISE 16

請先看 thesis statement 的關鍵字，然後由不同段落的主題當中，判斷哪一段的內容會破壞大 body 的「承」的工作？

題目 1.

作文題目	Key Words in Thesis Statement
Cynicism and Health（憤世嫉俗與健康）	stress（壓力） interpersonal relationships（人際關係） cancer（癌症） appreciation（感恩與珍惜）

根據作文題目與 key words，下列的段落主題若出現在大 Body 中是否適當？為什麼？

這一段落的主題是：	適合嗎？	不可取的原因
The importance of exercise	Yes / No	
How cynicism may cause stress	Yes / No	
Theories or experiments supporting how cynicism may cause stress	Yes / No	
How stress may cause cancer	Yes / No	
Statistics showing major causes of cancer	Yes / No	
A fact showing how cynicism affects interpersonal relationships	Yes / No	
Wise sayings supporting how appreciation helps avoid cynicism	Yes / No	
Experiments or statistics showing appreciative people tend to live longer	Yes / No	

題目 **2.**

作文題目	Key Words in Thesis Statement
The Boughs That Bear Most Hang Lowest （肚大才能容）	humility（謙卑） tolerance（容忍） forgiveness（寬恕）

根據作文題目與 key words，下列的段落主題若出現在大 Body 中是否適當？為什麼？

這一段落的主題是：	適合嗎？	不可取的原因
An example showing how humility allows for more accommodation	Yes / No	
Another example showing how arrogance hinders improvement	Yes / No	
A personal experience with being tolerant of someone	Yes / No	
The value of tolerance	Yes / No	
A story of how a famous entrepreneurs tolerates his critics	Yes / No	
The beauty of forgiving	Yes / No	
An example showing how a saint forgives his enemies	Yes / No	
An example showing how someone forgives then regrets	Yes / No	
An example showing how forgiveness is sweetly rewarded	Yes / No	

題目 1.

這一段落的主題是：	適合嗎？	不可取的原因
The importance of exercise	Yes / No	**完全文不對題**：全篇的主題是 cynicism 有害健康，這裡卻在談運動。
How cynicism may cause stress	Yes / No	
Theories or experiments supporting how cynicism may cause stress	Yes / No	
How stress may cause cancer	Yes / No	
Statistics showing major causes of cancer	Yes / No	**偏離主題**：雖然前一段提過「緊張可能促成癌症」，但是癌症並非這篇文章的主題，不適合佔用一整段的篇幅。
A fact showing how cynicism affects interpersonal relationships	Yes / No	
Wise sayings supporting how appreciation helps avoid cynicism	Yes / No	
Experiments or statistics showing appreciative people tend to live longer	Yes / No	

題目 2.

這一段落的主題是：	適合嗎？	不可取的原因
An example showing how humility allows for more accommodation	Yes / No	
Another example showing how arrogance hinders improvement	Yes / No	
A personal experience with being tolerant of someone	Yes / No	**偏離主題**：這只是個人的經驗，和「肚大能容」的整個大格局無關。除非意指自己的經驗證實「肚大能容」，但是即使如此，也並不專業。

The value of tolerance	Yes / No	
A story of how a famous entrepreneurs tolerates his critics	Yes / No	
The beauty of forgiving	Yes / No	
An example showing how a saint forgives his enemies	Yes / No	
An example showing how someone forgives then regrets	Yes / No	立場不穩：既然在全文的 thesis statement 當中已經表明認同「原諒」的美德，我們就不要節外生枝、自我矛盾。
An example showing how forgiveness is sweetly rewarded	Yes / No	

UNIT 17　起承轉合（三）要「轉」得溜

📄 文章之「轉」—— Transitions

　　好文章是一件生動而緊緻的作品，它是一連串的思緒像串珠一樣連結而成的，環環相扣，一個也不會走樣、更不會鬆掉。然而，當我們的思緒轉換時，文章如何圓潤地發展？例如，我們寫完了某一個觀念之後，該如何順暢地進入另一個觀點？或者，鎖定了某一件事的優點之後，如何順暢地討論它的缺點？為了避免 flow 的突兀，「轉」或「過渡」的角色這時就必須出現了，它就是轉折語（用於相異的看法）或過渡語（用於同質的看法），英文就是 transitional expressions。

　　換句話說，transitional expressions 的作用在於連接「相異」或「相同」的看法。

📝 有用的 transitions

表達「輕重緩急次序」的轉折語：

- **To start with,**（我從頭道來，……）
- **First, second, third, ...**
- **soon, then, meanwhile, later**
- **formerly**（前一個）
- **finally**（終於）
- **Last but not least,**（最後一個重點是……）
- **At first sight,**（第一次見面時，……）
- **theoretically**（理論上說來，……）
- **hypothetically**（假設上說來，……）
- **The priority of ... can be shown as follows:**（它的優先順序如下：……）
- **But the ... cannot be justified.**（但是即使如此，仍有不合理之處……）

「順勢」而為的轉折語：

- similarly（另一個類似的例子是……）
- furthermore（更進一步地說，……）
- In conclusion,（結論是……）
- consequently（因此……）
- conclusively（總結來說，……）
- logically（合理地來說，……）
- more significantly（更重要的是……）
- unexceptionally（下面這件事，是理所當然的……）
- unsurprisingly（這是意料之中的事……）
- supportingly（以下的例子，也將支持前面所說的這個看法……）
- accordingly（照著這個情況或數字……看來，我們不難猜測……）
- And that is not all.（還有其他類似的狀況，……）
- But he isn't alone.（除了他以外，還有人也如此……）
- More examples can be found in ...（還有很多例子提供各位參考……）
- But the tragedy didn't end here.（還有更慘的，……）
- History often repeats itself.（還有類似事件……）
- The ... is echoed with ...（事有「迴響」……）

「逆勢」而為的轉折語：

- on the contrary（反之，……）
- to our surprise（沒想到，……）
- surprisingly（沒想到，……）
- beyond our imagination（令人感到意外的是，……）
- Against his own will, ...（他並不願意去這麼做，但是……）
- Strikingly,（令人震驚的一件事是，……）
- Unfortunately,（不幸地，……）
- Disasters never occur alone.（真是禍不單行啊！除了前面發生的之外，還有……）
- But he/she has come a long way.（他很成功，但是他今天的成就得來不易，……）
- Against all (the) odds, ...（雖然勝算不大，他仍然……）

Transitions 可以自己獨立一段

在前一個單元有提到，在高級英文作文中，寫作的「邏輯不變、架構可以更靈活！」怎麼說呢？

所謂「邏輯不變」，就是思緒必然有始、有因、有果、有終，也就是「起、承、轉、合」。所謂「架構可以更靈活」，即如果「轉」的部分夠分量，甚至可自行獨立成一個段落！

例

題目 : An Unforgettable Experience

主文中的某一段：描述在山中迷路的恐懼！

↓ 下一段
（由恐懼**轉**到聽到直昇機的欣喜）

"We're saved!" cried our tour guide on hearing the chopper, whose noisy rotor blades sounded like heavenly music from above.

← 這一段因為內容夠強烈，所以全段獨立出來，完全做為上一段和下一段的 transition。

↓ 下一段
（由上直昇機之前的害怕**轉**到獲救之後的平安）

大家如何被救上直昇機以及獲救後的心情。

Ch
4

請嘗試分辨以下的 transition（轉折語）在上下文中是否適合，然後將 Yes 或 No 圈起來。

題目 1.：A Sad Experience

在大 body 中的前一段如下：

Topic Sentence
小 body
Main point: **I've been burdened with apprehension ever since.**   　　　　　　我自此愁腸百轉

以下的轉折語適合嗎？

↓

Transition: To start with,	適合嗎？ **Yes / No**
Topic Sentence	
小 **Body** 內容	內容
Main Point	

或

Transition: More examples can be found.	適合嗎？ **Yes / No**
Topic Sentence	
小 **Body** 內容	內容
Main Point	

或

Transition: Supportingly, …	適合嗎？ **Yes / No**
Topic Sentence	
小 Body 內容	內容
Main Point	

或

Transition: Disasters never occur alone.	適合嗎？ **Yes / No**
Topic Sentence	
小 Body 內容	內容
Main Point	

題目 2.：Child Education

在大 body 中的前一段如下：

Topic Sentence
小 body
Main point: **Group activities promote teamwork.** 　　　　　團體生活確實培養參與團隊的技巧

以下的轉折語適合嗎？

Transition: Supplemental education alone is not enough. 單靠補習教育是不夠的	適合嗎？ **Yes / No**
Topic Sentence	
小 Body 內容	內容
Main Point	

Transition: Statistics prove that group activities develop a sense of belonging and understanding. 數據顯示，團體生活可以提升我們在群體中的歸屬感，並使我們體諒別人。	適合嗎？ **Yes / No**
Topic Sentence	
小 Body 內容	內容
Main Point	

Transition: Statistically, parents choose courses from a plethora of programs.	適合嗎？ **Yes / No**
Topic Sentence	
小 Body 內容	內容
Main Point	

Transition: Statistics strongly support that children who feel comfortable expressing their ideas in a group are better equipped for career success. 數據強烈地證明，能夠在團體中表達想法的孩子，在事業上也較容易成功。	適合嗎？ **Yes / No**
Topic Sentence	
小 Body 內容	內容
Main Point	

題目 1.：A Sad Experience

在大 body 中的前一段如下：

Topic Sentence
小 body
Main point: **I've been burdened with apprehension ever since.**

以下的轉折語適合嗎？

Transition: To start with,	適合嗎？ Yes / **No**
Topic Sentence	原因：前段的結尾的「愁腸百轉」
小 Body 內容	↓如何憂愁？ To start with, (讓我一一數來，……)；接
Main Point	著就可以開始描述了。

或

Transition: More examples can be found.	適合嗎？ **Yes** / No
Topic Sentence	
小 Body 內容	原因：和前面「愁腸百轉」的意境突兀， 所以這個 linkage 不順暢。
Main Point	

或

Transition: Supportingly, …	適合嗎？ **Yes** / No
Topic Sentence	
小 Body 內容	原因："support" 這個字較為嚴肅強硬， 意境和上一段「愁腸百轉」的幽婉也不
Main Point	符，再次顯得突兀。

或

Transition: Disasters never occur alone.	適合嗎？ Yes / **No**
Topic Sentence	原因：前一段是「愁腸百轉」結尾，這
小 Body 內容	一段則表示還有更慘的。在氣勢上順暢 地帶出「這一段將更糟」的情景。
Main Point	

Ch
4

在大 body 中的前一段如下：

Topic Sentence
小 body
Main point: **Group activities promote teamwork.**

以下的轉折語適合嗎？

Transition: Supplemental education alone is not enough.	適合嗎？ **Yes / No**
Topic Sentence	原因：前一段的結尾是 group activities（群體生活）和 teamwork（團隊精神）的關係，這裡突然跳到 supplemental education（「補教」，例如 tutoring），破壞 flow，顯得突兀。
小 Body 內容	
Main Point	

或

Transition: Statistics prove that group activities develop a sense of belonging and understanding.	適合嗎？ **Yes** / No
Topic Sentence	原因：前一段的結尾是 group activities 和 teamwork 的關係，這一段 transition 提及「數據」如何 support 群體生活的主要性，立刻替這兩個段落先搭起橋樑，而使這兩個段落有順暢有力的 flow。
小 Body 內容	
Main Point	

或

Transition: Statistically, parents choose courses from a plethora of programs.	適合嗎？ **Yes** / No
Topic Sentence	原因：1. 前一段結尾是 group activities 和 teamwork，這一段卻跳到「如何選課程」，顯得突兀。
小 Body 內容	2. 如果把 transition 改成 "To ensure an optimal consequence.（為了確保最好的效益）" 就順暢地連結上一段，並替隨之而來的
Main Point	句子鋪好了路：參與團體生活的最佳態度。

Transition: Statistics strongly support that children who feel comfortable expressing their ideas in a group are better equipped for career success.	適合嗎？ Yes / **No**
Topic Sentence	原因：上一段的結尾是 group activities 和 teamwork，這一段緊接著用數字來支持群體生活的重要性。
小 Body 內容	
Main Point	

起承轉合（四）
水到渠成而「合」

📄 文章之「合」── Conclusion

　　任何完整的、有意義的思緒必然有始有終，否則就是白想一場。寫文章也一樣，有主題，有主文，還有結論。這一部分，在前面已經討論過了，我們這裡僅做個整理。

　　文章之「合」，就是結論。結論的宗旨就是回歸全文的主題，它告訴讀者：

我一開始就這麼說，現在事實證明，我的觀點是正確的！

　　thesis statement　　　　　　body　　　　　　conclusion

（也就是文章的 theme）

　　因此，「結論」就是把「主題」再次強調。

　　但是為了避免文字疲乏，用字遣詞不能一成不變，須有新氣象才好。結論該怎麼寫我們稍後再談，先來看文章必走的路徑。

📄 文章要怎麼「合」

　　一篇優質的英文作文無論在「文字」或是「思緒」方面，從頭到尾，是一個完整的「圓形」。我們用以下的圖形來詮釋，就更清楚了：

Thesis Statement	（像馬達一樣，發出力量，打出水流）
Body	（承受了馬達所打出的水流而陸續開花結果）
Conclusion	（收尾，回到 Theme）

接下來，我們要進一步認識它們三者之間的關係。

Thesis Statement 和 Body 的關係

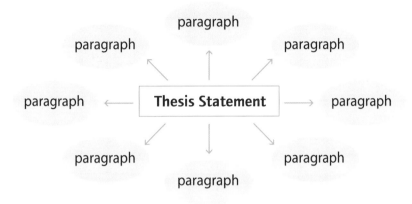

圓心：Theme
外圍：Body

文章之合

Body 和 Conclusion 的關係

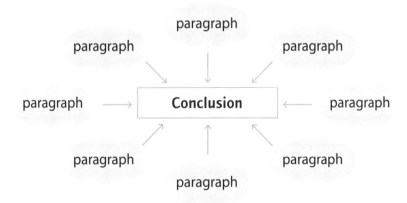

外圍：Body
圓心：Conclusion

以上這兩個圖的圓心其實是一模一樣的東西，在一篇優質的英文作文裡面，這兩個圓心的觀點、內涵、氣勢、意境、形式完全一樣，只是箭頭的方向不同，以及名稱

不同罷了。

為了保持連貫，我們就繼續用前面所提的四個最普遍的作文題目，完整地看看一篇英文作文如何寫得快又好。

首先，在高級英文作文中，第一段除了 thesis statement 之外，其前可以再加一個 lead。

Lead + Thesis Statement

我們想像一下：在不遠之處，有一個美麗的花園，外有圍牆，門上有一個小窗，我們可以從窗口望見裡面繽紛燦爛的花朵。英文作文就是要帶領讀者進入這個花園，細細地賞花。那麼，我們如何才能進入這個花園呢？在英文作文中，lead 就是那一條小徑，把我們帶到門口。Thesis statement 就是那道門，它上面的那扇窗（關鍵字）讓我們得以對花園一窺大概，卻又無法細細欣賞。Body 就是那個美麗的花園，它簇擁了花園裡的各種花朵，讓我們盡情地倘佯在花海之中。Conclusion 就是回到大門，門關上之後，回頭朝窗內再看一眼。

不過，有的花園有小徑帶路，有的花園則沒有小徑，圍牆就直接呈現在眼前，所以 lead 並非絕對必要。倒是在初級英文作文中，lead 往往免了，因為文字、意境、篇幅未臻成熟，lead 因此使不上勁。

為了多元化練習，以下，我們有時使用 lead，有時則不用 lead，而直接寫 thesis statement。

作文題目 1　My Best Friend

↓ 文章要「起」了

第一段 (Lead + Thesis Statement)

Like a beautiful melody and classic lyrics interweave an intoxicating song, a great sense of <u>humor</u> and loyal <u>friendship</u> exemplify my best friend, Tina.

＊前半句是 lead，套色字部分才是真正的 thesis statement。

關鍵字 humor、friendship

主軸與意境 Tina 如同一首美麗的歌曲，令人著迷。

繼續寫，文章要「承」了，裡面會有好幾
個「轉」（包括「轉折」與「過渡」語）

大 Body

1. 因為每個關鍵字都可以至少寫一段，所以主文至少可以寫兩段。
2. 主文的字數不限、段落不限。數十字至數萬字都可能成為佳作。
3. 每一段都鎖定主題，並加以發揮。
4. 每一段都深具內涵。
5. 寫這個題目，一定要融入情感，否則必定失敗。

文章要「合」了

Conclusion

Like a cellist plucks out an enchanting melody that can touch our soul, my soulmate plays her song with a friendly cheerfulness that enlightens my life.

Conclusion 的主軸和意境巧妙而完整地 echo with the thesis statement：

	全文的第一段 (Thesis Statement)	全文的最後一段 (Conclusion)
兩者形態一致 (consistent) 感覺柔順、 不會頭重腳輕。	一句話 + 真正的 thesis statement	一句話 + 真正的 conclusion
意境與文字 也一致 (consistent)	a beautiful melody _echoes with_	enchanting melody
	interweave（織出音樂）_echoes with_	plucks out（撥彈音樂）
	humor _echoes with_	cheerfulness
	friendship _echoes with_	friendly
	an intoxicating song _echoes with_	soulmate plays her song

作文題目 2 My Mother

↓ 文章要「起」了

第一段 (Thesis Statement)

★ 我們這次不用 lead

The <u>intelligence</u> and <u>altruistic maternal</u> love of my mother compliments her role as a <u>housewife</u>.

關鍵字 intelligence、altruistic、maternal、housewife

主軸與意境 母親雖是家庭主婦，卻兼具睿智與博愛。

↓ 繼續寫，文章要「承」了，裡面會有好幾個「轉」（包括「轉折」與「過渡」語）

大 Body

1. 因為每個關鍵字都可以至少寫一段，所以這篇文章的主文至少可以寫四段。
2. 主文的字數不限、段落不限。數十字至數萬字都可能成為佳作。
3. 每一段都鎖定主題，並加以發揮。
4. 每一段都深具內涵。
5. 寫這個題目，一定要融入情感，否則必定失敗。

↓ 文章要「合」了

Conclusion

I'm bestowed with a seemingly common yet most extraordinary mother who exemplifies the value of true wisdom and unselfish love.

Conclusion 的主軸和意境巧妙而完整地 echo with the thesis statement：

	全文的第一段 (Thesis Statement)	全文的最後一段 (Conclusion)
兩者形態 **consistent**	只有 thesis statement， 沒有另加 lead	只有 conclusion， 沒有另加 supplement
意境與文字 也 **consistent**	intelligence *echoes with*	true wisdom
	altruistic *echoes with*	unselfish
	maternal love *echoes with*	mother; love
	housewife *echoes with*	common mother

↓ 文章要「起」了

第一段 (Lead + Thesis Statement)

★ 這一次示範使用 lead，套色字部分才是真正的主軸。

Like chocolate chips in icecream or a square peg in a round hole, a mixed-cultural marriage can be <u>flavorful</u> yet unavoidably faces <u>conflicts</u>, ranging from <u>cuisine</u> to <u>family values</u>.

說明 Lead 使用的諺語 "A and B are like a square peg in a round hole." 意思是「格格不入」。

關鍵字 flavorful、conflicts、cuisine、family value(s)

↓ 繼續寫，文章要「承」了，裡面會有好幾個「轉」(包括「轉折」與「過渡」語)

大 Body

1. 每個關鍵字都可以至少寫一段，所以這篇文章的主文至少可以寫四段。
2. 字數不限、段落不限。數十字至數萬字都可能成為佳作。
3. 每一段都鎖定主題，並加以發揮。
4. 每一段都深具內涵。
5. 這個題目可加入情感，而成為一篇抒情文，也可以純論述而成為論說文，亦可兩者兼具，展現剛柔並濟的綜合文體。

↓ 文章要「合」了

Conclusion

As "the die is already cast," wontons and clam chowder can be equally delicious, and both core and extended family are equally valuable.

說明 也使用了諺語 "the die is already cast"，意思是「木已成舟」。

關鍵字 delicious、family、valuable

Conclusion 的主軸和意境巧妙而完整地 echo with the thesis statement：

	全文的第一段 (Thesis Statement)		全文的最後一段 (Conclusion)
兩者形態 **consistent**	一句話 + thesis statement		一句話 + conclusion
意境與文字 也 **consistent**	引用諺語： "Like a square peg in a round hole."	*echoes with*	引用諺語： the die is already cast
	cuisine	*echoes with*	wontons and clam chowder
	family values	*echoes with*	core and extended family

※ core family 小家庭；extended family 大家庭

作文題目 **4** My Definition of Beauty

↓ 文章要「起」了

第一段 (Thesis Statement)
★ 我們這一次不用 lead **Genuine <u>generosity</u>, true <u>mercifulness</u>, and unchallengeable <u>wisdom</u> accent the charisma of the <u>old age</u>—the image of real beauty.** 關鍵字 generosity、mercifulness、wisdom、old age 主軸與意境 感性與理性兼具。"generous、merciful、beautiful" 是偏感性的描述；同時 "generosity、wisdom、image" 則是偏理性的產物。（※ generosity 既理性又感性）

↓ 繼續寫，文章要「承」了，裡面會有好幾
↓ 個「轉」（包括「轉折」與「過渡」語）

大 Body
1. 每個關鍵字都可以至少寫一段，所以這篇文章的主文至少可以寫四段。 2. 短至數段、長至數萬段皆可。 3. 每一段都鎖定主軸 (the beauty of the old age)。 4. 深具內涵。 5. 寫這個題目須情感與評論兼具，才能同時展現理性與感性。

↓ 文章要「合」了

Conclusion

A portrait of an old gentleman whose eyes beam the glow of generosity, tenderheartedness, and wisdom would be a most beautiful piece of art about human life.

關鍵字 generosity、tender-heartedness、wisdom、beautiful

意境 兼具情感性與評論。

感性：portrait、generosity、tender-heartedness、art piece

理性：generosity、wisdom

Conclusion 的主軸和意境巧妙而完整地 echo with the thesis statement：

	全文的第一段 (Thesis Statement)	全文的最後一段 (Conclusion)
兩者形態 consistent	只有一個簡單句	只有一個簡單句
意境與文字 也 consistent	genuine generosity *echoes with*	(beam the glow of) generosity
	true mercifulness *echoes with*	(beam the glow of) tender-heartedness
	unchallengeable wisdom *echoes with*	(beam the glow of) wisdom
	real beauty *echoes with*	piece of art

　　所以，英文作文真的不難寫，只要隨著「起、承、轉、合」這個邏輯，就不會偏離主題，而且能創造圓順的 flow；也因為成功地鎖定了主題，而愈走愈深入，自然而然展現了綿密而邏輯的思考，最後自然水到渠成，成就了令人信服的結論。

　　總之，從一下筆開始就繞著 thesis statement，完整地鎖住主題，使 main idea 如影隨形，經由 body 的 powerful 卻 exquisite 的發揮，再產生了 conclusion，也就是把讀者帶回到文章一開始就主張的觀點。

　　好的文章必有極高的可信度和說服力，即使我們的讀者或許意見相左（例如論說文可能遭遇讀者持有不同的意見），但是因為文章的邏輯堅固、文筆優美、思緒細膩、數字和例子具有相當的說服力，作者的專業和努力必使文章不同凡響。

EXERCISE 18

請先看完以下的題目，再看每一題的 conclusion 是否完全搭配 thesis statement 和 body。

作文題目 1.：**On Negotiating**

↓ 「起」

Thesis Statement
Negotiating is an essential "give and take" skill to reach mutually acceptable agreements with colleagues, spouses, and even children. 「談判」是一種很有用的技巧，它包括了「給」與「取」，可以幫助我們和同事、配偶甚至孩子取得雙方皆認可的協議。

↓ 要「承」了

(Body) First Paragraph
主題：the definition of negotiation

(Body) 更多 Paragraphs
主題：the techniques of negotiation 這一部分可以有許多段落，例如： 1. Prepare the desired settlement point（準備心中的目標）至少一段 2. Identify the needs of the other side（了解對方的需要）至少一段 3. Ask questions（要會提問）至少一段 4. Listen（要會傾聽）至少一段 5. Stay issue oriented（不要被對方模糊焦點）至少一段 6. Control emotions（情緒要穩定）至少一段 7. Make concessions（要懂得讓步）至少一段 etc.

+

如果要寫更多 **Paragraphs**
舉例證明 the importance of negotiating
和 colleagues 的溝通至少一段
和 spouse 的溝通至少一段
和 children 的溝通至少一段

↓ 文章要「合」了

以下請作答：

這個結論好嗎？ Yes / No

Conclusion A
To sum up, negotiation plays a vital role in our lives, which is a job we must not ignore.

這個結論好嗎？ Yes / No

Conclusion B
Negotiation requires considerable effort, but the reward is definitely sweet!

這個結論好嗎？ Yes / No

Conclusion C
Collaborative negotiations, a process of exchange, get our needs met while preserving cordial interpersonal relationships.

作文題目 **2.**：**Advantages of Jogging**

↓ 「起」

Thesis Statement
Jogging conditions the heart and lungs, improves muscle tone and strength, and relieves pressure and stress—and just about anyone at any age can do it! 「慢跑」可以調節我們的心臟和肺臟，促進肌肉的訓練、提升肌力，而且還可以舒壓。最重要的是，這是不分年齡的運動！

↓ 要「承」了

Body
1. conditions the heart 至少一段（若要寫長一點，也可以「原因」寫一段、「例子」寫一段、「數據」寫一段）
2. improves muscle tone and strength 至少一段（也可同上面，寫好幾段）
3. relieves pressure and stress 至少一段（也可同上一段一樣，寫好幾段）

↓ 文章要「合」了

以下請作答：

這個結論好嗎？ Yes / No

Conclusion A
Jogging is indeed an effective form of exercise, even though it may result in joint problems.

這個結論好嗎？ Yes / No

Conclusion B
Just a good pair of running shoes can bring us effective and efficient cardiovascular, muscular, and bone fitness. Imagine the possibilities!

這個結論好嗎？ Yes / No

Conclusion C
If we wish to burn calories or prevent heart disease, jogging regularly is an excellent choice.

作文題目 1.：**On Negotiating**

這個結論好嗎？ Yes / No

Conclusion A
To sum up, negotiation plays a vital role in our lives, which is a job we must not ignore.

原因
1. 思想空泛、文字也太隨便。
2. 自說自話，腦中沒有一致性，也沒有 echo the thesis statement。

這個結論好嗎？ Yes / No

Conclusion B
Negotiation requires considerable effort, but the reward is definitely sweet!

原因
1. 這只是全文當中某一個小論點的結論（例如「談判」是辛苦的），分量不夠做全文的結論。
2. 未能 echo thesis statement。

這個結論好嗎？ Yes / No

Conclusion C
Collaborative negotiations, a process of exchange, get our needs met while preserving cordial interpersonal relationships.

原因 主軸、文字和意境均靈巧而完整地 echo the thesis statement。

thesis statement		conclusion
give and take	echoes with	process of exchange
mutually acceptable	echoes with	cordial interpersonal relationships
colleges, spouse, children	echoes with	interpersonal

作文題目 **2.：Advantages of Jogging**

這個結論好嗎？ Yes / No

Conclusion A
Jogging is indeed an effective form of exercise, even though it may result in joint problems.
原因 在 thesis statement 中提及 jogging 的優點，結論卻提到 jogging 有傷關節。如此結尾，顯得腦筋錯亂。

這個結論好嗎？ Yes / No

Conclusion B
Just a good pair of running shoes can bring us effective and efficient cardiovascular, muscular, and bone fitness. Imagine the possibilities!
原因 主軸、意境和文字均靈巧而完整 echo the thesis statement。

thesis statement		conclusion
heart and lungs	*echoes with*	cardiovascular
muscle tone and strength	*echoes with*	muscular and bone fitness

這個結論好嗎？ Yes / No

Conclusion C
If we wish to burn calories or prevent heart disease, jogging regularly is an excellent choice.
原因 並未完全 echo the thesis statement，顯得寫作的思緒不夠完整、也不細膩。

UNIT 19

內涵決定深度

英文寫作的內涵──主觀和客觀

我們從小就會哼唱「一閃一閃亮晶晶，滿天都是小星星」，它的曲調活潑、旋律優美、伴隨著我們的童年。但是經由莫札特寫成「小星星變奏曲」之後，主旋律依舊，內涵則因為十分地豐富，所以意境迴然不同，成為一首細緻、龐大、迷人的、被許多鋼琴大師演奏過的鋼琴曲。

我們常看到蓋房子，在同樣的地區，用同樣的價錢、同樣的時間，有些人蓋得平凡通俗，並不特別引人注意；有些人則可蓋出精巧脫俗的藝術品。

寫作也是一樣，同一個題目，有些人寫得幼稚，令人搖頭；有些人寫得平庸，讓人過目即忘；有些人則寫出深具內涵，令人讚賞的文章，三者的層次差距當然很大。

既然內涵如此重要，我們的作文豈能沒有它？那麼，內涵由何而來？又該如何去創造它？為了方便各位讀者學習，我把英文寫作的內涵分為主觀和客觀兩種：

主觀方面的 Input：

- 個人的**經驗**：少則一段，多則不限。
- 個人**對別人的觀察**：少則一段，多則不限。
- 個人的**看法和感動**（這個比較狹隘，因為它完全來自個人）：少則一段，多則不限。

缺乏內涵是許多人寫英文作文的致命傷。我常替報社及大學盃英文作文比賽服務，從中發現大部分的作品均偏向「主觀性」，使文章內涵因此欠缺深度和廣度。

寫英文作文絕對不可純主觀！人都是有限的，再聰明的人，思考必仍有所不足；再有知識的人，資訊必仍有所不足；再具人生經驗的人，經歷必仍有所不足。一篇好的作品，必須呈現廣度和深度，如果僅靠主觀方面的支柱，會呈現一面倒的單薄。

Ch

4

客觀方面的 Input：

這個可就豐富了，因為它走出了我們自己的世界，進入了所謂 "The sky is the only limit." 的格局，使文章立刻脫胎換骨。客觀的 input 包括：

- **例子**：在社會中，相關的例子太多了，我們在擷取例子的時候以愈出名的愈好。例如，要談到「愛」，與其舉自己的父母為例，就不如以 Mother Teresa 或證嚴法師為例。
- **數據**：數據來自研究，新聞刊物、書本、期刊、網路皆可提供豐富的數據。
- **網路**：網路是高級英文作文寫作的好幫手，它有各式各樣的資訊。
- **實人實地採訪**：Interview 的對象不限，可以是平凡人，也可以是文章的主角或有關的專家，只要他們言之有物，就可放入主文。
- **書籍**：書籍是作者的智慧結晶，很有貢獻。
- **論文**（它尤其提供豐富的數據）：論文是作者多方考證和研究的成果，有許多專業知識，可以使作文更顯專業。
- **詩詞**：詩詞橫跨古今而不墜，又是藝術的結晶，自有它迷人之處。
- **歷史**：歷史是一面鏡子，也是歲月的聚寶盒，有絕對的說服力。
- **別人的智慧之語**：自己不夠智慧，若是借用別人的智慧之語來支持我們的文章，也是智慧！

請想想看，文章的內涵是不是很容易就可以建立起來了呢？而且，愈長的文章，段落愈多、可涵蓋的深度與廣度愈多，自然而然地應該更具內涵，而不是時常聽到的訴苦：「要寫那麼多字！怎麼寫？」有了以上主觀和客觀的 input，我們可以確信英文寫作真的沒那麼難！短文長文都簡單！只要方法對了，何必搔破白頭呢？

接下來，請先看以下的範文。後面會有更清楚的說明。

The Beauty of Chinese Literature

A Chinese poet once said, "Artistic talent displays the landscape of the human heart, and landscapes are an artistic gift from Mother Nature."① Indeed the exquisite artistry and intertwined sentiments of Chinese poetry have penetrated Chinese culture for centuries.

Some poetry simply admires the beauty of nature:

> *Birds fly into the sunset glow;*
> *And rivers inlay the horizons aglow.②*
> 「落霞與孤鶩齊飛，秋水共長天一色。」——王渤

This 1,425-year-old poem reveals the beauty of nature in two extremes. First it focuses on the beauty of nature in motion. Next it shows the beauty of nature in a static state. A dynamic image is contrasted with a static one; birds gracefully flying into a hazy sunset versus a sleepy river reflecting the last light of the day. Both evoke a sense of natural beauty tied together by the setting Sun's waning glow.

Some poetry is metaphorical:

> *Beanstalks fervently burn to heat the fire;*
> *On the fire are beans in the pot.*
> *Beans utter sad calls,*
> *"You and I were once one,*
> *Please spare some mercy for me!"③*
> 「煮豆燃豆箕，豆在釜中泣：
> 本是同根生，相煎何太急！」——曹植

Ch
4

This 1,882-year-old poem is known as the Seven Pace Poem. In the late Eastern-Han Dynasty (circa AD 220), the king-to-be Cao Pi schemed to kill his extremely intelligent brother, Cao Zhi, by ordering him to compose a poem within seven paces. This is the poem that Cao Zhi came up with. It is particularly piercing because it is a metaphor for the relationship with his brother. The beanstalks and beans both come from one plant. They are one and the same, yet the beanstalks work fervently to heat the fire that burns the beans. It is a touching plea for mercy from one who has been wronged by his own kin.

A poem even changed Chinese history.

> *Gloriously, the sunset glows;④*
> *But the nightfall is close.*
> 「夕陽無限好，只是近黃昏。」——李商隱

This 1,266-year-old poem originally addressed human mortality and played on a deep sentimental attachment to life, but was appropriated by former Chinese leader Deng Xiaoping when his reform plan was boycotted by conservative political power-holders. Deng used the sentiments of past glory and loss that were already associated with this poem and transferred them to a patriotic context. He referred to the old, glorious China which had long been behind the bamboo curtain and which would soon meet the nightfall brought about by globalization and global competition. The only way to bring China back to glory was to adapt and reform. The indisputable truth of his message was heard by millions and quieted the opposition, removing the obstacles to reform and making China what it is today.

As in many poetic traditions, numerous Chinese poems are about love. The following contains a theme that has stricken many souls over the centuries:

> *Silkworms only die after the last mouthful of silk is spun;*
> *Candle tears only dry after the last inch of wick is burned.*⑤
> 「春蠶到死絲方盡，蠟炬成灰淚始乾。」——李商隱

This 1,266-year-old poem talks of the sacrificial love of parents and lovers. Countless romantic stories have powerfully illustrated such love. As an example, for Christians, love is best exemplified by the sacrifice of Jesus on the cross, who shed his last drop of blood for the sins of all humanity.

The place of poetry in Chinese history is irreplaceable. Not only do poems tell of the times in which they were created, but they also speak of things that are timeless and universal: love and loss; wisdom and art. Chinese culture is intertwined with its poetry, which can not only touch the heartstrings, but influence an entire nation.

① Li Yu, Qing Dynasty (1644-1911) poet.
② Wang Bao, Tang Dynasty (618-907) poet.
③ Cao Zhi, late Eastern-Han Dynasty (25-220) poet.
④ Li Shangyin, Qing Dynasty poet.
⑤ Li Shangyin.

下一頁起，我們將文章的結構標示出來，提供讀者作為對照。

The Beauty of Chinese Literature

↓ 開始「起」

(lead ▶) A Chinese poet once said, "Artistic talent displays the landscape of the human heart, and landscapes are an artistic gift from Mother Nature." (Thesis Statement ▶) **Indeed the exquisite artistry and intertwined sentiments of Chinese poetry have penetrated Chinese culture for centuries**.

↓ 開始「承」

大 Body
開始：

Some poetry simply admires the beauty of nature:

> *Birds fly into the sunset glow;*
> *And rivers inlay the horizons aglow.*

轉折語 ①

例一

「落霞與孤鶩齊飛，秋水共長天一色。」——王渤

(topic sentence ▶) **This 1,425-year-old poem reveals the beauty of nature in two extremes.** (小 body ▶) First it focuses on the beauty of nature in motion. Next it shows the beauty of nature in a static state. A dynamic image is contrasted with a static one; birds gracefully flying into a hazy sunset versus a sleepy river reflecting the last light of the day. (viewpoint ▶) **Both evoke a sense of natural beauty tied together by the setting Sun's waning glow**.

Some poetry is metaphorical:

> *Beanstalks fervently burn to heat the fi re;*
> *On the fi re are beans in the pot.*
> *Beans utter sad calls,*
> *"You and I were once one,*
> *Please spare some mercy for me!"*

轉折語 ②

例二

「煮豆燃豆萁，豆在釜中泣：
本是同根生，相煎何太急！」——曹植

(topic sentence ▶) **This 1,882-year-old poem is known as the Seven Pace Poem.** (小 body ▶) In the late Eastern-Han Dynasty (circa AD 220), the king-to-be Cao Pi schemed to kill his extremely intelligent brother, Cao Zhi, by ordering him to compose a poem within seven paces. This

Ch
4

is the poem that Cao Zhi came up with. It is particularly piercing because it is a metaphor for the relationship with his brother. The beanstalks and beans both come from one plant. They are one and the same, yet the beanstalks work fervently to heat the fi re that burns the beans. (viewpoint ▶) **It is a touching plea for mercy from one who has been wronged by his own kin.**

A poem even changed Chinese history.

> *Gloriously, the sunset glows;*
> *But the nightfall is close.*
>
> 轉折語 ③
>
> 「夕陽無限好，只是近黃昏。」──李商隱

(topic sentence ▶) **This 1,266-year-old poem originally addressed human mortality and played on a deep sentimental attachment to life, but was appropriated by former Chinese leader Deng Xiaoping when his reform plan was boycotted by conservative political power-holders.** (小 body ▶) Deng used the sentiments of past glory and loss that were already associated with this poem and transferred them to a patriotic context. He referred to the old, glorious China which had long been behind the bamboo curtain and which would soon meet the nightfall brought about by globalization and global competition. The only way to bring China back to glory was to adapt and reform. (viewpoint ▶) **The indisputable truth of his message was heard by millions and quieted the opposition, removing the obstacles to reform and making China what it is today.**

As in many poetic traditions, numerous Chinese poems are about love. The following contains a theme that has stricken many souls over the centuries:

> *Silkworms only die after the last mouthful of silk is spun;*
> *Candle tears only dry after the last inch of wick is burned.*
>
> 「春蠶到死絲方盡，蠟炬成灰淚始乾。」──李商隱

例四	(topic sentence ▶) **This 1,266-year-old poem talks of the sacrificial love of parents and lovers.** (小 **body** ▶) Countless romantic stories have powerfully illustrated such love. (**viewpoint** ▶) <u>**As an example, for Christians, love is best exemplified by the sacrifice of Jesus on the cross, who shed his last drop of blood for the sins of all humanity.**</u>
結論	↓ 開始「合」 The place of poetry in Chinese history is irreplaceable. Not only do poems tell of the times in which they were created, but they also speak of things that are timeless and universal: love and loss; wisdom and art. Chinese culture is intertwined with its poetry, which can not only touch the heartstrings, but influence an entire nation.

Ch

4

細膩的文字帶來感動

　　粗枝大葉的丈夫，常令妻子不安；細心體貼的丈夫，則讓妻子感到溫暖。生澀粗嘎的音樂，常令人心神難寧；細緻典雅的音樂，則令人陶醉。

　　英文作文完全一樣，細膩貼切的文筆立刻為作品帶來令人樂於細細品味的質感。

細膩的文筆從何而來？

　　其實在寫英文作文時，只要做到以下幾點，每一個人都可以擁有絕佳的文筆：

1. 字彙要細膩精巧

　　前面已經舉出英文作文最常見到的慣用語，我們隨後將更進一步，直接用替換法來示範如何讓我們的字彙變得更精緻巧妙。

2. 寫作要有感情

　　不帶感情而寫出的歌曲，難以感動人；不帶感情而演出的電影，也難以感動人。寫作何能例外？文章就像是一場演說、甚至是一篇告白，它和讀者應當有深切的心靈溝通。不用感情而寫出的文章，連自己都不覺得感動，又如何能夠撥動別人的心靈之弦呢？

3. 思想要純正

　　一個長相美麗、打扮精緻的女孩，如果沒有一個高貴的靈魂，就不會吸引人。同樣地，再優美的字彙詞藻，再細膩的感情，如果思想不正（例如怨天尤人、傳達不道德的看法、自私、狹隘、抄襲），就絕對無法展現令人如沐春風的氣質，寫了還不如不寫！

以下僅提供一些例子，大家還是要藉由大量的閱讀以汲取更多優美的字彙詞藻，只要努力，每個人都做得到。

📑 換成高手用字（一）：形容詞

中文	初級英語用字	寫作高手替換用字
清楚的	clear	**explicit** [ɪk`splɪsɪt]
多話的	talkative	**loquacious** [lo`kweʃəs], **bombastic**
好運的	lucky	**blessed, fortunate**
不好的	bad	**negative, odious** [`odɪəs]   **abominable** [ə`bɑmənəbl̩] 例 abominable behavior 就常在寫作中使用
光亮的	bright	**brilliant, luminous** [`lumənəs]
廣闊的	broad	**extensive, wide-ranging, widespread**
好管閒事的	nosy	**meddlesome** [`mɛdl̩səm]   **officious** [ə`fɪʃəs]
公然的；公開的	open	**undisguised** [ˌʌndɪs`gaɪzd] **thinly-veiled**
精緻的	fine	**exquisite** [`ɛkskwɪzɪt], **intricate** [`ɪntrəkɪt]
害羞的	shy	**bashful**
震驚的	shocked	**astonished, stunned, thrilled**
堅硬的	hard	**stiff**（硬實的）, **fortified** **rigid** [`rɪdʒɪd]（僵硬的）, **solid**（紮實的）
柔軟的	soft	**mild**（溫和的） **supple** [`sʌpl̩]（柔情的；唯唯諾諾的）  **pliable** [`plaɪəbl̩]（易折的；順從的）
微弱的	weak	**feeble, fragile** [`frædʒəl]
詳細的	detailed	**minute** [maɪ`njut], **particular** **elaborate**

中文	初級英語用字	寫作高手替換用字
確定的	true, assured	**definite**, **conclusive**, **irrefutable** **absolute**
有限的	limited	**confined**, **finite** [ˈfaɪnaɪt]
重要的	important	**crucial**, **essential** **imperative** [ɪmˈpɛrətɪv]（絕對重要） **significant**
很棒的	wonderful, excellent	**marvelous**, **ingenious** [ɪnˈdʒinjəs] **remarkable**
快樂的	happy	**cheerful**, **elated** [ɪˈletɪd], **joyful**
過時的	old-fashioned	**outdated**, **out-of-date** **obsolete** [ˈɑbsəˌlit], **outmoded**
富裕的	rich	**wealthy**, **affluent** [ˈæfluənt]
貧窮的	poor	**shanty** [ˈʃæntɪ], **scanty** [ˈskæntɪ]
可憐的	poor	**miserable**, **wretched** [ˈrɛtʃɪd] **pathetic**, **pitiful**
示範性的	showing	**exemplary** [ɪgˈzɛmplərɪ] **demonstrating**
瘋狂的	crazy	**insane**（指精神方面） **frenetic** [frɪˈnɛtɪk]（指交易、宗教） **radical**（激進的）
憤怒的	angry	**furious** [ˈfjʊrɪəs], **irritated**（被惹怒的）
關鍵的	key	**crucial**, **critical**, **decisive** [dɪˈsaɪsɪv]
卑鄙的	mean	**despicable** [ˈdɛspɪkəbl̩], **base** **contemptible**
有助的	helpful	**valuable**, **conducive** **advantageous** [ˌædvənˈtedʒəs] **beneficial**, **favorable**

中文	初級英語用字	寫作高手替換用字
有害的	harmful	**devastating** [ˋdɛvəsˏtetɪŋ]（害處極大的、具毀滅性的） **disastrous** [dɪzˋæstrəs] **traumatic** [trɔˋmætɪk]（會帶來創傷的） **pernicious** [pɚˋnɪʃəs]（很有害的） **catastrophic** [ˏkætəˋstrɑfɪk]（天災方面）
天生的	born	**congenital** [kənˋdʒɛnətḷ] **hereditary** [həˋrɛdəˏtɛrɪ]（遺傳的）
大膽的	bold	**audacious** [ɔˋdeʃəs], **daring**
聰明的	smart, bright	**intelligent**, **clever** **astute** [əˋstjut]（機靈的） **resourceful**（思想很快的） **shrewd**（精明的）
完美的	perfect	**flawless**, **impeccable** [ɪmˋpɛkəbḷ]
簡單扼要的	brief	**concise** [kənˋsaɪs], **succinct** [səkˋsɪŋkt]
根本的	basic	**elementary**（初步的） **primary**（根本而主要的） **fundamental**（基礎所需的） **underlying**（根本且十分重要的）
粗俗的	rude	**vulgar** [ˋvʌlgɚ], **uncivilized**
真的	real, true	**actual**（事實如此的） **genuine** [ˋdʒɛnjuɪn]（純正的） **authentic** [ɔˋθɛntɪk]（十分逼真的）
假的	fake	**phony** [ˋfonɪ] **pseudo** [ˋsudo]（冒牌、冒名的）
小心謹慎的	careful	**prudent** **provident** [ˋprɑvədənt]（深謀遠慮的）

Ch
4

中文	初級英語用字	寫作高手替換用字
務實的	practical	**pragmatic**
盛行的	popular	**prevalent** [ˋprɛvələnt], **widespread** **faddish** [ˋfædɪʃ]（成為風尚的）
美麗的；迷人的	beautiful, charming	**picturesque** [ˌpɪktʃəˋrɛsk]（美如畫的） **glamorous** [ˋglæmərəs] **breath-taking, stunning** **charismatic** [ˌkærɪzˋmætɪk]（有魅力的）
逼真的	real	**lifelike, authentic** [ɔˋθɛntɪk]
冷淡的	cold	**remote, detached** [dɪˋtætʃt]
有名的	famous	**prestigious** [prɛsˋtɪdʒɪəs] **illustrious** [ɪˋlʌstrɪəs] **reputable** [ˋrɛpjətəbḷ]
即將來臨的	coming	**upcoming, impending, approaching** **imminent** [ˋɪmənənt]（迫在眉睫的）
可疑的	suspicious	**skeptical, dubious**

請替換以下畫線部分的文字

① a <u>clear</u> voice → _____

② <u>bad</u> behavior → _____

③ <u>nosy</u> → _____

④ <u>soft</u> character → _____

⑤ a <u>detailed</u> description → _____

⑥ <u>important</u> → _____

⑦ a <u>mean</u> idea → _____

⑧ a <u>perfect</u> design → _____

⑨ a <u>fake</u> name → _____

⑩ a <u>coming</u> storm → _____

EXERCISE 20-1 參考答案

① (an) explicit

② abominable

③ meddlesome

④ supple

⑤ elaborated

⑥ crucial

⑦ despicable

⑧ (an) impeccable

⑨ phony

⑩ (an) approaching

　　形容詞在用字遣詞上占極重要的地位。其實，除了單字之外，複合字也是非常有力的形容詞。以下是很實用的複合形容詞，請務必要熟習並善用。

中文	善用複合形容詞
涵蓋範圍很廣的	**wide-ranging** 例 The plague, which covers a wide area, has killed 220 people. 　↓ 改為 The **wide-ranging** plague has caused 220 fatalities. [fəˋtælətɪ]
全國的	**nation-wide** 例 These contests are conducted throughout the whole country, and many people are participating. 　↓ 改為 These **nation-wide** contests have drawn numerous participants.
解決麻煩的	**trouble-shooting** 例 He always knows how to solve problems. 　↓ 改為 He is good at **trouble-shooting**. （或 He is a good troubleshooter.）
破紀錄的	**record-breaking** 例 His speed has broken the record. It only took him three minutes to complete the event. 　↓ 改為 His **record-breaking** speed was three minutes.
高調的	**high-profile** 例 Her high position in the government draws a lot of public attention. 　↓ 改為 She has a **high-profile** government position.

中文	善用複合形容詞
低調的	**low-profile** 例 In order to protect yourself, try not to draw too much attention to yourself. ↓ 改為 Keeping your actions **low-profile** is a good idea.
職位高的	**high-ranking** 例 He has a very high position in the government. ↓ 改為 He is a **high-ranking** official.
全面性的	**across-the-board / full-scale** 例 Please prepare this completely. ↓ 改為 Please make **full-scale** preparations.
危機重重的	**crisis-ridden** 例 The country is faced with many crises. ↓ 改為 The country is **crisis-ridden**.
飽受戰爭之害的	**war-ridden** 例 The Middle East has long suffered from wars. ↓ 改為 The Middle East is **war-ridden**.
債台高築的	**debt-ridden** 例 He owes people a lot of money. ↓ 改為 He is heavily **debt-ridden**.
是非分明的； 寫得清清楚楚的	**black-and-white** 例 What can and can't be done is written very clearly. ↓ 改為 The musts and mustn'ts are written in **black and white**. （名詞，中間不加 hyphen）

Ch
4

中文	善用複合形容詞
久被擱置的	**long-stalled** 例 He has delayed this proposal, which should be turned in tomorrow. ↓ 改為 This **long-stalled** proposal is due tomorrow.
以家庭為重的	**family-oriented** [ˈorɪɛntɪd] 例 In my sister's heart, nothing is more important than her family. ↓ 改為 My sister is **family-oriented**.
以事業為重的	**career-oriented** 例 John does everything for his career. ↓ 改為 John is **career-oriented**.
人口稀少的 （國家或地區）	**sparsely-populated** 例 Even though there aren't many people in the country, all of them look very happy. ↓ 改為 People in this **sparsely-populated** country seem content.
人口眾多的	**heavily-populated** 例 There are so many people living in India; meanwhile, India is becoming prosperous. ↓ 改為 **Heavily-populated** India is prospering.
彌補缺失的	**fence-mending** 例 We need several methods to solve this problem. ↓ 改為 Several **fence-mending** measures are required.
填鴨式的	**force-fed** 例 If students learn in a forced way, they will not be able to think creatively. ↓ 改為 **Forced-fed** education deprives students of their originality.

EXERCISE 20-2

請使用複合形容詞以及比較細緻的文字，重寫以下句子。

① Economists are trying very hard to face the global financial storm.

答案：＿＿＿＿＿＿＿＿＿＿＿＿＿＿＿＿＿＿＿＿＿＿＿＿＿

② It's not good if parents force their children to learn things.

答案：＿＿＿＿＿＿＿＿＿＿＿＿＿＿＿＿＿＿＿＿＿＿＿＿＿

③ Because of the small population, Canada welcomes people to immigrate there.

答案：＿＿＿＿＿＿＿＿＿＿＿＿＿＿＿＿＿＿＿＿＿＿＿＿＿

④ All husbands and wives should make the family first priority.

答案：＿＿＿＿＿＿＿＿＿＿＿＿＿＿＿＿＿＿＿＿＿＿＿＿＿

⑤ This country has so many crises that it may go bankrupt soon.

答案：＿＿＿＿＿＿＿＿＿＿＿＿＿＿＿＿＿＿＿＿＿＿＿＿＿

⑥ He does only things right and hates to be wrong.

答案：＿＿＿＿＿＿＿＿＿＿＿＿＿＿＿＿＿＿＿＿＿＿＿＿＿

⑦ We already stated the rules very clearly in the contract, and we should follow them.

答案：＿＿＿＿＿＿＿＿＿＿＿＿＿＿＿＿＿＿＿＿＿＿＿＿＿

⑧ China had so many wars during the Spring and Autumn Period (270-476 BC) that many suffered from hunger.

答案：＿＿＿＿＿＿＿＿＿＿＿＿＿＿＿＿＿＿＿＿＿＿＿＿＿

⑨ He works for the company, and his position is very high.

答案：＿＿＿＿＿＿＿＿＿＿＿＿＿＿＿＿＿＿＿＿＿＿＿＿＿

Ch
4

⑩ Even though he is very successful, he still remains humble and keeps to himself.

答案： _____

📖 EXERCISE 20-2 參考答案

（以下答案只是參考，讀者可由書本中找出更多的進階用法）

① Economists strive for fence-mending measures during the global financial storm.

② Force-fed education isn't recommended.

③ Sparsely-populated Canada recruits emigrants worldwide.

④ The married should be family-oriented.

⑤ This crisis-ridden company is faced with imminent bankruptcy.

⑥ He believes in keeping things black and white.

⑦ This black-and-white contract should be respected.

⑧ Hunger prevailed in the war-ridden Spring and Autumn Period of China.

（※ 在高級英文寫作中，各種資料都需嚴謹，才有 credibility。因此，「春秋時期」在英文作文中不可單獨出現，而需立即補上年代。）

⑨ He is a high-ranking employee in the company.

⑩ He is very low-profile about his success.

換成高手用字（三）：動詞

　　動詞是句子的靈魂，絕對不可隨便使用。以下動詞的意涵是英文作文經常需要用到的，請務必學會更多的替換字讓英文更進階。

中文	英語寫作常用字	寫作高手替換用字
問	ask	**inquire**
回溯	look back	**resound**（一邊追憶，一邊說出來） **recall**
花費	cost	**consume**
恨	hate	**loathe** [loð], **detest**
改變	change	**shift** 例 shift one's ground（轉變立場） **transform**（大轉變、脫胎換骨）, **alter**
抓住	catch, hold	**grip**, **grab**, **grasp**, **seize**
注視	look	**gaze**, **behold**
監督	monitor	**oversee**, **supervise**, **superintend**
想像	imagine	**fancy**, **visualize** [ˈvɪʒʊəˌlaɪz]
限制	limit	**confine**, **restrict**
動	move	**undulate** [ˈʌndjəˌlet]（一波波移動，例如稻田） **fluctuate** [ˈflʌktʃʊˌet]（上下波動；例如股市）
加強、強調	strengthen, emphasize	**enhance**, **intensify**, **heighten** **augment**, **reinforce** [ˌriɪnˈfɔrs]
淡化	play ... down	**dilute** [daɪˈlut]
舉行	hold	**put on**, **conduct** **stage**, **host**（舉辦宴會）
警告	warn	**exhort** [ɪgˈzɔrt]
告訴	tell	**notify** [ˈnotəˌfaɪ], **inform**

中文	英語寫作常用字	寫作高手替換用字
丟臉	lose face	**be disgraced**, **be embarrassed**
加速進行；促成	speed up	**accelerate** [æk`sɛləˌrət] **facilitate** [fə`sɪləˌtet]
抵抗	fight against	**confront** **resist**（主動地抗拒） 例 resist temptations **withstand**（被動地抗拒；奮力站穩地抵擋） 例 withstand natural calamities [kə`læmətɪ] **rebound**（反彈）
避免	avoid	**shun** [ʃʌn], **avert** [ə`vɝt]
罵	scold, blame	**rebuke**, **condemn**, **chide** [tʃaɪd]
講述	talk about	**depict** **broach** [brotʃ]（開始講述） **recount**（限定講述已發生之事） **delineate** [dɪ`lɪnɪˌet]（描出輪廓） **elaborate**（詳述） **portray**（細細地描述）
修正	correct	**redress**, **amend**, **rectify** [`rɛktəˌfaɪ]
實現	come true	**materialize** [mə`tɪrɪəlˌaɪz] **realize**
停止	stop	**halt**, **cease**, **pause**
妨礙	hinder	**hamper**, **impede** [ɪm`pid]
令人害怕	scare	**intimidate**, **frighten**, **petrify**, **terrify**
超越	pass	**overwhelm**, **overshadow**（令別人遜色）
對……有害	harm	**plague** [pleg], **injure**
跌落	fall	**tumble**（亦指心情、股價……）

中文	英語寫作常用字	寫作高手替換用字
應付	handle	**manage**, **tackle** [ˋtækḷ]
交出	turn in	**submit**
預見	predict	**foresee**, **envision** [ɪnˋvɪʒən]
支持	support back up	**bolster**（有聲援之意） **buttress**
增加	increase add	**intensify**, **boost**（快速增加） **raise**, **augment**, **multiply**
減少	decrease	**dwindle** [ˋdwɪndḷ], **dilute** [daɪˋlut] **curtail**（削減） **alleviate** [əˋlivɪˌet]（減輕） **downsize**（減少規模）
確定	assure	**confirm**, **define** **affirm**, **acknowledge**
假設	suppose	**assume**, **presume** **hypothesize** [haɪˋpɑθəsaɪz]
破壞	break	**mar**, **wreck** **sabotage** [ˋsæbəˌtɑʒ]（暗中破壞） **undermine** [ˌʌndəˋmaɪn]（由根基來破壞） **paralyze** [ˋpærəˌlaɪz]（使整個癱瘓）

Ch
4

請將畫線部分替換成較精緻的文字。

① look back at the past → _____

② completely change → _____

③ strengthen → _____

④ play the scandal down → _____

⑤ fight against someone → _____

⑥ fight against the fire → _____

⑦ blame someone → _____

⑧ pass someone's performance（超越）→ _____

⑨ turn in the key → _____

⑩ suppose I am right → _____

EXERCISE 20-3 參考答案

（以下答案只是參考，讀者可由書本中找出更多的進階用法）

① recall

② transform

③ intensify

④ dilute

⑤ confront

⑥ withstand

⑦ condemn

⑧ overshadow

⑨ submit

⑩ presume

換成高手用字（四）：動詞片語

　　因為動詞非常重要，所以我們寫作時也常用動詞片語來表達。請各位比較之後，努力熟記，讓它成為自己的寫作資產。

中文	常見英文用語	較精緻的替換用語
有明亮的前景	have a bright future	**expect broad prospects**
提出意見	give opinions	**air views** **voice opinions**
放寬限制	loosen limits	**ease restrictions**
提出……問題	ask the question about	**raise the issue of**
對……有影響力	have influence on	**wield influence over**
寄望於……	put one's hope on	**peg one's hope to**
使希望破滅	break the hope	**shatter the hope** **dampen the hope** **disillusion**
擺脫……	get away from …	**dissociate oneself from …**
消除歧見	stop different opinions	**iron out conflicts**
對……施壓	put pressure on …	**exert pressure on**
到最高點	go to the top	**reach the zenith**
獲利	make money	**reap profit**
儲存能量	save power	**gather momentum**
守信用	keep a promise	**honor a pledge**
有權去……	have rights to …	**be entitled to**
發起抗爭	start a fight with	**lodge a protest against**
不顧……的面子	don't care about the face of …	**disregard** 某人的 **sensibilities**

Ch
4

📑 換成高手用字（五）：名詞

中文	常見英文用語	較精緻的替換用語
在……方面	side	**respect**, **aspect**, **dimension**
光輝	light	**radiance**, **brilliance**, **glow**
幻想、幻覺	imagination	**illusion** [ɪˋljuʒən], **fantasy** **reverie** [ˋrɛvərɪ], **mirage** [məˋrɑʒ]
工具、手段	tool	**means**（方法） **instrument**（工具、方法） **implement** [ˋɪmpləmənt]（手段、方法）
煩惱	worry	**apprehension** **misgiving**(s)（可數名詞）
故事	story	**plot**（強調故事內容） 例 This movie has a sad plot. **anecdote**（軼事）, **legend**（傳說）
甜言蜜語	sweet talk	**blandishments** [ˋblændɪʃmənts]
細節	details	**particulars**, **elaborations**
重點	point(s)	**essential**(s), **gist**(s) [dʒɪst] **focal point**(s)
動力	power	**impetus** [ˋɪmpətəs] **momentum** [moˋmɛntəm]
關聯	relationship	**context** [ˋkɑntɛkst], **connection**
視野	view	**vista** [ˋvɪstə], **vision**
活力	energy	**vitality** [vaɪˋtælətɪ] **dynamics** [daɪˋnæmɪks]
會議	meeting	**symposium** [sɪmˋpozɪəm]（大會） **forum**（論壇）, **seminar**（座談會） **conference**（大會）, **assembly**（大會） **conclave** [ˋkɑnklev]（祕密會議，尤指教宗選舉）

中文	常見英文用語	較精緻的替換用語
地位	position	**status**（身分、地位）
喊人	call	**beckon**（用手勢喊人）, **summon**（傳喚）
情形	situation	**scenario** [sɪ`nɛrɪ‚o]
玩笑	joke	**prank**（也可指「惡作劇」）, **zest**
談話	talk	**dialogue**
層面	level	**dimension**, **facet** [`fæsɪt]
標準	standard	**criterion** [kraɪ`tɪrɪən]（複數形是 criteria）
變化	change	**transformation**（徹底的改變） **cataclysm** [`kætə‚klɪzəm]（劇變） **reform**（改革）
旁觀者	watcher	**onlooker**
對未來的展望	future	**outlook**
方法	way method	**means**（方法） **strategy**（策略） **maneuver** [mə`nuvə]（策略） **implement**（手段） **scheme**（計謀） **mechanism** [`mɛkə‚nɪzəm]（機制）
請求	ask	**request**, **plea**

Ch
4

EXERCISE 20-4

請將下列文字替換成較精緻的文字。

動詞片語

① give opinions → _____

② ask the question about → _____

③ get away from（擺脫）→ _____

④ go to the top → _____

⑤ keep a promise → _____

名詞

⑥ sweet talk → _____

⑦ worry → _____

⑧ energy → _____

⑨ level → _____

⑩ big change → _____

EXERCISE 20-4 參考答案

① air views

② raise the issue of

③ dissociate oneself from

④ reach the zenith

⑤ honor a pledge

⑥ blandishments

⑦ apprehension

⑧ vitality

⑨ dimension

⑩ transformation

　　副詞的力量很大，只要用得靈巧，往往一個字就代替了一整句話，所以各位如果要寫進階英文，就須流利地使用副詞。以下彙整的這些副詞，它們對高級英文寫作大有助益。

中文	善用副詞
好像是	**seemingly** 例 That girl seems frustrated, and she doesn't talk. 　　↓ 改為 That **seemingly** frustrated girl remains quiet.
靠一己之力	**single-handedly** 例 He caught the thief all by himself. 　　↓ 改為 He **single-handedly** caught the thief.
明確地	**specifically** 例 He made it very clear that he would like to order that dish. 　　↓ 改為 He **specifically** ordered that dish. 　　　　　　　　　　　　　那道菜
斷然地	**categorically** [ˌkætəˋgɔrɪklɪ] / **flatly** / **sternly** 例 She refused his proposal without hesitation. 　　↓ 改為 She **flatly** refused his proposal. 　　　　　　　　　　　　求婚
名義上來說	**nominally** [ˋnɑmənḷɪ] 例 You can say that he is the master of dancing. 　　↓ 改為 He is **nominally** the dancing master. 他是名符其實的舞蹈大師。

中文	善用副詞
令人懷舊地	**nostalgically** [nɑˋstældʒɪkəlɪ] 例 When I saw this town, I couldn't help but think of the old days, which made me cry. ↓ 改為 This town **nostalgically** brought me to tears.
相反地	**contrarily** [ˋkɑntrərɪlɪ] 例 I thought he loved her; on the contrary, he hated her. ↓ 改為 Instead of loving her, he **contrarily** hated her.
在意料之中地	**unsurprisingly** 例 As we all expected, he married her. ↓ 改為 **Unsurprisingly**, he married her.
在物質上來說	**materialistically** 例 Even though he is rich, he is not happy. ↓ 改為 He is **materialistically** rich, yet spiritually poor.
不甘願地	**reluctantly** 例 Even though he didn't want to go, he still went. ↓ 改為 He **reluctantly** went.
再三地	**repeatedly** 例 I've told them over and over again not to touch that. ↓ 改為 I've **repeatedly** warned them to stay away from it.
本質上來說	**essentially** 例 The English language itself is quite interesting. ↓ 改為 English is **essentially** interesting.

中文	善用副詞
令人注目地	**conspicuously** 例 That neon sign is so bright that draws everyone's attention. ↓ 改為 That neon is **conspicuously** bright.
不需爭辯的事實	**indisputably** 例 He is so generous that no one would argue it. ↓ 改為 He is **indisputably** generous.
量很可觀地	**substantially** 例 I've cut down the money I spend. ↓ 改為 I've **substantially** reduced my expenses.
明確地說	**explicitly** 例 He explained very clearly the reasons why we must work hard. ↓ 改為 He **explicitly** indicated the reasons we must work hard.
暗示性地說	**implicitly** 例 He tried to ask her out, but he didn't say it clearly. ↓ 改為 He **implicitly** asked her out.
比較起來	**comparatively** 例 Among all the girls, she is especially tall. ↓ 改為 She is **comparatively** tall among all the girls.
依數據上來看	**statistically** 例 According to statistics, global warming is becoming worse. ↓ 改為 **Statistically**, global warming is worsening.

Ch
4

中文	善用副詞
依事實上來看	**realistically** 例 It is true that many people aren't happy. ↓ 改為 **Realistically**, many people aren't happy.
令人鼓舞的是	**encouragingly** 例 He finally succeeded, which encouraged many people. ↓ 改為 **Encouragingly**, he finally succeeded.
令人灰心的是	**discouragingly** 例 They didn't show up, which discouraged many people. ↓ 改為 **Discouragingly**, they didn't show up.
難以避免地	**inevitably / unavoidably** 例 Living in this dirty city, he finally got sick. ↓ 改為 He **inevitably** got sick living in this polluted city.
以藝術的角度來看	**artistically** 例 Even though it is second-hand, it looks beautiful from the point of view of art. ↓ 改為 It is second-hand yet **artistically** beautiful.
以科學的角度來看	**scientifically** 例 It has been proven by science. ↓ 改為 It has been **scientifically** proven.
理論上來說	**theoretically** 例 The theory may be right. ↓ 改為 It's **theoretically** correct.

中文	善用副詞
假設說	**hypothetically** 例 Your suggestion may be helpful, but it's only a hypothesis. ↓ 改為 Your suggestion is **hypothetically** helpful.
從觀念上來看	**conceptionally** 例 Many Chinese people think that Confucianism is very important. ↓ 改為 **Conceptionally**, many Chinese people esteem Confucianism.
從宗教的觀點來看	**religiously** 例 According to Christianity, people should love their enemies. ↓ 改為 **Religiously** speaking, Christians should love their enemies.
在傳統上	**traditionally** 例 It's a Chinese tradition to be nice to parents. ↓ 改為 **Traditionally**, Chinese esteem filial <u>piety</u>. 孝道
由歷史的角度上來看	**historically** 例 China has gone through many wars. ↓ 改為 **Historically**, China has been war-ridden.
如夢似幻地	**dreamily** 例 She danced with him, which was like a dream to her. ↓ 改為 **Dreamily**, she danced with him.
難以下決定地	**hesitantly** 例 He couldn't make up his mind if he ought to tell him the bad news or not, but he finally hold him. ↓ 改為 **Hesitantly**, he informed him of the bad news.

Ch
4

中文	善用副詞
基本上	**fundamentally** 例 Love and trust are the most basic and important elements of marriage. ↓ 改為 Love and trust are **fundamentally** important to marriage.
只是臆測地、推理地	**speculatively** 例 Experts are guessing that the economy will recover in Q3. ↓ 改為 **Speculatively**, experts indicate that the economic recovery may arrive in Q3. （※ Q3 = the third quarter 第三季）

請運用副詞重新撰寫句子。

① That girl looks happy, and she loves dancing.

答案：_____

② They didn't tell anyone but her the good news.

答案：_____

③ People call him an expert, but he's just an amateur.

答案：_____

④ Even though he is not interested in washing dishes, he still washed them.

答案：_____

⑤ She is very tall, which often draws people's attention.

答案：_____

⑥ She has tried twice to remind him.

答案：_____

⑦ In the real life, most married couples aren't happy.

答案：_____

⑧ We assume that is correct.

答案：_____

⑨ Even though he couldn't make up his mind about whether he should quit his job, he finally quit.

答案：_____

⑩ He wasn't sure if he was correct, but he still made a conclusion with what he knew.

答案：_____

📖 **EXERCISE 20-5 參考答案**

（以下答案只是參考，讀者可由本書中找出更多的進階用法）

① That seemingly happy girl loves dancing.

② They specifically informed her of the good news.

③ He's nominally an expert but actually an amateur.

④ Reluctantly, he washed the dishes.

⑤ She is conspicuously tall.

⑥ She has implicitly reminded him twice.

⑦ Realistically, successful marriages are rare.

⑧ That is hypothetically correct.

⑨ He hesitantly resigned.

⑩ Speculatively, he drew a conclusion.

【一】試著將色字部分換成另外的字吧！

① 她說話清楚。

She speaks clearly.

↓ 改成

_____

② 他看起來心情很好。

He looks very happy.

↓ 改成

_____

③ 我需要一個詳細的報告。

I need a detailed report.

↓ 改成

_____

Ch
4

④ 我是個過時的老太太。

I'm an old-fashioned older woman.

↓ 改成

_____

⑤ 我們的想像力被教育制度限制了。

Our imaginations have been limited by the educational system.

↓ 改成

_____

⑥ 他的幽默感是天生的。

He was born with a sense of humor.

↓ 改成

_____

⑦ 這是基本的要求。

This is the basic requirement.

↓ 改成

_____

⑧ 中國飽受戰爭之苦。

China has suffered from wars.

↓ 改成

_____

⑨ 她以家庭為主。

She puts her family first.

↓ 改成

_____

⑩ 我們必須加強他的注意力。

We must improve his concentration.

↓ 改成

_____

【二】改寫句子

① 我們中國人習慣在過年的時候放鞭炮。

We Chinese are accustomed to setting off firecrackers to celebrate Chinese New Year.

改寫：_____

② 他一直避免談論這個話題。

He tries not to talk about this topic.

改寫：_____

③ 第八屆選美比賽將在一個非常美麗的國家公園舉行。

The 8th-annual beauty contest will take place in a very beautiful national park.

改寫：_____

④ 你好沒禮貌，真讓我丟臉。

You are so rude that you've made me lose face.

改寫：_____

⑤ 他雖然在國家位居要職，卻失職了。

Even though he has an extremely important position in the country, he didn't do a

good job.

改寫：_____

⑥ 我們城市的人口很少，所以人力短缺。

The population is very small in our city; therefore, we are short of labor.

改寫：_____

⑦ 她天生就是音樂家。

She was born to be a musician.

改寫：_____

⑧ 這是一個紀錄片，內容是舉例說明世界暖化的危機。

This documentary demonstrates the crisis of global warming with examples.

改寫：_____

⑨ 在這最重要的時刻，她失蹤了！

She disappeared at the most important time!

改寫：_____

⑩ 他毫無保留地展現對她的愛，使她流下淚來。

He fully displayed his love for her, making her cry.

改寫：_____

Ch

4

【一】

① explicitly

② elated

③ elaborated

④ obsolete

⑤ confined

⑥ He has a natural sense of humor.

⑦ fundamental

⑧ war-ridden

⑨ She is family-oriented.

⑩ intensity

【二】

① Traditionally, Chinese set off firecrackers during the Lunar New Year.

② He is shunning this issue.

③ The 8th-annual beauty contest will be staged in a picturesque national park.

④ Your rudeness has disgraced me.

⑤ He betrayed his indispensable position in the country.

⑥ Our sparsely-populated city is short of manpower.

⑦ She is a natural musician.

⑧ This exemplary documentary alerts us about global warming.

⑨ She disappeared at a crucial moment.

⑩ His undisguised love for her brought her to tears.

Appendix

引用睿智之語
是明智之舉

✅ 可以增加文章價值的諺語

　　想寫出一篇讓人印象深刻的好作文，就少不了放入幾句諺語來支持自己的看法。本書挑選出的諺語不但實用，用字又簡單，只要多看幾次，就可以把它們靈活運用於作文之中，增加文章的價值。

　　首先，我們得先了解在文章中加入諺語的方法：

① 獨立成句

Opportunity seldom knocks twice. If you don't take this chance, you might have none ever.

機會不待人。如果你不把握這次機會，或許你再也不會有。

② 用連接詞連接

IBM offered Jennifer a good job, and she took it right away because opportunity seldom knocks twice.

IBM 提供珍妮佛一個工作機會，她立刻就答應了，因為機會很少敲兩次門。

③ 當作引言插入

"Opportunity seldom knocks twice," as the old saying goes. Don't give up the chance or you'll regret it.

如同這句諺語所言：「機會很少敲兩次門」。不要放棄這個機會，否則你一定會後悔。

　　接下來讓我們一起用填空的方式來完成下面的 99 則實用諺語吧！在練習填入單字的時候，建議可以拿張紙將頁面右半邊的答案遮住，試著依諺語的中文意思或括號裡的提示來猜出正確的答案！

一 激勵 & 鼓勵的諺語 (Inspiring and Encouraging)

1. 打鐵趁熱。
   Strike while the <u>iron</u> is <u>hot</u>.
                     鐵   熱

   strike (v.) 鑄造
   Ans.: iron; hot

---

2. 善用機會；趁機行事。
   Make _____ while the sun shines.
            乾草
   〔趁有太陽時把草曬乾。〕

   hay (n.) 做飼料用的乾草
   Ans.: hay

---

3. 有時候，吃虧就是占便宜。
   Sometimes the best _____ is to lose.
                        獲得
   〔有時候，最好的收穫就是失去。〕

   Ans.: gain

---

4. 否極泰來。
   Every _____ has a _____ lining.
            雲   銀色
   〔每一片雲都有銀色滾邊。〕

   lining (n.) 內襯
   silver lining 比喻陽光從雲後
   面所襯出的光芒，讓雲朵看
   來像裹上了銀色滾邊。
   Ans.: cloud; silver

---

5. 雨過天青。
   After a _____ comes a _____.
            暴風雨   平靜
   〔暴風雨過後就會風平浪靜。〕

   Ans.: storm; calm (n.)

---

6. 留得青山在，不怕沒柴燒。
   While there is _____, there is _____.
                    生命   希望
   〔有生命，就有希望。〕

   Ans.: life; hope

---

7. 每個人都有出頭的機會。
   Every _____ has its _____.
            狗   日子
   〔每隻狗都有得意的一天。〕

   Ans.: dog; day

---

8. 好酒沉甕底；好戲在後頭。

The best fish swim near the _____.
底部

〔最好的魚游在最靠底部的地方。〕

Ans.: bottom

---

9. 深藏不露；大智若愚。

_____ waters run _____.
靜止的　　　　　　　深

〔靜水深流。〕

Ans.: Still; deep

---

10. 要以智取，不以力奪。

One good _____ is better than a hundred strong
頭

_____.
手臂

〔一顆好頭腦勝過百隻強壯的臂膀。〕

Ans.: head; arms

---

11. 滴水穿石。

_____ dripping w_____ a_____ the stone.
持續不斷的　　　　磨損【片語】

〔持續的水滴可以將石頭磨損。〕

dripping (*n.*) 水滴
Ans.: Constant; wears away

---

12. 積少成多；鐵杵也能磨成繡花針。

_____ strokes fell _____ oaks.
小小的　　　　　　巨大的

〔小刀小刀的砍伐也能砍倒大樹。〕

stroke (*n.*) 砍
fell (*v.*) 砍倒
oak (*n.*) 橡樹
Ans.: Little; great

---

13. 失敗是成功的基礎。

Failure is the _____ of _____.
基礎　　　成功

failure (*n.*) 失敗
Ans.: foundation; success

---

14. 沒有熱誠，難成大事。

Nothing _____ was ever achieved without _____.
偉大的　　　　　　　　　　　　　熱衷

achieve (*v.*) 達成
Ans.: great; enthusiasm

15. 不畏艱難，勇敢面對。

Take the ＿＿＿＿ by the ＿＿＿＿.
　　　　　　公牛　　　　　　　　角

〔要制伏公牛，得抓住牠的角。〕

Ans.: bull; horns

16. 遲做總比不做好。

Better ＿＿＿＿ than ＿＿＿＿.
　　　　遲　　　　從來沒有

Ans.: late; never

17. 聊勝於無。

Something is ＿＿＿＿ ＿＿＿＿ nothing.
　　　　　　　勝過【片語】

〔有總比沒有好。〕

Ans.: better than

18. 結局好，則一切都好。

All's ＿＿＿＿ that ends ＿＿＿＿.
　　　好　　　　　　　　　好

Ans.: well; well

19. 學無止境。

Live and ＿＿＿＿.
　　　　　學習

Ans.: learn

20. 成敗靠自己。

Sink or ＿＿＿＿.
　　　　游泳

〔要不就沉下去，要不就游起來。〕

sink (v.) 沉入
Ans.: swim

★ 注意到第 19、20 兩則諺語的共通性了嗎？這兩個諺語都刻意使用了同一個字母開頭的字，像 sink 跟 swim 都是使用 s 開頭的字。這種形式的諺語不僅簡單好記，也可創造出一種押頭韻的趣味呢！

有時候韻不押字首，但會押在字尾（押尾韻）或一個字當中的母音：比如 think 和 speak 押尾韻 [k]（Think today and speak tomorrow 要深思熟慮），而 sight 和 mind 押母音 [aɪ]（Out of sight, out of mind. 眼不見為淨）。

接下來的內容裡也會出現很多有押韻的諺語，若能多留意這種在諺語當中的巧妙安排，不但能藉此增添學習的樂趣，還可強化我們對諺語的記憶力。

二 告誡 & 建議的諺語 (Admonishing and Advising)

21. 半瓶水響叮噹。

_____ vessels make the most _____.
空的　　　　　　　　　　　　　　　聲音

〔空瓶可以發出最響亮的聲音。〕

vessel (*n.*) 容器
Ans.: Empty; sound

---

22. 老狗學不了新把戲。

You cannot teach an _____ _____ new tricks.
老的　　狗

〔你無法教會一隻老狗新的花招。〕

trick (*n.*) 花招；把戲
Ans.: old dog

---

23. 江山易改，本性難移。

A leopard cannot change his _____.
斑點

〔美洲豹身上的斑點是無法改變的。〕

leopard (*n.*) 美洲豹
Ans.: spots

---

24. 積習難改。

Old _____ _____ hard.
習慣　　死；消逝

〔老習慣不容易消失。〕

Ans.: habits; die

---

25. 人多嘴雜。

Too many _____ _____ the broth.
廚師　　搞砸

〔太多廚師就會搞砸一鍋湯。〕

spoil (*v.*) 搞砸
broth (*n.*) 用肉和蔬菜煮成的湯
Ans.: cooks; spoil

---

26. 說的比做的容易。

_____ said than done.
較容易的

Ans.: Easier

---

27. 身體力行；言行一致。

_____ what you preach.
實踐

preach (*v.*) 說教
Ans.: Practice

---

28. 說得到，也要做得到。
Deeds, not _____.
　　　　　話語
〔要的是行動，不是言語。〕

deed (n.) 行動
Ans.: words

---

29. 小時了了，大未必佳。
Today a _____, tomorrow a _____.
　　　　　男人　　　　　　　老鼠
〔今天是男子漢，明天是膽小鬼。〕

Ans.: man; mouse

---

30. 三思而後行。
_____ before you leap.
　看
〔先看好再跳出去。〕

leap (v.) 跳躍
Ans.: Look

---

31. 按部就班。
_____ before you _____.
　走　　　　　　　　跑
〔學跑之前，要先學會走。〕

Ans.: Walk; run

---

32. 熟思而後言。
_____ today and _____ tomorrow.
　想　　　　　　　　說
〔今天想好，明天再說。〕

Ans.: Think; speak

---

33. 煩惱無濟於事。
_____ is no cure.
　擔心
〔煩惱不是解決問題的方法。〕

cure (n.) 處理問題的對策
Ans.: Care

---

34. 要以智取，不以力奪。
_____ trouble trouble _____ trouble troubles you.
絕對不要 （動詞）（受詞）　直到　（主詞）（動詞）（受詞）
〔不要打擾煩惱，直到煩惱打擾你。〕

Ans.: Never; till

35. 不要本末倒置。

Don't _____ the cart before the _____.
　　　　　放　　　　　　　　　　　　　馬

〔別將馬車放在馬的前面。〕

cart (*n.*) 給馬、牛拉的運貨車
Ans.: put; horse

---

36. 好奇心會害死一隻貓。

_____ killed the cat.
好奇心

Ans.: Curiosity

---

37. 乞丐沒有選擇的權利。

_____ can't be choosers.
乞丐

〔此諺語亦有「飢不擇食」之意。〕

Ans.: Beggars

---

38. 忍耐是痛苦的，但它的果實是甜美的。

Patience is _____, but its fruit is _____.
　　　　　　　苦的　　　　　　　　　　甜的

Ans.: bitter; sweet

---

39. 量入為出。

Cut your coat _____ _____ your cloth.
　　　　　　　　根據【片語】

〔有多少布料，就做多少衣服。〕

Ans.: according to

---

40. 量力而為。

Don't _____ off more than you can _____.
　　　　　咬　　　　　　　　　　　　　　咀嚼

〔不要咬下多過於你能嚼的。〕

Ans.: bite; chew

---

41. 貪多必失。

Grasp all, _____ all.
　　　　　　失去

grasp (*v.*) 抓住
Ans.: lose

42. 己所不欲，勿施於人。

Do unto _____ as you would have them do unto you.
　　　　　其他人

Ans.: others

---

43. 盡人事，聽天命。

_____ proposes, _____ disposes.
　人　　　　　　　　神

propose (*v.*) 計畫、盤算
dispose (*v.*) 處置、安排
Ans.: Man; God

---

44. 不要打如意算盤。

Don't _____ your _____ before they are hatched.
　　　　　數　　　　　　小雞

〔在小雞還沒孵出之前，不要數你的蛋。〕

hatch (*v.*) 孵化
Ans.: count; chickens

---

45. 為無法挽回的事而懊惱，是沒有意義的。

It's no use _____ over spilt milk.
　　　　　　哭

〔牛奶已灑出，哭也無用。〕

spilt (*adj.*) 已灑出的
Ans.: crying

---

46. 木已成舟；覆水難收。

What's done cannot be _____.
　　　　　　　　　未完成的

Ans.: undone

---

47. 不要孤注一擲；要會分散風險。

Don't put all your _____ in one _____.
　　　　　　　　蛋　　　　　籃子

〔不要將所有的蛋都放進同個籃子。〕

Ans.: eggs; basket

---

48. 凡事不可貌相。

You cannot tell a book by its _____.
　　　　　　　　　　　封面

〔光看封面無法得知一本書的內容。〕

Ans.: cover

---

49. 不要以貌取人。

Never _____ a person by his _____.
        評斷   外貌

Ans.: judge; appearance

50. 中看未必中用。

_____ that glitters is not _____.
  所有的   金子
〔所有會閃爍的東西未必都是金子。〕

glitter (v.) 閃閃發光
Ans.: All; gold

51. 美貌是膚淺的。

_____ is but _____ deep.
  美麗   皮膚

Ans.: Beauty; skin

52. 眼不見，心不念；久別情疏。

Out of sight, out of _____.
                      心念

sight (n.) 視線範圍
Ans.: mind

53. 過去就讓它過去。

Let bygones be _____.
                往事

bygone (n.) 往事
Ans.: bygones

54. 絕不念舊惡。

Forgive and _____.
              忘記
〔原諒並遺忘。〕

forgive (v.) 原諒
Ans.: forget

55. 欲速則不達。

Haste makes _____.
              浪費

haste (n.) 慌忙
Ans.: waste

56. 養育重於生育。

_____ is above _____.
  滋養   天性

Ans.: Nurture (n.); nature

312

57. 一分耕耘，一分收穫。

As you _____, so shall you _____.
　　　　　　播種　　　　　　　　　　收穫

Ans.: sow; reap

---

58. 不勞則無獲。

No pain, no _____.
　　　　　　收穫

Ans.: gain

---

59. 不浪費，不匱乏。

_____ not, want not.
浪費

Ans.: Waste

---

60. 不入虎穴，焉得虎子。

Nothing ventured, _____ _____.
　　　　　　　　　　沒有東西　收穫

〔不冒險，則無獲。〕

venture (v.) 冒險
Ans.: nothing; gained

---

61. 失之毫釐，差之千里。

A _____ is as good as a _____.
　　疏失　　　　　　　　　　　英哩

Ans.: miss; mile

---

62. 事出必有因；無風不起浪。

Where there is _____ there's _____.
　　　　　　　　　煙　　　　　火

〔有煙就有火。〕

Ans.: smoke; fire

---

63. 禍不單行。

Misery loves _____.
　　　　　　同伴

〔痛苦喜歡找同伴。〕

Ans.: company

64. 機不可失；福無雙至。

Opportunity seldom _____ _____.
敲打　　兩次

〔機會很少會敲兩次門。〕

opportunity (*n.*) 機會；良機
Ans.: knocks; twice

---

65. 一個巴掌拍不響。

It takes _____ to tango.
兩個

〔兩個人才有辦法跳探戈。〕

Ans.: two

---

66. 集思廣益；三個臭皮匠，勝過諸葛亮。

Two _____ are better than one.
頭

〔兩個頭腦勝過於一個。〕

Ans.: heads

---

67. 如果一件事值得做，就值得做好。

If a _____ is _____ doing, it is _____ doing well.
事情　　值得　　　　　　值得

Ans.: thing; worth; worth

---

68. 在商言商；公事公辦。

_____ is _____.
做生意　　做生意

Ans.: Business; business

---

69. 入境隨俗。

When in _____, do as the _____ do.
羅馬　　　　　　羅馬人

〔到了羅馬，就做羅馬人會做的事。〕

Ans.: Rome; Romans

---

70. 做而學，行而知。

In _____ we learn.
行動

Ans.: doing

三 人 & 生活的諺語 (People and Life)

71. 情人眼裡出西施。
    _____ is in the eye of the beholder.
    　　美麗

    beholder (*n.*) 觀看的人
    Ans.: Beauty

72. 人要衣裝，佛要金裝。
    Fine _____ make fine _____.
    　　　羽毛　　　　　　　鳥
    〔漂亮的羽毛造就出一隻漂亮的鳥。〕

    fine (*adj.*) 美好的
    Ans.: feathers; birds

73. 禮多人不怪。
    Courtesy _____ nothing.
    　　　　　花費
    〔禮節不需花半毛錢。〕

    courtesy (*n.*) 禮節；禮貌
    Ans.: costs

74. 人非聖賢，孰能無過。
    _____ Homer sometimes _____.
    　　甚至　　　　　　　　　　　打瞌睡
    〔就連荷馬也有打瞌睡的時候。〕

    ★ Homer 是一位偉大的古希
    　臘詩人
    Ans.: Even; nods

75. 知錯能改，善莫大焉。
    A _____ confessed is half redressed.
    　　錯誤
    〔承認錯誤，就是改正了一半。〕

    confess (*v.*) 承認；供認
    redress (*v.*) 改正；矯正
    Ans.: fault

76. 愛屋及烏。
    Love me, _____ _____ _____.
    　　　　　愛　　我的　　狗
    〔愛我，也要愛我的狗。〕

    Ans.: love my dog

77. 龍生龍，鳳生鳳。
    Like mother, like _____. (Like _____, like son.)
    　　　　　　　　女兒　　　　　　父親

    Ans.: daughter; father

78. 神通廣大。

He has _____ in the _____ of his _____.
　　　　　　　眼睛　　　　　　後面　　　　　　頭

〔他的後腦有長眼睛。〕

Ans.: eyes; back; head

79. 五十步笑百步。

The _____ calls the _____ black.
　　　鍋子　　　　　　茶壺

〔鍋子嫌茶壺黑。〕

Ans.: pot; kettle

80. 見仁見智。

One man's _____ is another man's _____.
　　　　　　肉　　　　　　　　　　　毒藥

〔同樣的東西，對甲是肉，對乙是毒。〕

Ans.: meat; poison

81. 物以類聚。

Birds of a _____ flock _____.
　　　　　　羽毛　　　　　一起

〔同樣羽毛的鳥會聚集在一起。〕

flock (v.) 聚集
Ans.: feather; together

82. 英雄所見略同。

Great minds think _____.
　　　　　　　　　相似地

Ans.: alike

83. 時間會證明一切。

Time will _____.
　　　　　說明

〔時間會說明一切。〕

Ans.: tell

84. 變化帶來生活的樂趣。

_____ is the spice of _____.
多樣化　　　　　　　　　生活

〔變化是生活的調味料。〕

spice (n.) 香料；調味料；樂趣
Ans.: Variety; life

85. 知足就是幸福；知足常樂。

Content is _____.
　　　　　 幸福

content (n.) 滿足
Ans.: happiness

---

86. 天下無不散之筵席；好景不常在。

All good things come to an _____.
　　　　　　　　　　　　　　結束

Ans.: end

---

87. 沒有十全十美的人生。

There is no _____ _____ a thorn.
　　　　　　　玫瑰　　沒有

〔沒有不帶刺的玫瑰。〕

thorn (n.) 刺
Ans.: rose; without

---

88. 百聞不如一見。

_____ is believing.
看見

Ans.: Seeing

---

89. 條條大路通羅馬。

All roads _____ to Rome.
　　　　　　通往

Ans.: lead

---

90. 塞翁失馬，焉知非福。

(Something is) a _____ in disguise.
　　　　　　　　祝福

〔（某事）是化了裝的祝福。〕

disguise (n.) 偽裝；掩飾
Ans.: blessing

---

91. 患難見真情。

A friend in _____ is a friend indeed.
　　　　　　需要

〔在需要幫助的時候會給予協助的朋友，才是真正的朋友。〕

indeed (adv.) 真正地
Ans.: need

---

92. 死無對證。

_____ men tell no tales.
死亡的

tell tale 說故事
Ans.: Dead

93. 有生就有死；不要害怕死亡。

Dying is _____ _____ _____ living.
跟……一樣的自然

〔死亡就跟活著一樣的自然。〕

Ans.: as natural as

94. 人人皆有一死。

All _____ are mortal.
　　人

mortal (*adj.*) 會死的
Ans.: men

95. 金錢萬能；有錢能使鬼推磨。

_____ _____.
金錢　　說話

〔金錢會說話。〕

Ans.: Money talks

96. 需要為發明之母。

Necessity is the mother of _____.
　　　　　　　　　　　發明創造

necessity (*n.*) 需要；需求
Ans.: invention

97. 薄利多銷。

_____ profits, _____ returns.
小的　　　　　　快的

profit (*n.*) 利潤
Ans.: Small; quick

98. 血濃於水。

_____ is thicker than _____.
血液　　　　　　　　　　水

thick (*adj.*) 濃厚的
Ans.: Blood; water

99. 人非孤立於世的。

No man is an _____.
　　　　　　島嶼

〔人非孤島。〕

Ans.: island

☑ 有助於英文寫作的智慧語

寫英文作文時，若適時地引用智慧之語，絕對是明智之舉，它對寫作者的貢獻是：

☞ 我們雖然可能平凡，但是引用智者的看法，我們的文章也具有智慧。

☛ 我們雖然可能平凡，但是連如此有智慧之人也贊同我的看法，可見我也不算太差！

但是，不用永遠停留在 A friend in need is a friend indeed. 或 Make hay while the sun shines. 的階段。我們強烈期盼讀者多背一些詞藻優美、令人眼目一新的西方常用睿智話語，為英文作文增值增色。

接下來，讓我們一起用填空的方式來完成下面有助於英文寫作的智慧之語吧！在練習填入單字的時候，建議可以拿張紙將頁面右半邊的答案遮住，試著依智慧語的中文意思或底下的提示來猜出正確的答案！

---

1. 十年樹木，百年樹人。
   It _____ three _____ to make a _____.
   　　　花費　　　　　　代　　　　　　　　紳士

   Ans.: takes; generations; gentleman

---

2. 事實勝於雄辯。
   _____ speak _____ than _____.
   　行動　　　　比較大聲　　　　字

   英文須活用，"Actions speak louder than words." 亦可用於「身教重於言教」。
   Ans.: Actions; louder; words

---

3. 木已成舟，為時已晚。
   The _____ is _____.
   　　　骰子　　被擲出去了

   cast 的動詞三態同型
   Ans.: die; cast

---

4. 言多必失。
   The _____ talks at the _____ _____.
   　　　舌頭　　　　　　　腦袋的　成本

   Ans.: tongue; head's; cost

---

5. 盡人事，聽天命。

___ ___, ___ ___.
男人　謀劃　神　處理

Ans.: Man; proposes; god; disposes

---

6. 魚與熊掌難以兼得。

___ one's ___ and ___, too.
留住　　蛋糕　　吃掉它

〔蛋糕吃了就留不住了；若要留下蛋糕，則又不能吃。〕

Ans.: Have; cake; eat it

---

7. 自己闖天下。

___ a ___ for oneself.
燒　　路徑

Ans.: Blaze; trail

---

8. 多此一舉。

___ ___ to Newcastle.
帶著　煤炭

Newcastle 是英國的產煤區
Ans.: Carry; coals

---

9. 三個和尚沒水喝。

Two is ___, three is ___.
作伴　　　　一群人

〔兩個還能作伴，如果人多了，就不那麼親了。〕

Ans.: company; a crowd

---

10. 殺雞取卵。

Kill the ___ that ___.
鵝　　　　下金蛋

Ans.: goose; lays the golden eggs

---

11. 持續到最後的，才是贏家！

He who ___, ___.
笑到最後　　　笑得最久

Ans.: laughs last; laughs longest

---

12. 人各有所好。

One man's ___ may be another man's ___.
肉　　　　　　　　　毒藥

Ans.: meat; poison

13. 江山易改，本性難移。

    You can't _____ an _____ new _____.
    　　　　　　　　教　　　老狗　　　把戲

    亦可說 "A leopard can't change his spots." 花豹改不了斑點。

    Ans.: teach; old dog; tricks

---

14. A 和 B 格格不入。

    A and B are like a _____ in a _____.
    　　　　　　　　　　　方木釘　　　　　　　　圓洞

    亦可說 A & B are like a 圓木釘 in a 方洞。

    Ans.: square peg; round hole

---

15. 聊勝於無。

    _____ is better than _____.
    半條吐司麵包　　　　　　　　　啥都沒

    a loaf 是一條吐司麵包；bread 是麵包包括吐司麵包；toast 則是烤過的吐司麵包。

    Ans.: Half a loaf; none

---

16. 一樣米養百樣人。（這世界無奇不有。）

    It takes _____ _____ to make a world.
    　　　　所有的　種類

    Ans.: all; sorts

---

17. 好酒沉甕底。

    The best _____ swim near the _____.
    　　　　　魚　　　　　　　　底部

    fish 是集合名詞，不加 s，動詞仍使用多數。

    Ans.: fish; bottom

---

18. 如人飲水，冷暖自知。

    _____ knows where the _____ _____ like the
    沒人　　　　　　　　　鞋　　打腳

    _____.
    穿的人

    Ans.: No one; shoe; pinches; wearer

---

19. 我內心百感交集。

    I'm _____ with _____ feelings.
    被纏繞著　　　　一大堆

    Ans.: tangled; a multitude of

---

20. 平時不做虧心事，半夜敲門心不驚。

    A good _____ is a soft _____.
    　　　　良心　　　　　　枕頭

    Ans.: conscience; pillow

---

21. 集思廣益。

Two _____ are better than one.
　　　腦袋

Ans.: heads

---

22. 深藏不露。（或大智若愚）

_____ waters run _____.
　靜止的　　　　　　　深

waters 表示河水、湖水、海水
Ans.: Still; deep

---

23. 名師出高徒。

Like _____, like _____.
　　　老師　　　　學生

或是「笨老師教出笨學生。」
Ans.: teacher; pupil

---

24. 捨近求遠。

_____ far and wide for what _____.
　追尋　　　　　　　　　　　　躺在手邊

Ans.: Seek; lies close at hand

---

25. 知足常樂。

_____ is better than _____.
　滿足　　　　　　　　財富

Ans.: Content; riches

---

26. 酒後易失言。

There's many a _____ between the _____ and the
　　　　　　　　溜掉　　　　　　　　嘴巴
_____.
杯子

Ans.: slip; mouth; cup

---

27. 醉翁之意不在酒。

Many kiss the _____ for the _____ _____.
　　　　　　孩子　　　　　護士的　緣故
〔藉著探望孩子之便而接近護士。〕

Ans.: child; nurse's; sake

---

28. 天下沒有不散的筵席。

Even the _____ day must have an _____.
　　　　　　 最長的　　　　　　　　　　 結束

Ans.: longest; end

29. 以柔克剛。

A _____ and _____ approach can _____ a man of
　 柔軟的　　　　微妙的　　　　　　　　卸除武裝

his _____.
　　壞脾氣

Ans.: soft; subtle; disarm; hot temper

30. 最危險之處也就是最安全之處。

The _____ place is under the _____.
　　　 最暗的　　　　　　　　　 蠟燭台

〔蠟燭台上有火光，所以非常明亮，下面卻被燭台擋住了，十
分陰暗。〕

Ans.: darkest; candlestick

31. 肚大能容。

The _____ that _____ hang _____.
　　 樹枝　　　　 生得最多　　　　 最低

Ans.: boughs; bear most; lowest

32. 君子之交淡如水，水長流。

A _____ between keeps friendship _____.
　 樹籬　　　　　　　　　　　　 青綠

Ans.: hedge; green

33. 吃得苦中苦，方為人上人。

_____ leads to _____.
　逆境　　　　 繁華

Ans.: Adversity; prosperity

34. 萬事起頭難。

All things are _____ before they are _____.
　　　　　　　　 難　　　　　　　　　 容易

Ans.: difficult; easy

35. 不經一事，不長一智。

A _____ into a _____, a _____ in your _____.
    摔跤   坑   收穫   智力

Ans.: fall; pit; gain; wit

36. 半瓶水響叮噹。

Empty _____ make the most _____.
      容器   聲音

Ans.: vessels; sound

37. 無風不起浪。

There is no _____ without _____. / Where there's
        煙   火

_____, there's _____.
  煙   火

Ans.: smoke; fire; smoke; fire

38. 賠了夫人又折兵。

Went for the _____, but got _____.
         羊毛   剃毛

〔原本去偷羊毛，結果自己被剃毛了！〕

Ans.: wool;
shorn (shear-shore-shorn)

39. 一失足成千古恨。

One wrong _____ may bring a great _____.
        步   摔跤

Ans.: step; fall

40. 玉不琢，不成器。

The finest _____ must be _____.
       鑽石   切割

Ans.: diamond; cut

41. 五十步笑百步。

The _____ calls the _____ _____.
    平底鍋   茶壺   黑

Ans.: pot; kettle; black

42. 開卷有益。

Reading is always _____.
       有助益的

Ans.: beneficial

43. 樂極生悲。

_____ has a _____ in his _____.
歡樂　　　　刺　　　　　　尾巴

Ans.: Pleasure; sting; tail

44. 水能載舟，亦能覆舟。

The wind that _____ the _____ also _____ the
吹熄　　　　蠟燭　　　　　燃起

_____.
火焰

Ans.: blows out; candle; kindles; flare

45. 法網恢恢，疏而不漏。

_____ has a long _____.
正義　　　　　　手臂

Ans.: Justice; arm

46. 近朱者赤，近墨者黑。

Keep good men _____ and you shall be the _____.
同伴　　　　　　　　　　　　　數目

〔與好人作伴，你就會成為衆數之一分子。〕

Ans.: company; number

47. 羨慕無助於事（羨慕令人心中難受不已）。

_____ has no _____.
羨慕　　　　假日

Ans.: Envy; holidays

48. 長江後浪推前浪。

The new _____ are _____ the old ones.
世代　　　　勝過

Ans.: generations; excelling

49. 樹大招風。

A tall tree _____ much wind.
抓住

Ans.: catches

50. 凡事都是別人錯，自己從不錯。

A bad _____ always _____ his _____.
工匠　　　　責怪　　　　工具

Ans.: craftsman; blames; tools

51. 引狼入室。

_____ the _____ to keep the _____.
　　安排　　狐狸　　　　　　　鵝

鵝的單數是 goose；變化同「牙齒」：tooth → teeth

Ans.: Set; fox; geese

52. 不入虎穴，焉得虎子？

Nothing _____, nothing _____.
　　　被冒險　　　　被收穫

Ans.: ventured; gained

53. 小心駛得萬年船。

_____ is the _____ of _____.
　小心　　　父或母　　安全

Ans.: Caution; parent; safety

54. 一言九鼎。

Promise is _____.
　　　　欠債

Ans.: debt

55. 人人平等，不要歧視人。

A _____ may look at the _____.
　貓　　　　　　　　　國王

Ans.: cat; king

56. 會欺負人的絕非大丈夫。

A _____ is always a _____.
　惡霸　　　　　儒夫

Ans.: bully; coward

57. 本末倒置。

Put the _____ before the _____.
　　　馬車　　　　　馬匹

Ans.: cart; horse

58. 天有不測風雲。

It's the _____ that always happens.
　　無法預知的

the + 形容詞 = 集合名詞，表示全部。例：the elderly 老人；the weak 衰弱之人；the poor 窮人

Ans.: unforeseen

59. 事後諸葛。

It's easier to be _____ after the _____.
　　　　　　　　睿智的　　　　　　事件

Ans.: wise; event

60. 冰凍三尺，非一日之寒。

_____ was not built in a day.
　羅馬

Ans.: Rome

61. 第一印象最重要。

First impressions are _____ the _____.
　　　　　　　　　　一半　　　　　作戰

Ans.: half; battle

62. 親兄弟，明算帳。

Short _____ make long _____.
　　　帳　　　　　　　朋友
〔帳算得勤快，反而有助於友誼。〕

Ans.: accounts; friends

63. 愈得不到的東西愈珍貴。

_____ fruit is sweet.
被禁止的

Ans.: Forbidden

64. 巧婦難為無米之炊。

You cannot make _____ without _____.
　　　　　　　　磚頭　　　　　稻草

古時的磚頭是稻草做成的
Ans.: bricks; straw

國家圖書館出版品預行編目(CIP)資料

英文寫作高分指引 / 郭岱宗, 鄒政威, 盧逸禪作：
-- 初版. -- 臺北市：波斯納, 2020.05
  面：　公分

  ISBN 978-986-98329-1-5（平裝）

  1. 英語　　2. 作文　　3. 寫作法

805.17   109005768

English Writing Guide 英文寫作高分指引

作　　者／郭岱宗、鄒政威、盧逸禪
執行編輯／朱曉瑩

出　　版／波斯納出版有限公司
地　　址／台北市 100 館前路 26 號 6 樓
電　　話／(02) 2314-2525
傳　　真／(02) 2312-3535
客服專線／(02) 2314-3535
客服信箱／btservice@betamedia.com.tw
郵撥帳號／19493777
帳戶名稱／波斯納出版有限公司

總 經 銷／時報文化出版企業股份有限公司
地　　址／桃園市龜山區萬壽路二段 351 號
電　　話／(02) 2306-6842

出版日期／2020 年 6 月初版一刷
定　　價／520 元
I S B N／978-986-98329-1-5

English Writing Guide 英文寫作高分指引
Copyright 2020 by 郭岱宗、鄒政威、盧逸禪
Published by Posner Publishing

貝塔網址：www.betamedia.com.tw

喚醒你的英文語感！

Get a Feel for English!

喚醒你的英文語感！

Get a Feel for English !